C000187084

Reader feedback, especially reviews (hint hint),
is a writer's lifeblood. I'm contactable on the
usual suspects:

Facebook (@Woolrich.writes)
Twitter (@PeterWoolrich)
Instagram (woolrichwrites)

My author website is:
www.peterwoolrich.com

"A 21st Century twist on *Sons and Lovers*. Heart-rending."

Karen Kanter, Author of The Laughing Ladies

"A suitcase full of memories leaking all over the floor."

Rob Young, Hollywood script writer

"Brutally honest. Funny. Poignant."

David Llewelyn, former Conville and
Walsh talent spotter

A Corroded Soul

PETER WOOLRICH

The Book Guild Ltd

First published in Great Britain in 2023 by
The Book Guild Ltd
Unit E2 Airfield Business Park,
Harrison Road, Market Harborough,
Leicestershire. LE16 7UL
Tel: 0116 2792299
www.bookguild.co.uk
Email: info@bookguild.co.uk
Twitter: @bookguild

Typeset in 11pt Minion Pro

Printed and bound in Great Britain by 4edge Limited

ISBN 978 1915352 248

British Library Cataloguing in Publication Data.
A catalogue record for this book is available from the British Library.

For Tracey.
Without whom this wouldn't have been possible.

Special thanks to David Llewelyn, Tom Johnson,
and Rob Young, whose belief kept me going.

Narcissistic personality disorder: characterised by an excessive preoccupation with personal adequacy, an excessive need for admiration, vanity, and the inability to see the damage they are causing themselves and others.

CHAPTER 1

One of the few things I'm sure about is my mother's dead. At least I think she is.

Bodily, she's been gone for about a week. I saw her. Marble cold. False teeth jutting like a salmon's jaw.

Muriel would be mortified if she knew how she looked. Keeping up appearances was important to her. Make that *vital*.

But if she's no longer here, how come my mother dictates my every move? My every thought. As in life as in death, I suppose.

Am I my own man or hers?

It's fine by me if I'm hers. It'd excuse a litany of crimes. Against humanity, supermarkets, and charity shops.

I shouldn't exaggerate. Against humanity suggests mass murder or ethnic cleansing. All I've done is upset a few people. Still, it seems a bit harsh to be hated so much.

It's true about the supermarkets and charity shops, though. Along with dentists, chandleries, and neighbours, both domestic and foreign, I've stolen from them. I've put everything from an organic chicken to a windlass in my pocket. Not literally.

CHAPTER 2

Sitting in Muriel's chair, I rest my fifty-year-old hands where hers have worn the orange geometric fabric, and I feel closer to her than when she was alive.

An enlarged version of her is bearing down on me from the sideboard, frowning from the mantelpiece, attempting a thin-lipped smile from the sewing box she'll never open again.

The photographs have been positioned around our parents' front room by my older sister Jane. She's keen to preserve our mother's presence. I'm not and can't wait to bury her.

A wood pigeon waddles back and forth on the lawn outside the bay window. Single-minded in its pecking, shimmering neck mechanical, unlike me, it's got purpose. The bird disappears into the grass that Jim, my father, has let grow. Without his wife telling him what to do, he's doing nothing.

In the glazed corner cabinet I know my mother's left me, mistaken in the belief I like it, yellowing glue weeps from the fractured back leg of a ceramic Shetland pony. My parents stopped collecting holiday souvenirs when we moved to the 'New House' in Fairfield Close thirty-five years ago.

Tomorrow I'll be back in London, the funeral done and dusted. Ashes to ashes. "If I never see Stoke Blakely again, it'll be too soon."

"Are you talking to yourself again, Daniel? You're supposed to be taking the dog for a walk," Jane shouts through the door I've just closed.

"They'll be here in a minute." I assume she's referring to the expected handful of extended family mourners.

I reach for the photo album Jane unearthed from the attic and deposited on the coffee table. Flicking through the musty smell of Connah family history, a buckled image catches my eye.

One of the lick-and-stick hinges is missing, and my infant self is clinging to the page dressed in my sister's hand-me-down bathing suit. It's a wonder I'm not gay though I wouldn't rule it out.

I can still hear my father's voice as the Polaroid whirs from the camera nearly half a century ago. "At least try and look happy. We're on holiday, supposed to be enjoying ourselves," are familiar words.

I'm crouching beside my mother on a deserted beach. The tide, along with the other vacationers, has long departed. Sand furrows continue across mine and

Muriel's faces; hers partially obscured by wind-blown hair. Lug worms coil at our feet.

I turn the photo over where Jim's sloped handwriting tells me what I want to know:

Mother and Crybaby Daniel, aged two.
Southport 1964.

The clatter of breakfast plates in the kitchen makes me look up, and Christmas stares back at me from an image on top of the music centre. Four children, twelve years apart, are opening brightly wrapped presents.

I'm seven years old, staring at a gift tag I know I'll have read over and over, wanting to believe its sentiments. *Very much love, Mother* wasn't something I heard every day.

An unspoken truce was called on 25 December though it rarely lasted beyond lunchtime. A broken toy, or Jim forgetting the trifle's hundreds and thousands, might cause hostilities to be resumed, along with any number of other things. If I'd felt loved for that one day, I might have felt better about the other 364.

Will I be able to forgive Muriel when she's lowered into the ground? I hope not. Fifty years of neglect is hard to bury. Maybe I really am the 'nasty piece of work' she said I was.

Reaching for a picture of her seated in the chair I now occupy, the smell of decay entrenched in the fabric, I peer into Muriel's mud-brown eyes and ask, "Was I born bad, or did *you* make me this way?"

Maybe a last walk round the village will reveal some answers.

CHAPTER 3

"Woolworths, is it?" I ask Jane, who's admiring her hat in the hall mirror.

"No, it flippin' well isn't. It's Dorothy Perkins and cost twenty pounds, if you must know."

"I could have made you one for less than that. Any chance we might finish our little chat later?"

"About as much chance of you showing some respect."

"*Respect*? Since when were we, especially *you*, shown any respect?"

"Don't start that again, or Dad'll hear. He's doing what you should be doing. Getting ready upstairs."

"It's not even light yet!"

John, my older brother, pauses doing the washing up. "For the first time in his life, Daniel's right, Jane. The cars won't be here 'til 11.30."

"They'll be early, knowing my luck. Where's Terry?" Jane's husband tended to disappear at Connah family gatherings. The lucky bastard.

"*Cars* as in the plural? There's only about five of them?" I want to call the mourners 'vultures', but now's not the time. "Why can't they walk?"

My spaniel, Ben, demands his morning walk by pawing the paint off the back door. "Get down. We're going." My voice makes him scratch even harder. "Don't miss me too much," I call over my shoulder.

"If you see Terry, tell him to get a wiggle on." Jane's husband dropped my sister off first thing this morning, then sped off, saying he had an errand to run.

"I'll come with you as far as the Co-op," John says, grabbing his jacket. It must be obvious I want to be alone, but I forget my brother has the emotional range of a psychopath.

"If you must, but if there are any women out there, you might have to fight them off with a stick. I'm looking particularly gorgeous this morning." My inferiority complex heightens when I'm with John.

"I don't think you being mobbed by rampaging women is going to be a problem, Danny Boy." I know he's right, though it doesn't stop me from glaring at him.

In reality, I diverge from public opinion that says I'm handsome. My lips curl rather than smile; forehead high; nose Roman. And my jawline, albeit chiselled, sports eleven o'clock rather than five o'clock shadow.

I double pace to keep up with my brother walking down the drive, stiffening my six-foot-one frame in a bid to match his additional inch. We both pretend not to notice Jane rapping on the window, warning us not to be late. "Gets more like Mother every day," John and I chorus, looking at each other in a rare moment of unity.

A divorcé, John has a new Scottish girlfriend who didn't fancy meeting the Connah clan 'at such a sensitive time'.

Fairfield Close is a cul-de-sac of near-identical, semi-detached brick houses. Muriel ensured ours was a cut above the rest by instructing Jim to attach diagonal lead strips to the windows. She said it was 'real class'. The rest of us cringed.

My mother saw our *new* house in Fairfield Close as a step down from the *old* house in Crow Park Crescent, where I grew up, a fact she never tired of telling my father.

John and I don't speak again until we reach the early morning slumber of Main Street. A blast of winter cold sees me raise my knock-off Hugo Boss coat collar.

"I see you're doing alright for yourself," John sneers, or so it seems to me.

"Alright just about covers it, but you're only as good as your last story in my game." I soften my tone in a bid to have a conversation.

"You know Mother kept all your old newspaper cuttings, don't you? If you can call the *Daily Mail* a newspaper." His breath pushes against the chilled air. His words incite resentment.

"Jesus. I haven't worked for them for twenty years. Have you never heard of forgive and forget?"

"No. The point is you were her favourite."

"*ME*? *You* were Mr Golden Balls. 'Take this fiver, John'. 'Smoke my fags, John'. It used to drive me and Margaret mad. Speaking of the devil, where is she?"

I notice my brother's nape-length hair is whitening like a birch tree, the liver spots on his neck more pronounced, skin looser. It's what the future holds for me.

"God knows. Margaret's a law unto herself." John and my eldest sister aren't close, but you could say that about all of us.

"I gather she'll be at the church with Sandra. Mother'll turn in her coffin if she sees them."

Margaret's an even blacker sheep than me. She left her husband and two children for built-like-a-docker Sandra years ago. Our family condemned my sister for abandoning her young family. I regarded her living a lie the greater crime.

An eleven-year age gap meant Margaret and I weren't close growing up, though my squeals of delight when she defied our mother meant she saw me as an ally. She, and eventually me, left the village, and Muriel, as soon as we could.

Stoke Blakely, a clean, tidy, and boring commuter village twelve miles east of Nottingham, is where I spent my childhood in the 1960s and '70s.

Back then, the railway station didn't have a waiting room, the library and Post Office closed on Tuesday afternoons, and Greasy Norma was fined for gobbing in the chip oil to test if it was hot enough.

Variously known as 'Stokie' or 'Blakers', it acts as a makeshift market town for a string of smaller villages dotted throughout the Trent flood plain.

The river's whorls and flows border meadows where Friesians dine on buttercups, daring each other closer to match day fishermen who scold them away. North of Main Street, behind several rows of red-roofed houses, rises one side of the Trent valley.

Its wooded slopes provided an adventure playground for youngsters brave enough to rope-swing over Dead Man's Pond. Unlike the other children, I went the extra thrill-seeking mile by flinging frog spawn into scattering girls' hair.

As John and I progress along Main Street, I see the hand-painted metal sign pockmarked by stone-throwing children that continues to boast Stoke Blakely once won a Best Blooming Village award. It was so long ago that most of the gardeners are now pushing up daisies themselves.

When I moved to the village as a four-year-old, the remnants of a mining generation hung on in several sooty terraces. But, as Blakely became more desirable, its working-class residents were thought less so, their homes demolished to make way for grander properties hidden behind hedges.

In the early '70s, when I was still in shorts, the village's social divide was most evident in the two pubs whose windows I peered through. The Fisherman's Arms pulled pints of foul-smelling Shipstones for its male-only customers, while the Red Lion popped crimped lids off Babycham bottles for the ladies.

Blakely's smoky terraces were a memory by the time I was ten, and even the Fisherman's Arms sold prawn cocktail crisps.

We migrated to the village from Warwickshire when my father improved his social standing by landing a job with the Knitting Lace Training Board, though none of us took the trouble to ask him what it was he did.

With my mother proclaiming she'd finally 'arrived' in what the estate agent called a 'sought-after location', Jim moved his wife and four children into Stoke Blakely's upper reaches.

Ours was the last house on the road, and it bordered fields and woods where I could steal birds' eggs and climb trees.

White shells glued onto a turd-coloured plate, a souvenir from a day's outing to Skegness, announced we lived at number 17 Crow Park Crescent. I can visualise the house's dimpled, buff-coloured bricks that longstanding questions are driving me towards.

My formative years, if you can call them that, were spent under number 17's sharply pitched roof.

CHAPTER 4

"**A**re you ignoring me, Daniel?"

"Sorry, John, I was away with the fairies." In truth, being back in my childhood village is reigniting unwelcome memories.

"Speaking of fairies, your dog's pissing on Gervase's ornamental bay tree." John's a distraction, if nothing else.

"Ben, come here."

"You could always put him on the lead."

"I could put you on one as well. Did Gervase – that can't be his real name – do Mother's Land Girl curls?"

"They cost Dad a fortune, whatever they were."

"Maybe she should've fed us properly, instead."

"We didn't starve." John's look says he doesn't know what I'm talking about.

"Speak for yourself." I watch an acned youth pushing a trolley of Mother's Pride bread into the Co-op. "Talk about ironic."

"I think you'll find ironic is the wrong word, though I wouldn't expect anything less from a journalist." Is John jealous, or does he really not like me?

My brother's voice trails off as his long-legged stride carries him across Main Street. "And don't be late. Jane's upset enough as it is." His shout causes heads to turn.

My food-pricked mind drifts to a place I'd rather not go as I continue to walk. I'm eight years old, sick, and off school with a fever, searching the kitchen cupboards.

"I'm hungry," bellowed through the kitchen wall, elicits no response from my mother. "There's nothing for lunch."

"Use whatever's in. Costs me a ruddy fortune going to the shops just for you. Anyway, Bob's on in a minute." Bob Langley is a matter of life and death for Muriel. A glint in the eye of the housewives' choice presenter moistens lips long presumed dry.

"I'm going to tell Dad you don't feed me. I know he gives you money to look after me." Silence. "**I WISH YOU WERE DEAD**." I shout through the same door Jane did an hour ago.

I thump down the only ingredients I can find onto the worktop. Blood and tomato sauce spurt across my pyjamas when my hand slips opening a can of baked beans.

Inhaling snotty tears, I yell in my unbroken voice, "Ruddy fat cow. As soon as I'm old enough, I'll leave and never come back. Then you'll be sorry."

"That's what you think," is what I think I hear in reply.

Standing on tiptoe, I stir a raw egg into the now bubbling baked beans, followed by a handful of cornflakes, a Dairylea triangle, and four-day-old Mother's Pride. 'Use whatever's in', she said. So I did, then took a perverse pleasure in eating the stand-a-spoon-up-in gloop.

A shoulder barge jostles me back to the present. "Wotchit, mister." The newspaper boy isn't much bigger than his bag, which most likely contains my own printed words.

Steadying myself on the frostbitten pavement, Gervase glowers at me as he pours a jug of water over his pissed-on plant. I offer him a wave that could be an apology or a *fuck you*.

Muriel paid the stylist's inflated prices for the kudos of being seen to walk through his door, and I shudder at the thought of her airs and graces. A brisk, haughty walk to the shops saw a Hermès scarf trail behind a Jaeger blouse. A set of freshwater pearls and a Harris Tweed skirt completed my mother's 'real elegance' outfit.

Although Jim's salary ensured Muriel's wardrobe was far from extensive, any unfashionable repetition went unnoticed because she so rarely went out. Back behind closed doors, the garments were swapped for a Crimplene housecoat.

My mother had two ways of looking at people. Up and down. She had acquaintances but no friends.

"Sound like anyone you know, Ben?" A knowing stare says he does. "Alright. Don't rub it in. You're a dog."

Listening to her stories, Muriel's proudest hour was being crowned Mansfield May Queen. It was a teenage moment, it appeared to me, that she continued to live in. The family home was her kingdom, children and husband loyal subjects, or so she liked to think. Her governing tactics were simple: Divide and rule.

Muriel contrived to keep her four children apart, whispering conspiratorial words into our ears about the others' treachery. Equally important was maintaining a distance between our father and us. My phone conversations with Jim rarely lasted longer than the minute it took my mother to snatch the receiver out of his hand. To this day, I barely know my brother and sisters or my father.

Perhaps by the time I came along as the unplanned last in a line of four, Muriel's mothering instincts were exhausted, if they ever existed. She was the matriarchal pivot on which everything rested, her mood a storm cloud waiting to burst over whoever pricked it first, usually Jim, then me.

I'm aware, mainly because I heard it often enough, that Muriel envisaged a very different outcome for herself. It was one built on wartime promises of silk stockings, cigarettes, and funny-tasting chocolate from tall, tailored men who knew how to dance and French kiss.

As a child, I pictured sassy GIs offering my mother the sort of Hollywood life she'd seen on the big screen, open-mouthed as the velvet curtains drew back and Fred Astaire glided across the stage.

Wrapped in her own uniformed embrace, I imagined Muriel had found a leading man, one who'd take her away from Mansfield's backstreets and me. When curiosity took me to those streets a few years ago, Hermès scarves weren't prevalent.

A couple of doorstep cronies, integral to the grid of two-up two-downs, told me how twenty or more children used to play in the cut-throughs and alleyways. Skipping ropes thwacked, sandals tap-danced through hopscotch squares, and cricket stump dustbins rattled, or so they said.

It's hard to envision my mother as a child – young, vibrant, happy – and I ask the cronies if they'd known her.

"Who wants tah know?" the stouter of the women challenged.

"My name's Daniel, Muriel Jessop's youngest. She married Jim Connah."

"Are ya nah, well we ne'er played wi' 'er. She wer a bit too 'igh and mighty if y'ask me." I chuckle as a more familiar Muriel reappears.

"Mind, want easy fer 'er lookin' atter poorlie sister. Polio, think it woh."

I'd like to hear more about the polio-stricken sister I know nothing about, but the first biddy's on an unstoppable roll. "Where she live now, anyroad? Buckingham Palace?

"She's working on it, but until then, she's in Nottingham." A sense of disloyalty towards my mother surprises me.

"'er father did alrite for 'im sen. Moved famly tah posh haus ont other side a tram line. Not upsettin' yer, am I? We calls a spade a spade rahnd 'ere."

"Not at all," I semi-lie. "She never talks about any of this."

"Aye, I bet she don't."

I'm told my maternal grandfather, Reuben, pulled himself up by the bootstraps he wore delivering milk churns on a horse and cart. Admiring the stern young man's work ethic, it appears the Co-op elevated him to Master Baker.

After the five-strong Jessop brood moved to a nearby tree-lined street, Murial occasionally sauntered back to her old neighbourhood. Chin a few degrees above horizontal, vowels exaggerated, the capital letters in her father's title went to her head, or so the gossips had it.

Muriel took to performing Bible readings at the church hall, going on to gain a First Class 'summat or other in proper speakin'", which I take to mean elocution. Fee-paying book-laden pupils then ambled down Muriel's path in search of similar improvement themselves.

"There's nowt yer mam liked mor than sahnd on own voice tha's fer schure." I relish how freely backstreet tongues wag.

The blabbermouths have it that Muriel was driven by ambition towards the Brittanic Insurance Company, where there was an opportunity for a flirty brunette to be promoted. Within six months, she was Typing Pool Supervisor with her own set of keys and access to the stationery cupboard.

As guns began to thunder in Eastern Europe, Muriel stepped up to entertain the troops with Vera Lynn classics and the occasional ditty. She met Jim while manning a tea and cake stall. His ardour, it appears, was aroused at first sight. Muriel kept her options open.

"Reckon she thaght Jim a-bit, yer know, straight buht sted-y, like," the first neighbour suggests. A glance says she's considering my feelings.

"She means Jim wah borin," the second counters. "Maybes why Muriel spent soh much time wi Americans."

"Dirren stop 'er lerrin' Jim 'av kiss-n-a-cuddle in clockrum thou. Keep 'im innerested, jus' in case, like." The first woman has given up considering my feelings.

Mansfield, I'm told, was flooded with gum-chewing GIs in pressed cotton shirts and open-top jeeps. Generous Uncle Sam rations meant the men weren't in need of handouts, yet they queued for Muriel's treats. Jim's orange squash went unnoticed.

Muriel's reputation spread, and before long, she was out from behind the tea urn, entertaining the two armies with more risqué performances and a shapely leg. "Warden, daff bugger, thought Muriel wer boostin' morale," crony one says, lifting her ample bosom.

I'm assured, I assume by way of compensation, that my mother wasn't the only woman to enjoy the GIs' attentions, though most suppressed their yearnings slightly longer, it seems.

Initially concerned about losing the local men they'd already snared, it wasn't long before some of the other women were discovered in the back of Blitz Buggies, canvas hoods up.

The biddies inform me that Muriel maintained Jim's wounded affections over the next four years, enticing him back each time he withdrew his engagement proposal. But as the guns fell silent and the GIs broke camp, so my mother's suitors became less handsome.

Diverting to Jim, who the neighbours are equally knowledgeable about, they describe him as a polite and thoughtful young man, if not a little dull, who lived in his God-fearing father's hook-nosed shadow.

During the war years, Alfred Thomas Connah tolerated his son's ambition to be an engineer, mainly to avoid the draft, but once peace was declared, he had other ideas. Descended from a long line of evangelists, Alfred was adamant his only male offspring would divine for celestial glory by becoming a priest.

"Wanted tah pack Jim off tah re-ligious school sumwhere neer Burm-ing-am. Be gone three yeer, 'e would." Biddy two appears to feel for my dad.

Jim's imminent departure presented Muriel with a dilemma. Either she relinquished his five-year-long advances – which might save her from a far-flung mission when he was ordained – or she lived in the hope that her US colonel reappeared, as promised in his one and only letter.

One of Muriel's three sisters was the apparent source of much of the cronies' information, though whether out of spite, I don't know. Either way, my mother's dilemma was decided for her with the clear parental hint that it was time for her to fly the nest and make her own.

The gossips claim that Muriel's greatest concern was turning into an old maid without a shelf to sit on. So, she borrowed her future sister-in-law's wedding dress and prayed she didn't become a twenty-eight-year-old pastor's wife living in purgatory.

But God turned a deaf ear to the unhappy bride's prayers and shunted her off, or Overdale Seminary College did, to the Gorbals where a baptism of fire awaited her in Glasgow's razor-gang slums.

In *his* letters home, Jim let it be known that even though he and his now pregnant wife were dependent on charity, they led a 'fulfilling life' administering to those worse off than themselves.

In *her* letters, Muriel complained of gritting her teeth over a two-ring stove as Alka-Seltzer proved an ineffective remedy against morning sickness.

Listening to the biddies' recollections, I can almost see the colour bleed from my mother's life as Jim's cassocks hang alongside bleached towelling nappies on the washing line.

CHAPTER 5

I'm eight years old when Dad tells me about his time in the pulpit. We were, unusually, alone in the car after the christening of my parents' first grandchild, courtesy of my sister, Margaret. Muriel had stayed behind, insisting more pictures be taken of her holding the baby outside the church.

Waiting to pull out of the car park, Jim doesn't react to the motorist flashing his headlights then honking his horn, arms gesticulating.

"Dad ... Dad, that man who was letting you go said a naughty word." Jim is wearing the same distant look whenever he slips into the past, a criminal offence as far as my mother is concerned.

Sitting in the car, the Mark I Cortina's roof fabric stained with Jim's forty-a-day John Player Special habit, I'm moved to ask if he's alright. What happens next is stored in my memory, there to be selected like a jukebox record.

"Are you okay, Dad. You look a bit, sort of, sad."

A scented pine tree dangling from the rear-view mirror keeps time as the car crunches through the gears.

"Who do they think they are with their hellfire and brimstone? Flaming hypocrites, the lot of them."

"Who, Dad? Who are flaming hipnocrits?"

"All that talk about giving when all they do is take. Claptrap and hot air, that's all religion is. Be good and go to heaven, be bad and go to hell. *Pah*. I don't know what's worse."

I've seen Jim lose his temper, usually when my mother pushes him too far, but nothing like this. Lighting one John Player Special with another, the veins on his hands are like bruised, swollen rivers.

Addressing no one in particular, he reveals how his dreams of becoming an engineer were thwarted by his father marching him off to a different kind of war. An onward Christian soldier, the battleground is a cauldron of Glaswegian violence where humanity lives on its knees.

I try to keep up as Jim tells me how, as a twenty-four-year-old vicar, he gave communion to a congregation of impoverished parishioners drained by greater daily suffering than the Good Lord himself could endure. As he tried to punctuate the misery of smacked-out stairwells, his sunny countenance dimmed, was how I understood it.

"It was hard to keep my faith when children were hungry. We had very little – which was hard on your mother being a newlywed – but we were rich compared to them."

As I got older, it occurred to me that Jim was relieving himself of a burden carried without expression for twenty-five years. I listen, as intently as an eight-year-old can, to my father telling me how he and his disaffected wife battle on until the product of their honeymoon fortnight in an Isle of Wight guesthouse arrives.

Margaret is a sickly baby whose incessant wailing prevents Jim from hearing himself think for a further two years, by which point my mother is pregnant again, this time with John.

Over the years, I've interpreted what Jim said, but what has struck me most is a telegram he received one winter's day.

PAUL **STOP** KILLED **STOP** MOTORCYCLE ACCIDENT **STOP** CONDOLENCES **STOP** MOTHER

Paul Eggerstone had been Jim's closest friend at Overdale Seminary College. The younger man, a bishop's son, was assigned the more genteel parish of Harrogate while my dad was shipped off to Glasgow.

The men exchanged weekly letters, Paul fortifying my father's wavering faith when it might have been more charitable to let it lapse.

His twenty-four-year-old friend's demise under the wheels of a bus hit Jim hard, and heading south to conduct the memorial service, he questioned his holy orders. The doubt continued as he stood behind the funeral lectern.

"I was just going through the motions, saying the words without believing them. I wanted to say what a warm, generous man Paul was who saw God's work as helping people, not dressing up in fancy costumes. If only I'd …"

Later in life, I understood that Dad wasn't just mourning Paul Eggerstone, but his only remaining friend since marrying Muriel, who put the brakes on 'such nonsense'.

"Instead of saying how kind Paul was, I heard myself talking about his sinful body and repentant soul. The words stuck in my throat, especially seeing his mother and father sitting in the front pew. I couldn't lie to them, so I said I was sorry and stepped down. The ministers were furious, which was the only good thing about it."

It's the first time I see Jim as an adult with frailties rather than just a henpecked husband and disappointing father.

"But that's great, Dad. It makes you a superhero like Batman... or James Steen."

He turns to look at me with a wistful smile. "I don't know about that, son. Your mother deserved better. She could have had anyone she wanted, especially during the war. I've always known I was second best."

Reflecting on my childhood as a fifty-year-old man, I suspect I've inherited another unwanted parental hand-me-down. Jim's low self-esteem

CHAPTER 6

A queue of 4x4s is choking Main Street, exhaust fumes troubling the air as outlying village school-run mums simmer behind tinted windows. The millennials want the baby boomers out of the way.

I squint into the Red Lion where I'd enjoyed, then regretted, so many lock-ins. The carpets once stained with a thousand spilt pints are now glossy floorboards. Next door, the lime tree outside the post office, which I remember bending to breaking point as a sapling, now casts winter shade over the row of shops.

'*Is that* …? It is, it's her. She hasn't changed a bit. She looked sixty when she was twenty.' I'm struck by the usual dilemma of whether to declare myself or to keep walking.

"Excuse me. Mrs Simpson, is that you? You won't remember me, but …"

"Of course, I remember you, Daniel. You're not easily forgotten." I brace myself. "I'm only teasing. It's been a long time. How are you? I was sorry to hear about your mother. I know how close you two were."

"*Erm*, thanks." Perception is a curious thing.

"Jim told me how proud she was of you. He said your name was in the newspapers, and you'd even been on TV. Have you really? The funeral's today, isn't it? I wanted to attend, but …"

"Sorry, I'm a bit … shocked."

"I'm sure you are. It's a terrible thing to lose a parent. They say time's a great healer though."

"It's not that. It's seeing you. I wasn't expecting it. I … You remembered my name after forty years or more."

"I'd recognise you anywhere, Daniel. By the way, it's Miss Davies, not Mrs Simpson."

"*Sorry*?"

"It's Miss Davies. I never married, but please call me Wendy."

"But we always thought Mr Simpson was the postmaster and you were the mistress."

"So did he."

Her comment's at odds with her appearance. A hedgerow wren fearful of being noticed, Wendy's bucolic cheeks and pinched expression look as if they'd shatter if harshly spoken to. A lonely ache in her bones seems to weigh her down.

Time's stood still for her: peach blouse tucked into pleated skirt; dough-coloured tights; sensible shoes. Even the jade brooch on her full-length woollen coat appears the same.

Wendy's voice, kind yet inconsequential, is identical to how I remember, maybe a little weaker, harder to hear as she chirps about Caroline Curtis's father selling the horses' field to Crichton Estates; his palm crossed with silver and a mock-Tudor mansion – my thoughts not hers.

"What happened to Caroline?" I venture.

"*Ah*, yes. You could have been sweethearts, but she thought you didn't like her." Wendy was everyone's confidant, it seems. "She married and moved to the Norfolk Broads, then divorced, which seems to be the way these days."

'What might've been,' I wonder, envisioning Caroline, my first crush, astride Charlie, her salt-and-pepper maned horse.

Wendy informs me how otters have been reintroduced to the banks of the Trent, somehow aware I used to fish there, her knowledge unnerving.

I point at the Post Office window display that I'm sure hasn't been altered in 40 years; faded jigsaws, plywood dinosaurs, and Manila envelopes with string wound flaps. "You're not still serving oiks like me in there, are you?"

Blinking, she retrieves a glance from over my shoulder. "Goodness me, no. I left the village not long after you did. I only came back quite recently. Mr Simpson died of a heart attack, and his wife sold the business. I was just popping in for a stamp and some wine gums."

It's now or never. "You know I took things from the shop … lots of things, actually. I stole from you, that's what I did, and I'm sorry. You were always so nice to me."

"I know you did, Daniel. Sweets, pens, even a model aeroplane. And what did you do with all those pencil cases?"

"If you knew, why didn't you stop me … or call the police? I always felt so guilty afterwards. I couldn't help it, still can't …" It's an admission too far, and I interrupt myself. "I feel even worse now you've told me."

"Don't. Let's just say it was my little way of getting even with old man Simpson. He couldn't understand why he never made any money." Wendy giggles behind a wool-mittened hand before changing the subject.

"Do you remember all those airmail letters your mother sent you? When Jim came in to post them, we laughed about the price of the postage to … where was it? Thailand? Then Hong Kong and Australia. How is Jim, by the way? I often think of him."

"Bearing up. There's something I've wanted to ask you, Mrs … Wendy, though it's probably unfair of me to bring it up after all this time."

I've been haunted by the image of a dribbling, lopsided child coming out of the post office for four decades. Tumbling off the school bus, I'd mimicked the boy's Frankenstein walk and strangled speech, unaware that the boy's mother was standing behind me.

When I finish telling Wendy the story, I reach down and stroke Ben to hide my discomfort. "Basically, I wasn't a very nice person – still aren't in many ways. Do you happen to know where the boy lives so I can apologise?"

Lifting my head with her hand, she says, "I saw you do it, Daniel. It was hot, and the door was open. The boy's name was Callum. He was always smiling, despite having cerebral palsy, and probably thought you were being funny – even if his mother didn't.

"The family moved away when Callum died." She hesitates before saying, "Don't be too hard on yourself. It was a long time ago. You weren't much more than a child yourself. Anyway, it was nice to meet you again. And Daniel …"

"Yes."

"You always seemed such a lost little boy. I hope you're not anymore. Anyway, you must have lots to do. I'll look out for you on the television. Oh, and I'll say a little prayer for your mum. What time's the funeral?"

"Twelve."

"Goodbye, Daniel. Tell Jim I'll be thinking of him. We were quite close once. Is that your dog over there? It's about to … oh dear." Wendy hurries inside the shop where she'd worked for thirty years.

✳

My descent into the criminal underworld begins with taking coins from Muriel's purse. She deserves it for not looking after or listening to me. At least that's the way I see it.

Waiting for her to vacuum the stairs or answer the phone, I scurry into the front room and slide under the music centre. Heart pounding in my ears, I worry the devious cow will leave the hoover running and catch me.

Belly crawling between the wall and her chair, my mouth as dry as the veneer of dust where the vacuum doesn't reach, I enter a forbidden world.

Smelling my mother's perfume as I stretch for her handbag, I freeze when it suddenly goes quiet. Then, ears primed, carpet static bristling round my bare knees, I analyse the silence until the Electrolux resumes its humdrum work, and I move in.

Dampening the handbag's *click* with my left hand, I snake two fingers inside, probing for Muriel's chafed leather purse. Bronze coins are pennies from heaven for bubblegum machines.

I progress to silver sixpences, shillings, and half-crowns; purchasing power for Marathon bars, Mintolas, and Tutti Frooties. I'm worthless, as my mother would say, no more.

By the time I reach my bedroom, each stolen coin feels like a sin, and I promise to replace them with my pocket and paper round money, knowing I won't.

I placate my conscience with undeniable logic. What was the point of spending my own money, I reason, if I can use somebody else's? Someone like my cow of a mother, for instance.

Before long, I cut out the middleman by putting the stolen sweets straight into my pocket alongside the coins. Anyone can buy things. Colouring sets and board games are a natural extension of my endeavours, which is when I discover another use for my satchel. But still, I want more.

The fivers and tenners I need as a teenager for moped petrol, scrumpy, and soft porn mags are beyond the limit of Muriel's purse. So, knowing Dad's wallet is in an inside pocket, I watch him return from work and hang his suit jacket on a dining chair before assisting Muriel with dinner.

The problem is that the chair is in plain view of the lounge and the front windows, which increases the chance of getting caught. It's an important lesson: the greater the risk, the greater the return.

Stealing marks me out as a free man, a stand-alone 'I' rather than a conformist 'we'. Better an individual than a part of a sum I detest goes, and still does, my thinking.

Although the tussle between post-robbery guilt and self-justification always subsides, a voice continues to nag. I tell it that 'wrong' is just a word, but it won't listen. Maybe I was born bad and always will be. I steal because I have to. Choice isn't an option.

In my mid-teens, I politicise my larceny by imitating another Nottingham lad called Robin Hood, depriving the rich to feed the poor – or at least me.

Into adulthood, I'm incensed by the price of an organic chicken that's robbery by any other name, so I level the playing field by placing 'reduced' stickers, unpeeled from elsewhere, over the full price. Seventy-pound toilet seats are obscene, so why not put them in a twenty-pound box and head for the checkout?

I filch, rag, and swipe, and if there are consequences in this life or the next, then so be it. If Judgement Day's coming, I might as well carry on impressing and disgusting myself in equal measure; my morality twisted.

To this day, have I ever profited from honesty or found it the best policy? No.

But however I rationalise my deviancy, I can't escape the demon demanding to know the reason why I'm a thief. Maddeningly, the only person who might provide an answer is taking her secret to the grave.

On the morning of my mother's funeral, I'm taking a last walk around where I was raised to see if she's left any clues.

CHAPTER 7

I'm in the heart of the village, and staring at the church hall across the road returns me to being a six-year-old glared at by a grim-faced Methodist banging out *Jerusalem* on an old piano. I can feel her peering over her glasses at my flushed face, huffing as I stumble over the words. The following Sunday, I cut my bow tie's elastic and refuse to return.

My fifty-year-old gaze seeks out the narrow strip of land that used to exist between the church and its spiked perimeter fence. The weeds have been sprayed, poisoned heads wilting, but otherwise, it's the same.

"Could they still be there?" I ask Ben. "Might even be worth a bob or two." My spaniel cocks a quizzical ear whenever I talk out loud, which is often. The gate creaks as I enter consecrated ground.

In the far corner, next to a drain, I scuff the ground with my boot. It's where I buried the bagful of Matchbox cars I pilfered from the post office four decades ago, but my Omega tells me I'll have to search another day.

Noticing Wendy direct an envelope at the mouth of the post box, I wave a final acknowledgement, which she doesn't see. Strange how she said she and Jim had been close.

✖

'Perhaps it was Sarah's fault I became a criminal,' I muse, crossing back over Main Street.

Sarah Jenkins – a tearaway I'd encountered in the new comprehensive system where relative middle-class politeness was thrown into a lion's den of working-class hostility – was my first love.

While her shoplifting skills were superior to mine, and she might have inspired me to raise my game, stealing had run through me like a screw thread long before I met her.

Every Saturday morning after ice skating lessons, the thirteen-year-old girl with twenty-year-old curves presented me with stolen tokens of her affection. Her desire to give dovetailed nicely with my desire to take.

Sarah's offerings included Peter Frampton's live double album, a pair of six-button Oxford bag trousers, and a Meccano set. It wasn't my style to tell her I admired her ingenuity.

We kissed in the ice rink's dim concrete walkways. The reek of semen-stained pants, half-eaten burgers in Styrofoam cartons, and decomposing vermin heightened our sense of unassailable togetherness.

Frequently stopping for tongue-probing snogs, we made our way to the stadium's shadowy upper reaches, where an asbestos roof met the top tier of seats. From here, Sarah roared abuse at less able skaters on ice the colour of soaking socks.

I'd never been happier or more forlorn. Emptiness always at the heart of me.

Sarah laughed in the face of danger – her own or anyone else's. At home, she ducked and dived, helpless against father and son's closing-time stench of fag ends and curried chips.

Her 1970s glamour girl looks, excitable nature, and burgeoning breasts had no reason to expect a protective arm or social care. Marred by authority, her fear of it was spent, empowering her by closing her down. The quickest route to respect was defiance, so if life said 'No', she smacked it in the face and moved on.

But I discovered a chink in her armour. A carelessly tossed playground word unresolved by the school bell plunged her into a whirlpool of despair, the starting gun for my favourite game.

"The little madam's been on the phone six times already," Muriel huffs as I walk through the door, certain that there'll be another *dring*.

"*Ooo*, that'll be her again." I'm convinced my mother's upset by the attention I'm getting more than anything else. "Tell her if she doesn't stop calling, I'll be along to see her mother. Where does she live anyway?"

It's time to bait the trap.

"On Top Valley estate in a council house with no curtains. Her dad's a binman, and her mum's a skivvy."

"No wonder she's a hussy. If you don't stop seeing her, there'll be trouble, and then you'll have me to answer to."

If only Muriel realised that trouble is what I want.

"You've never met her, so how do you know she's a hussy?"

"Because she's common as muck, that's how. And don't you backchat me, my lad, or you'll get what's coming to you."

"What's that?"

"Some of this, that's what." She pulls back her hand. "Now go and tell her to STOP calling this house. Or else."

I hear Sarah's sobs even before I pick up the receiver. I feel for her, but it's too soon to put her out of her misery. The limits of her idolatry have to be tested first.

"Hello," I say enthusiastically before dropping a tone. "Oh, it's you. What do you want?"

"Specting sum uver slag, was ya? I wan' you an' am gerrin on bus tah cum see ya."

"You can't."

"Why not? I can, am gunna."

"You didn't want to see me at lunchtime, so why you bothered now?" I ask, winding the spring. "I'm about to have my tea, and Mum won't let you in. She says you're a hussy."

"She wah? I'll kill fuckin' bitch. Anyroad, did wanna see ya lunchtime but goh purrin dension. Tried get aght winda but wer locked. Nurse 'ad tah put bannage on me 'and when tried smashin' it."

"Then why arrange to meet down fag bank? I was there. You can ask Lorraine Thingy. No way you got detention. Who off?"

"Arse-breff Gibson."

"I don't believe you, what for?"

"Fer smackin' Karen Fletcher, thas wha'."

"What you do that for? Karen's alright."

"Thas why I 'it 'er."

"What?"

"Cos fancies you an' you fancy 'er, an' all."

Long silences punctuate the next forty-five minutes (as they did most evenings during our eleven-month affair) until Muriel, tutting in the background, grabs the phone. "Daniel's got to go. He's having his tea."

"'K-off y'owd bag."

✖

Sarah was instrumental in my sexual awakening, which went something like this:

Age seven, I hump a cushion while watching Diana Rigg in her *Avengers* catsuit. Muriel barges in, snatches the cushion, and tells me I'm disgusting.

Age eight, I spy on Caroline Curtis with one hand down my pyjamas as she gallops round the horses' field.

39

Age nine-and-a-half, I pore over Jim's copy of *Fiesta* magazine hidden behind the hot water tank, incapable of increasing the stickiness on its pages.

Age nine-and-three-quarters, I hide in the airing cupboard, watching my sister use the loo. I really am disgusting.

Age twelve, I wank myself raw behind the hawthorn hedge where I'd found a bagful of Swedish porn.

Age thirteen, I watch my semi-flaccid penis disappear into Sarah and shoot my first watery cum.

This last encounter is particularly eventful.

After Sarah coerces a couple of inches of my reluctant member inside her alarmingly hairy orifice, our post-coital awkwardness is cut short by the sound of her parents' Reliant Robin thumping up the kerb.

"Geroff fer 'e kills both on us." Then, leaning over the bed in search of her pants, I get my first glimpse of a real vagina which is when time stutters to a halt, trapping me between two worlds.

If I was now a man, it didn't feel like it. For starters, I wasn't sure if what had come out my knob was sperm. Surely *that* couldn't make a girl pregnant, become a human being? *Me.*

But what if she *is* pregnant and I have to marry her? She's underage, and they could send me to prison. I wish she hadn't made me do it. I want to go home.

Then again, I had now fucked a girl, banged her good and hard like it said in Dad's magazine. My friends aren't to know I'd slipped out after two or three plunges, and I'll still be the first boy in school to lose my cherry. So why do I feel like a five-year-old who wants his mum?

What if she tells everyone I hadn't done it before and, worse, I haven't got any pubes? I could always get in before her and say *she* was the worst lay *I'd* ever had and that her fanny stank of fish.

Looking down, I panic. What's that crumbly stuff on the end of my willie? Has she given me VD? People say she's had loads of sex, and Tracey Carter once called her a 'cock sucker', whatever that is.

I ponder how to describe the crinkly folds of excess skin I'm staring at. Muriel's old leather purse or a City Ground hot dog with onions? *Jesus*. How many other knobs have been up there?

A different sensation swamps me. If Sarah's done it with other people, then I'm nothing special, and she's dirty. Daniel4Sarah4evernomore.

Should I tell her I love her? Then again, how many other blokes have told her that? And vice versa? If I say it, I'll just be another, in my case, undersized notch on her bedpost.

I have images of men thrusting their extended lengths in and out of her, a masochistic thrill I rerun in my bedroom and use to demean her outside of it.

Pulling down her tank top, she spits, "I told yer, gerraght 'fer 'e batters both on us." I've never seen her nervous, let alone terrified, before.

I glance from door to window and back again, stupefied by indecision. Should I stay and protect

41

Sarah, take on her father? Not bleedin' likely. Her dad and brother are both psychos.

Undoing the window latch, I pray the corrugated plastic carport will take my weight. A flattened Reliant Robin will only add to my problems.

Hanging on to the windowsill, I see Roy's slippered foot push open the door, steam from a cup of tea entwining with the smoke from the fag permanently stuck to his bottom lip.

"E'yar luv, bought ya nice cuppa. Wah the …?" The sound of cracking plastic sees Roy spring his whippet-like frame over to the window. "Cum 'ere, yer little bleeder. I'll 'ave yer bollocks fer garters."

When I thud to the ground, legs buckled, I hear him yell, "Sarra, gerrover 'ere, nah."

✕

Sarah and I were a demolition derby, two spheres colliding and melding into one, before disintegrating in a display of somersaulting parts. When 'game over' flashed on the screen one of us hit replay.

Our resentful natures were less lonely together than apart, challenging each other's commitment to danger as well as each other, absorbing one another like a tree does barbed wire.

The grazes of *my* suffering were rendered insignificant by Sarah's scars; she the only one whose needs exceeded mine. As she put it, "We'ez a modun day Rodeo an' Julie or summat." Opposing currents calm raging seas, or so it seemed.

We relished our equally cursed and blessed immorality, though we struggled to contain it within our relationship. Recriminating strife that said we didn't belong together voiced itself in menacing rows and rigid silences. The same routine plagues me to this day; long car journeys silent until I erupt into an invective of 'why don't you say something interesting?'

Sarah disappeared the day after her father was fired, leaving me reassured and devastated. Knowing I could, even unhappily, coexist with someone comforted me, though her loss threatened my ability to carry on.

Without her, I willed the hands of classroom clocks to move faster, freeing me from the drone of another obsolete teacher. Good or bad, Sarah made things happen.

Life, devoid of her devotion, or the goosebumps of her unpredictable behaviour, was unbearable. But, whatever its name – passion or possession – it allowed me to breathe, and I needed more.

As a grown man, I might be expected to call our teenage affair 'puppy love', but I won't because it's defined all my relationships since; each one a little less pure.

For me, Sarah was a diehard romantic whose spirited personality found its way through unknowable darkness, and I'll never forget her. The rumour mill had it that she progressed from Lowdham Grange borstal to HMP Nottingham.

Was Sarah's crime, as far as I was concerned, to be born female, the same sex as my mother and therefore to be battled with? Was I as unappreciative of her, at least to her face, as my mother was of me? Revenge by any other name.

Or are those just excuses for a rotten nature? Maybe my mother didn't love me because I was unlovable. In which case, I'm doomed.

CHAPTER 8

I return an inquisitive gaze from a cross-armed woman leaning against a doorway. Gold letters spell 'Supa Clean' on the large windows either side of her.

Middle-aged, the woman nods in my direction with a flicker of recognition. If it's who I think it is, time's not been kind.

"You still a hotshot reporter in London?" my infant school classmate Gail Mills shouts with a seeming sneer. Several stones have added themselves to an already hefty frame.

"More tepid than hot, Gail. You're looking … well. What you up to?"

"Same old, same old. Hear about Rob Dyson? Dead. Heart attack. Two kids. Only forty-seven." I have no idea who she's talking about.

"That's terrible. Tell his wife … whatshername, I'm sorry?"

"I would if she hadn't left him ten year ago. You know Wendy Davies moved back to the village, don't cha?"

"I do, actually. I've just seen her. Why do you mention it?"

"No reason. See yer later." A warm tang, as strong as Gail's comment is suspicious, wafts across the road.

Supa Clean occupies the site of the old Co-op where I remember sugar and tea being weighed into brown paper bags; carbolic soap and candles reached by a wooden ladder; paraffin sold by the gallon. It closed not long after I arrived in Stoke Blakely as a four-year-old, revamping as a travel agent that Muriel predicted wouldn't last. She said that about everything.

I search for Smelly Eric's rag-and-bone yard, but he's been consigned to the scrap heap himself, and a metal-roofed medical centre stands where his horse and cart once did. "Balloon fer yer scrap," he used to leer down at me from his perch, Steptoe-like.

Where Larch Lane starts to climb, the old people's home appears less and less cared for. Stuart Lockerby, who regularly threatened to 'cave my head in', once threw my football boot into the old fogeys' garden, though it was the back of *my* head that Muriel slapped. Even when innocent, I was presumed guilty.

When I reach the brow of the hill, my heart sags. In the years since I've walked this way, Stoke Blakely Infants has sold off its playing fields. Where I used to play football, horizontal children are staring at flat-screen televisions behind triple-glazed windows. On the grass that's now asphalt was where I'd disguised my lack of footballing talent – feeble strikes trickling wide of open goals – behind a confident swagger. To my amazement, it'd duped gullible managers into thinking I was useful. I'd been taught another important lesson: appearance is king.

Gripping the school's meshed enclosure that I half expect to be electrified, I see my seven-year-old self hanging from the gym's 1960s wall bars, arms aching.

The gym also served as a morning assembly hall where my sniggers – 'Our Father who farts in heaven hollow be your name' – were met with cane on outstretched palm. Headmaster Dobbs, a lean man with stooping neck, took the view that if you cried, you got another. *Ow.*

As an adult ruminating on who and why I am, I'm convinced my parents saw it as the school's responsibility to teach me right from wrong, and vice versa, leaving me to fall between the crack.

Perhaps with me being the fourth in line, the runt, Jim and Muriel were tired of being moral guardians, though considering my siblings' behaviour, it seems more likely they never bothered. Why? Only they can say.

✕

I can still smell the gym's waxed herringbone floor that at 12.30 hosted a dozen low dining tables. Chairs scraped, and plates clattered while juniors served infants their midday meal.

As juniors, my best friend, Martin, and I took the view that bigger kids deserved bigger portions, so we spat on our fingers and stuck them into favourite puddings. The younger kids' yelps of disgust only heightened our delight.

Mrs Chambers, a rosy-faced dinner lady, who smelt of freshly baked bread, oversaw, or in Martin and my case not, the lunchtime chaos. Her reassuring scent contrasted with skid-marked shorts, spilt bottles of free milk, and fish-and-chip Fridays.

Shaking the fence, I lament what's become of the football pitch, netball court, and sand pit. It's where my seven-year-old self swung The Killer, a vinegar-soaked, oven-roasted conker I was forced to retrieve from a bed of nettles after Muriel slapped my legs for stinking the kitchen out; welts on top of rashes.

Reliving these memories is like watching my young life play out on stage, unsure how many acts are left, knowing that my time there, once so vital, now amounts to nothing more than a few unnoticed hand movements; *tick, tock*.

CHAPTER 9

Releasing my grip on the fence, I whistle Ben, who reappears, tail wagging, from a nearby garden. "Jane will have a fit if we're late," I tell him.

I'm nearly at my childhood home where, unlike my sister, I want to confront the past. I need answers, like whether my now-dead mother is responsible for my corroded soul.

But my schooldays aren't yet ready to let me go. Seeing the Portakabin that'd served as a temporary classroom forty years ago, I'm back in 1972, pursuing Steve Sharpe out the door. He's the same age but half my size.

Variously known as Trampo or Stinko, Steve's got stained Ken Dodd teeth, a runny nose, and a perma-stench of having 'let-off'.

The Sharpes didn't belong in Stoke Blakely. They were poor.

It's play day, and the boy with a skew-whiff tie, not

having a toy of his own, grabs my Etch A Sketch. "Gis a go."

"Give it back, or I'll smash yer fat ugly face in," I snarl, letting loose a girly swing that misses.

"*Scrap. Scrap. Scrap!*" shriek a dozen ten-year-olds. "DAN-NY, DAN-NY, DAN-NY. STIN-KO TRAM-PO, STIN-KO TRAM-PO. Face smashed in. Face smashed in."

Steve pushes his way through the mob, speeds across the playground, vaults the perimeter fence, and disappears into the grounds of Colworth Hall. Although the Palladian mansion is reduced to a pile of rubble and the site declared out of bounds, impromptu football matches are played there, jumpers for goalposts.

I have the physique but not the courage to leap the fence, so I go the long way round, spurred on by a chanting horde of classmates and my wild-armed teacher, Miss Phipps.

With the Etch A Sketch under his arm, Steve vanishes through a doorway in the walled garden that leads to an unmade lane, which gives me an idea. If I cut through Mrs Ledley's shrubbery and cross the horses' field, it'll bring me out halfway up the track where I can launch an ambush.

But I underestimate the will of a hunted man, and Steve avoids my lunge by a shirttail then powers to the top of the hill. Looking back, he flashes me a toothy grin, two boys locked in eye-to-eye combat under a tree canopy.

Ner, ner, ner. PC Flower's panda car overwhelms the birdsong, and I wonder where he's going.

"Ruddy Norah, what if he's after me?" I say aloud. "I wouldn't put it past Dobbsie to call the police." Whatever trouble I'm in has just multiplied.

I'm about to shout a peace offering when Steve taunts me with a hands-on-hips chortle, turns, and leaps Dead Man's Stile. Pride dictates I resume the chase. PC Flowers' siren ups the ante.

Changing his mind, Steve retraces his steps, then picks up the footpath leading to the far end of the village. He's had it now. That path's overgrown with brambles.

I almost feel sorry for him as I close in, fists clenched, until he shoves the Etch A Sketch into his elasticated shorts and charges head-first into the thorns, serrated wounds cut into his arms and legs.

Stumbling out the other side, Steve pushes a handful of elderberries into his mouth, spraying the bushes with Ribena-coloured juice as he whoops. I tiptoe along the same prickly path, then hurtle after him down the steepest field in the village, squelching through cow pats at the bottom.

"Got you, you thieving gyppo," I shout as Steve twists his ankle in a hoof hole, face contorted with pain. But I lose my nerve, confronted by what to do next. Do I even know how to smash his face in, and what if he's stronger than he looks?

Steve saves me a decision as he gets to his feet, scrapes the mud off his school uniform, and limps on, me sauntering after him, knowing he's nearly home and dry.

On the Sharpes' uneven driveway, an old Vauxhall Viva sits on concrete blocks, and I watch Steve place the Etch A Sketch on the car's roof. His look says trouble is coming both our ways.

Hearing PC Flowers's radio crackle at the end of the road, I grasp my toy and leg it in the opposite direction, half-wishing I'd let Stinko keep it. I can get another. He can't.

✖

As a fifty-year-old man, I attribute denying Steve my Etch A Sketch to a sense of entitlement, perhaps a legacy from Muriel that what's mine is mine.

She certainly begrudged Jim the things she didn't have, but, as I turn to leave my school days behind, I'm convinced February 3, 1962, my birthday, spawned a monster.

CHAPTER 10

I've been confounded by injustice for as long as I can remember. My first memory is being left under a willow tree in an old-fashioned pram. Realising I'm alone, I throw my best friend, a rag doll golly with fuzzy, black hair and fire engine red lips, out through the collapsible hood.

When my mother doesn't respond to my distress calls, I scream the air out of my tiny lungs. With my face turning a bruised shade of purple, I'm left abandoned until my sister, Jane, comes home from school inquiring about my whereabouts.

I'm not sure if the unjust, which I associate with disappointment, replaces hope, or if I didn't have any to begin with. What I do know is that my anticipation of things going wrong, or at best being mediocre, has made my life a lot more difficult.

I often ponder what it takes to be happy. Even saying the word gives me a chill. *Happy. Happy. Happy.*

Why does everyone pretend to be 'happy' when they're obviously not?

I equate happiness with popularity, one signposting the other, which, it seems to me, requires three ingredients. They are the ability to:

1. Laugh at unfunny jokes.
2. Regurgitate inane trivia.
3. Believe everything will be alright when it clearly isn't.

I've tried following the recipe, but it always comes out wrong. The masses have an uncanny ability to spot and repel interlopers, though it's annoying how they can see through me but not themselves.

I've been subjected to cold shoulders since childhood; my entreaties to wary mothers asking if their son can come out to play were met with, "Not today, love. He's busy."

Ostracism continues into adulthood when my phone rings about as often as a dinner party invite drops through the letterbox.

So rarely does anyone request the pleasure of my company that on Monday mornings, I'm unable to join in the coffee machine banter about drunken weekends or Barcelona stag-dos. Instead, I console myself by insisting the loss is theirs not mine and that my day will come. Which it doesn't.

Compounding my sense of isolation is that on the occasions I find myself in social situations, usually by inviting myself, I can't wait to leave anaesthetised by the dreary minutiae of people's lives; astounded that they're deaf to their own irrelevance.

Am I a misfit or just socially inadequate? A consequence perhaps of no one coming to the family home for tea, lunch, or dinner. My social skills were gleaned from shouting matches or silent mealtimes. For this, I lay the blame squarely at my parents' – particularly Muriel's – door.

I tend to occupy the bathroom at the few parties I attend. Sitting on a closed toilet seat, I listen as knocks become bangs. When I eventually open the loo door, I complain of curry to an impossible beauty I don't know how to talk to, then find my way to a coat-strewn bedroom where I resist the temptation to rifle through pockets.

Next, I rummage through kitchen drawers for an imaginary corkscrew, open and shut cupboards in search of a glass, then scour the fridge for something to drink. Anything to pass the time and appear involved.

I might make a passing comment to a fellow partygoer about the finger buffet being 'quite a spread', then pile food I'm too inhibited to eat onto a paper plate; chicken legs and baked potatoes resistant to my plastic cutlery, falling to the floor. Embarrassment, or worse, being laughed at, is my least favourite demon.

Scanning for imaginary friends in roomfuls of people, a nod or 'hello' is as far as any conversation goes. Finally, I seek out a refuge of last resort; the garden shed. Chastising myself, I summon the capacity, in later years via a rolled up £20 note, to engage, emerging to attach myself limpet-like to a luckless victim. Should my nerve desert me completely, I head for the exit, often before I've arrived.

I still have no control over my state of mind. Is mental illness, along with a glazed corner cabinet, part of my inheritance, my internal turmoil either high or extreme?

While other people can command an expression of interest, or at least fake it, my face refuses to lie, the severity of my ever-changing moods there for all to see. People stick to me like leaves on my coat. The next time I look, they're gone.

And so I sit alone in my south London flat, hating myself for watching television or lingering for hours in a scalding hot bath. Yet, if the doorbell rings, I panic and pretend I'm not in.

✖

As a fifty-year-old, it's no consolation that my morbid fear of social interaction comes from my mother. My father, who the family considers ineffectual, is the only gregarious one among us. Always ready to chat with strangers unless my mother's tuts warn him off, many seem to enjoy his company.

Thinking about it, two family members, Uncle Des and Aunty Mary, did attempt to maintain a family connection.

I'm nine years old when I meet them for the first time, although only because my mother's younger brother and his wife call in after unexpectedly finding themselves in Nottingham.

Roly-poly jolly, the couple are how I imagine relatives should be, especially when they offer me ten pence for every bag of horse manure I shovel up from the horses' field.

Even as a child, I find it amusing that while horse poo for the roses might be hard to come by in central Birmingham, Des and Mary's otherwise pristine Rover will reek by the time they get home. What I suspect are their ulterior motives, i.e. instilling in me a work ethic for financial reward, makes me like them even more.

To my glee, they establish a routine of coming round for tea on the last Sunday of every month, each visit bemoaned by Muriel as she waves them goodbye. "I don't know why they bother coming; we've nothing to talk about."

"But they're really nice," I protest. "You don't like *anyone*."

"Well, don't think they come to see *you*. They just want you out of the way, that's all." After three visits, Uncle and Aunt bother no more, my social education at an end.

After resenting my mother for decades, walking in the village where I grew up, I recognise my own behaviour in hers and wonder if her insecurities were as firmly rooted as mine.

I do venture out as I get older, though I'm largely dependent on a series of overly dedicated girlfriends who fall at my feet like broken waves.

But no matter how hard I strive for romantic compatibility on weekends away, I await the moment when my tolerance of the intolerably dull snaps, and another liaison goes to glory in a blaze of inane chit-chat.

As a fifty-year-old, I'm convinced my stronger than any drug conversation craving results from sneering silence at home, though I still question whether an intelligent conversation is too much to ask.

Something, *anything*, to relieve the tedium of hearing about work or faceless people I've never met nor want to. Am I alone in desiring to dredge the emotional depths, or just a fantasist? One speaks for many when she says, "Don't think big things." So I settle for a blow job instead.

I stand by my conviction that partners saying what they mean, the truth that dares not speak its name, along with good sex, is the only route to a love worth having. Laughably, my earnestness seems to arouse the very women whose shallowness repels me, so I take what I can and live with the solitude.

In my twenties, and now a journalist, years went by, hours passing like days until I was presented with another silent sacrificial lamb. Numbing my mind with cocaine and bottles of Pils was the only way to quieten my dissatisfaction and provide me with a degree of temporary, though sky-high, confidence.

I've been a malcontent aged five to fifty. Pleasure dissipates before it begins. Travelling, for instance, results in meeting the same small-minded people in a different place, which, after a while, isn't different anymore. The only benefit is that it takes me away from where I am.

While I might experience a certain exaltation about going on holiday, say, it's dampened by the prospect of being back at my desk, and all that's changed is that my clothes need ironing. I bypass great expectations and go straight to bleak house: bankrupt, with no prospect of time off for good behaviour.

On a good day, I can laugh at myself. Appalled by my self-absorption bordering on narcissism, I tell myself to grow up and think about those less fortunate than me. The problem is that I can't think of anyone.

I don't consider myself more disaffected than other people; I simply counter one philosophy with a contrary one. It keeps me alive but makes having an opinion almost impossible.

While spilling my emotional guts or speaking my perverted mind isn't the road to widespread acceptance, it's marginally preferable to saying nothing at all. The way I see it, most people talk to use up their oxygen allowance.

On the plus side, the disconnection I feel on a bad day is the root of self-satisfied conceit the next. Rolling in the stench of my otherness, I'm euphoric that the run-of-the-mill isn't for me.

My lifetime ambition is to find a place I don't want to leave, and when I find it, I'll laugh at those I've left behind.

CHAPTER 11

Whistling Ben, I glance behind to see Stoke Blakely's angled rooftops, the Red Lion's simulated Tudor chimneys projecting above the rest. Behind them is where Wendy Davies used to live alone in a maisonette.

Seeing the pub transports me inside. I'm in there with my brother, who's making a sporadic visit from Scotland three decades earlier.

"I'm telling you. Pa was a vicar. Ask Jane," he persists. My pretend ignorance about our father is designed to wind John up.

"Jesus, you're right. I'd forgotten," I concede. "Didn't he quit after his best friend was killed in a car accident or something? I think I called Dad a superhero which seems unlikely."

"You always did have a vivid imagination. It's probably why you became a hack."

"I'm not a hack; I do investigations. You're a childminder, aren't you?"

"Social worker."

"Like they've got a great reputation."

"Shall I give you a family history lesson, or not?"

It seems that after our father cast his wife and two children, Margaret and John, out from behind the church's cold though protective walls, they wandered aimlessly around the north of England.

Jim's search for a less spiritually draining vocation took them to one cheerless town after another. While he dallied with youth unemployment, welfare, and homelessness, Muriel's wardrobe shrank from scant to threadbare, her temperament curdling as they went.

"We ended up in a freezing cold and full of damp two-bedroom flat above a bookies. Ladbrokes, I think it was, in Skerne Park, Darlington."

I can tell from John's distressed expression that he's back in the flat, shivering. "Mother, poor cow, stood on a stool using a scouring pad on the mould that kept coming back in the kitchen. And the pilot light blew out on the boiler every time the wind blew." I've never seen my brother appear so distant as he wanders down Bad Memory Lane. "And *then*, get this, Jane came along."

Doctor Mustafa, a cheerful man who pulled off children's noses, was a regular visitor, it seems, and suggested the best cure for Baby Jane's respiratory problems was a change of address.

John tells me that Muriel's coping mechanism was not to talk to Dad for days on end, interspersed with bouts of venomous anger.

"No change there, then," I interrupt.

My brother, still in his reverie, disregards my attempted humour.

"Things sort of got better when Dad landed his first proper job at Paignton and Barlow. It was on a massive site in Flintbury Heath, Warwickshire, full of old warehouses and dying vats where me and Margaret got up to no good."

According to my brother, Jim fell into personnel without getting up again for the next thirty years. Although his pay didn't much improve, the new position came with a fourth-hand car and the old foreman's lodge. It was also where I came into being.

Sidcup Lodge, with its multitude of blocked-up chimneys but no central heating, had sat vacant for eighteen months. "The living room and two of the bedrooms had coin-operated three-bar fires that were about as much use as lighting a candle," remembers John.

He tells me he got stuck in the lodge's heatless box room, Margaret begrudgingly shared a bed with Jane, and my cot went in with our parents.

"Do you remember flying through the French doors?" he smirks, clearly delighted. "There was blood everywhere."

"Strangely enough, I do." A long gulp of my pint slips me into the past.

I see my four-year-old self playing horses with Dad, skipping rope for reins, as we canter round the sparsely furnished front room laughing – until one end of the rope slips through my hands.

Thinking it's part of the game and that I'm a toy aeroplane flying through the air, I remember not wanting the sensation to end. Then my memory goes blank like our black and white television being turned off. The next thing I know is that I'm on the lawn, Jim's furrowed brow hunched over mine.

"I helped wrap you in a white sheet that was soaked in blood by the time Dad carried you out to the car. You were nearly brown bread, which would have saved everyone a lot of trouble." I might be imagining it, but John's smirk appears forced this time.

"You did say you're a social worker, right? As in taking care of people."

"That's me."

"God help us."

John reveals how Jim fed me onto the back seat, which is when, according to him, I really started to howl. "They were still picking bits of glass out your head for months afterwards," he relishes telling me.

"Know what the funniest thing of all was, though? Dad literally going hopping mad when his boss made him pay to get the car cleaned."

Stroking my chin, I reply, "I'll tell you what the funniest thing of all is. The number of easy lays I've had because of this scar on my chin. You wouldn't believe the stories I've made up about how I got it."

"And you're not a hack!"

As far as I can tell, during the five years we live in Flintbury Heath, John and Margaret – if not the best of friends – form an alliance against the rest of us, watching each other's backs as they pocket whatever they can.

Jane, it seems, acts as gofer and stool pigeon for any misdemeanours that can be passed on to her. When I'm old enough to run, I'm press-ganged into doing the same.

My older brother, or so he boasts, and sister spend weekends and school holidays in Paignton and Barlow's dyeing yards, flicking fag ends and gobbing greenies into giant vats of cobalt and magenta. When the thrill of breaking into the factory wanes after they can't get any of the machinery to work, they tumble bales of cotton into the canal instead.

One especially hot summer's day, all other means of entertainment exhausted, John and Margaret seek our mother's permission to take Jane and me "out to play."

"Do whatever you want as long as you keep out of my way, but make damn sure you're not late for tea."

A branch railway line runs from the loading bay to the town's main sidings, along which my sister and I lag behind our guardians. "Hurry up, slow coaches, or we'll tie you to the tracks and watch your heads get chopped off," John taunts, slicing a hand across his throat.

Even as a four-year-old, I know the goods yards are out of bounds and that the two older children have only been there once before, daunted by the lines of rails stretching towards a huge, darkened engine shed that casts a permanent shadow.

Hoisting me over a white wood and metal gate with a round red STOP sign in the middle, John tells me to "shut your snivelling gob, or I'll fill it."

"Put me down, you stinking piece of pooh, or I'm telling. We're not a–llow–ed in here. I'm fright–end and want to go home. PUT ME DOWN."

"What's that, you snotty little ape? You want me to let go of you? Okay, but don't blame me if you get hurt."

"What are you doing? Don't, or I'll *falllll*." My head hitting the ground sends a crow flapping from a nearby telephone wire. "You big fat pig dog. Look at my hands. They're bleeding. Wait till I tell Mum – and Dad when he gets home."

"He already is home, you idiot. It's Saturday. Now shut up and get going, or we'll leave you behind to get splattered." John lolls his tongue out the corner of his mouth.

Emboldened by the absence of immediate danger, Jane and I hop, skip, and jump from one sleeper to another, thrilled by the echoing *clanks* lobbing rocks into open-topped rolling stock.

"Come over here, Danny Boy. If I lift you up, you can climb the ladder like a big boy and see what's inside the truck."

Raising me by the waist, John guides my outstretched hands to the first rung. Recoiling at the cold metal, I shriek, "I'm not going up there. It's too high."

"Watch it, you little bleeder. You just kicked me in the knackers." Wriggling free, I run to Jane, who's making a daisy chain.

"Loony, throw that stupid thing away and come over here," Margaret orders. Side-by- side you wouldn't think they were sisters. Dad's tall, slim build is evident in Margaret, who, although not a beauty, possesses a confidence local lads like.

Nine-year-old Jane is shorter, rounder, closer to my mother's appearance, whose destiny appears to be superimposed on her daughter, drawing her breath, draining her vitality.

The two sisters – Jane's disposition fragile, Margaret's ironclad – do have something in common. Each wears a primary-coloured Alice band to distract attention from the lifeless hair stuck to their heads.

I watch as Jane hangs her daisy chain over some switching gear and saunters over to her older siblings.

"Now then, Loony," says John. "I'm going to lift you, and then you're going to climb the ladder to see what's inside the truck. And don't say you won't because you know what'll happen if you do."

Squinting in direct sunlight, Jane nods her compliance and reaches for the initial rung. "Alright, but I don't want to be late home for tea, and I *don't* want to get into any more trouble." I watch open-mouthed as my sister climbs, then doubles over the lip of the truck out of sight.

"Fuckin' Ada," Margaret blurts. "You've done it this time, Johnny. She's fallen in. *Jane*, are you alright?"

Rolling an old oil barrel across two sets of tracks, John upends it, grabs the ladder, and calls Jane's name as he peers in the truck. I can tell by the way he's moving his head that he can't see her.

"Are you in there, Jane?" I hear the sound of shifting coal and fear for my sister's life.

"Gordon Bennett. I can only see the whites of your eyes. Mother'll kill you when she sees the state of your new dress – and if she doesn't, I will. Look at the state of my new tee-shirt. You're a Loony; that's what you are."

"Loony, Loony, Loony." Margaret and I chorus, banging the truck's sides.

Later, Jane tells me how she thought disappearing into the wagon and pretending to be dead would make the rest of us miss her. When she saw John, she really wished she was dead, knowing he was only Beelzebub's deputy. The real devil was waiting for her at home in a Crimplene housecoat.

"Right, you're gonna stay in there till I say you can come out, which'll probably be never," John tells my sister before descending the ladder and kicking over the oil drum to prevent Jane's escape.

"I'm hungry," I whine, growing bored of throwing stones at a disused signal box. "We'll miss tea if we're not careful."

As Margaret shatters the last remaining window, she cheers and remembers her younger sister. "Hadn't we better let her out?"

"Isn't that where we left her?" I shout. "Over there, where the train's moving."

"Holy crap, Batman. Where are they taking her? We're in for it now, Mags."

"Not *we*, Johnny boy. *You*. I told you not to leave her up there."

"No, you didn't."

I try to keep up with my brother and sister as they pelt after the runaway locomotive curving twenty or thirty wagons round a bend. Jane's sitting on top of the last one, and I return her frantic gestures with a low wave. "Bye, Jane. Say hello to Jesus for me."

John swings me onto his back, and his lengthy stride carries us to the white metal gate, then gallops along Paignton and Barlow's deserted service roads. Gasping, he debriefs me as we go.

"Repeat back to me what happened like I told you."

I know my brother's life is in more danger than mine because not even Muriel can blame a four-year-old for abandoning their sister on top of a coal train.

Shielded behind the gatekeeper's hut opposite the house, we wait for Margaret, who's stopped to smoke a fag end she found on a windowsill. "Have you two got your story straight?" she coughs.

"Ask this pillock," John answers, shoulder barging me into the cabin.

"Jane in-shited we go and play where the trains are," I say, in my best grown-up voice.

"It's not inshited, you cretin. It's *insisted*. In-Sis-Ted. Oh, forget it. Just say Jane said we had to."

As we step off the pavement, Jim appears in the doorway wearing a battered gardening hat. Muriel's voice bellows along the carpetless hallway behind him.

"Go and find the blighters and tell them there's hell to pay. Tea's ruined – and take that stupid hat off," she barks, slamming the door.

I run across the road, wrap my arms round the top of Dad's legs, and howl a torrent of words into his trousers.

"*Whoa*, what's this? I can see Bonnie and Clyde over there, but where's Jane?"

"She's dead."

"WHAT?"

"John and Margaret made us go to where the trains are and made Jane climb on top of the coal lorry and drove off."

"Do you mean a lorry or a train? Where? In the goods yard? Who drove it off? WHERE'S JANE?"

"She's sitting on top of some coal in the railway truck. They've taken her away. *Will* she die? It wasn't my fault, honest. It was John and Margaret, but really John."

"Jesus Christ, those coal trucks go to Longlockton power station. All of you, in the car. NOW."

I'm allowed in the passenger seat as we drive along

the road parallel to the sidings, four faces scouring the industrial landscape on the other side of a wire fence.

"Nothing's moving. We'll go across to the main entrance." I notice Jim using the cigarette he hasn't finished to light another.

Parking in a lay-by, Dad walks towards the donkey-jacketed security guard waving him away. "You can't come in 'ere, mate. It's private property."

"Hello, yes, sorry. *Erm*, are any trains going in and out today? It's the youngest, you see, train mad he is."

"This 'ere's a goods yard, not a chuffin' trainspotters' convention," the dumpy man objects, scrutinising the car. "Anyhow, like I said, you can't come in."

Jim uses his left hand to block his view of Muriel standing in the house doorway and speeds the Triumph Herald's faded paintwork through Paignton and Barlow's gates.

Staring out the window, I debate whether Dad's loyalty should be to a wife who yells at him or his children. I settle on the latter because he brought us into the world without asking.

Watching him hunched over the Austin 1100's steering wheel, knuckles white, Jim doesn't need telling he'll be held responsible for one of his children going missing.

Seemingly emboldened by Muriel's enraged image, Jim pulls the car alongside the white wooden gate John toppled me over.

"Daniel, stay in the car. Margaret and John, come with me. It doesn't bear thinking about if Jane ends up at the power station."

Following them, a late ray of sunshine glints off the security guard's safety jacket, and I hear my father beg, "Please don't turn around."

"Over there," Margaret calls. "They're the trucks John made Jane climb into."

"Thanks, Sis." My brother's middle name should be Sarkie.

"If you're sure, Margaret, duck down, so we don't get seen."

Dad flinches, touching a stationery wagon's wheel. "This one's been moved. Quick, which one did you put her in?" I clap, thinking Jim's like John Wayne.

The truck's steel walls protect Jane from what lies ahead, and hearing her hum *Yellow Submarine*, I wonder if she really wants to get out as my father climbs the ladder.

I object to relinquishing the passenger seat to Jane, who resists Jim's attempts to wipe her face with a spat-on hankie. "All of you, think about what we're going to tell your mother. We've been gone two hours."

"I've got an idea, Dad."

Margaret leans into the gap between the front seats. "I'll give Jane a bath, then put her to bed. John, you go to your room, and when I'm done, so will I. Dad, you tell the old co... mum you couldn't find us because we were playing in the woods, but you've given us a good telling-off and sent us to bed without any tea. Wait. That's not right. I'm starving."

Jim checks the time. "Right, she'll be watching *Coronation Street*, so you lot go around the back and in through the French doors.

I watch Dad's shoulders rise as he takes a breath, grips the lounge's brass-effect doorknob, and then wipes the grease mark off with his sleeve.

"Muriel, love, are you there? Only me." I've scooted over the road to peek through the ajar lounge window.

"Don't you 'love' me," she hisses without turning from the television. "And be quiet."

As the Milk Tray ad music plays, Muriel detonates.

"Where the ruddy hell have you been?" Unable to withstand her fury, a hairpin releases a Land Girl curl. "Now, look what you've done."

Adjusting her hair gives Jim an opportunity to plug the building head of steam. "But love ... the children, they're alright."

"Beggar the blasted children. What about tea? It's ruined. I'll be jiggered if I'm making any more."

"How about I fetch us some fish and chips – from the one you like in town?" Seemingly pacified by the thought of a nice bit of rock salmon, Muriel concedes a few decibels. "You've been gone more than three hours."

"Not quite, love ..."

"Be quiet." Vera Duckworth is back in the Rovers Return, and real-life has to be suspended. I watch Jim's shoulders slump with relief before tightening again.

"Don't think you've heard the last of this," my mother snaps as an afterthought. "I don't believe a word."

For once, I imagine Jim's grateful to eat dinner in silence, worried he might be found out for handing four extra portions of chips through Margaret's bedroom window.

As an adult querying my life, can I blame Muriel for our cruelty to Jane? Probably not because children left to their own devices can be adult-like vicious. Then again, she encouraged us to be rivals rather than brothers and sisters.

CHAPTER 12

Margaret has clashed with authority for as long as I can remember, especially my mother's. My eldest sister has a natural aversion to discipline. Doing what she's told doesn't make sense. Or so I've noticed over the years.

She isn't dim because she's closer to the bottom of the class than the top; she just doesn't see the point. In time, I come to recognise a visceral intelligence making her closer in temperament to Muriel than she'd like.

The full force of my sister's personality comes to the fore as a 15-year-old when, as I race around the house, I'm entertained by the increasing intensity of mother and daughter rows.

Plus, she's the only one who sticks up for me.

"Why don't you leave Daniel alone? He's only four," she yells at Muriel while I nod in the background. "You're making all our lives hell, especially Dad's. None of us will speak to you again at this rate."

Muriel winces before resuming her armour-plated exterior. It reminds me of a cowboy pulling an Indian's arrow from his body.

"Don't you threaten me, young lady. Wait 'til you see what it's like when you're a mother." If she had told us, we might have understood.

Muriel and Margaret vie for family control until, aged sixteen, my sister makes her first bid for freedom. It comes shortly after Jim's change of job sees the family move from Flintbury Heath to Stoke Blakely.

John and I challenge our mother as far as we dare, but Margaret's in another league. Swearing and spitting, the two women are one-too-many cats in the same alley. The school career advisor's solution is for Margaret to bide her time with a secretarial job until she finds a husband, but the idea doesn't appeal to her.

Margaret sees her vocation as drinking in the Fisherman's Arms then swimming across the Trent's treacherous currents in front of an applauding gang who commandeer the pub for weekend booze-ups. I watch the Polish-born leader strip off and join my sister from the top of the rec's slide.

Bimbolyn is thought to be the bastard son of Mr Kowalski – who lives alone in a crumbling pile at the top of the village – and is said to carry a sawn-off shotgun in the lining of his sheepskin coat.

Whatever Bimbo's heritage, Margaret becomes acquainted with the back seat of his glacier blue Ford Anglia, the reputed setting for any number of unrecorded conceptions. But one August night, Margaret doesn't come home. Or the next.

"Perhaps we should think about calling the police, love? Report her missing in case she's run away," I overhear Jim suggest to Muriel.

"What the devil for? She'll be back soon as she realises which side her bread's buttered." My five-year-old self wills my sister to keep on running, wondering if my mother longs to do the same.

I watch the bags under Jim's eyes sag as his daily routine of finishing work, eating his tea, and then scouring local villages takes its toll. Muriel says he's wasting everyone's time.

On day four, sitting on a police station bench listening to Margaret being listed as a missing person, I've no idea what sort of 'game' my sister might be on when the sergeant suggests it.

While Jim combs the streets, Muriel stays at home 'in case the phone rings', which also ensures she doesn't miss an episode of *Corrie*, though Jack and Vera get interrupted when Jim bursts through the door one Friday evening.

It seems Margaret's best friend, Val, tells Jim she's seen someone in town who thinks Bimbo lives on the fifth floor of a Hyson Green tower block that even I know is on the wrong side of Nottingham's tracks.

Margaret later relates to Jane, who relays it to me, how Jim climbed eleven flights of stairs before a near skeletal girl of indeterminate age responds to his inquiries. Years later, piecing together snippets of information enables me to paint a picture.

✖

"Hello. Is your mummy in?" Jim inquires. Continuing to stare, the girl purses her lips. "I'm looking for my daughter, Margaret. Have you seen her? Please, I've searched everywhere."

"Lydka, come inside. There's a good girl."

"Excuse me, Lydka." Jim pushes past and feels his way down a narrow hallway towards the voice escaping from under a door at the far end, which he flings open.

Body warmth, lingering cigarette smoke, and council-controlled central heating disorientate Jim as he enters a bedroom. The click of a bedside lamp and guttural snarl shock him back to reality.

"Be fuckin' off, old man? Get out house before breaks fuckin' legs," a lean though muscular older lad threatens, raising his naked torso from under a sheet. A pair of Y-fronts lies next to a mattress on a stained cord carpet.

"Bimbo, wait. Don't hurt him. It's my dad. He won't leave without me, no matter what you do. I can't stay here. It stinks."

That night, I listen to my parents' raised voices through the bedroom ceiling. It's obvious, even to a five-year-old, that something serious has happened, but no matter how many doors I put my ear to, I can't discover what.

Margaret quits the village to work as an au pair in north London less than a year later, and to everyone's surprise, including her own, she thrives. Although pleased for my sister, I'm aware there's now one less line of defence between me and Muriel.

My eldest sister tires of the capital's anonymity after eighteen months. Preferring to be noticed, she dyes her hair lilac and returns to Nottingham, where she shacks up with Lenny Shaw after a two-day binge in Yates Wine Lodge. A panel beater, he's got his own flat in Clifton, a defeated council estate on the edge of town.

Soon after, aged eighteen, Margaret gives birth to Katie, which is when history repeats itself, and her problems really start.

CHAPTER 13

A fifty-year-old man, I'm snapped back to the present by stepping on a small frosted branch not far from the old family home. My spaniel, Ben, knows that the fields and woods lie ahead. His look tells me to hurry up, but a hawthorn bush reminds me of where I first found disappointment in success.

Heading home down the unmade lane after an unsuccessful hunting trip with my catapult, I spot the white rump of a bullfinch.

Even now, I haven't a clue what possesses me to reach for the weapon tucked into the waistband of my shorts. To satisfy a hunter's ego, exert an influence I don't have elsewhere, or because I'm evil, all cross my mind.

I watch, motionless, as the bird settles on a twig twenty feet away, an impossible distance for my homemade device. Yet, conflicted by the elation of a prize-winning shot and the inevitability of failure, I sight its pink breast, pull back the inner tube, and let fly. *Thwack*.

In the instant between the conker-sized stone striking the creature's plumage and the force of nature deciding its fate, I beg for divine intervention.

"Please let it live, God. I promise I'll be good and pray every night before bed. *And* I won't steal anymore and do as I'm told."

God's thumb hovers as I wait to see if he'll be my, and a little bird's, saviour or condemn it to death and me to hell. I've never felt as naked as I do this spring afternoon when God's thumb points downwards.

Running to the house, I empty my football badges out of their shoebox and refill it with Muriel's cotton wool, the bird's final resting place already damp with my tears.

I return to the bird's motionless body, hoping that God has performed a miracle as he did for his own son. Instead, a single drop of blood is congealing on its beak, its warmth almost gone.

My eyes are now swollen with shame as I lay the creature down, seal its tomb with the cardboard lid, and lower it into a shallow grave.

I mark the spot where innocence is lost, soft tissue turned to bone, with a Remembrance Day poppy.

The child who kills the thing it supposedly loves, am I an abomination or doing unto others what's been done unto me? Try as I might, I know it is the former.

*

I've met God on several occasions. Each time, whether by coincidence or not, I'm at death's door.

My relationship with the big man is particularly difficult because I don't believe He exists. His invention deserves to be crucified, but I'm confounded by the fact I've been in His presence, saved when I should have been taken.

I first cross paths with Him during a Friday evening visit to see Grandad Connah. My parents insist our weekly trudge is to pay Grandad our respects, though, I suspect it's an insurance policy to safeguard they're taken care of in the old man's will.

Alfred Thomas Connah lives in a creepy Victorian Gothic house with his church-mouse wife, Mavis, and their backward daughter, Ethel, who runs down the drive to gather me into a tremulous ocean of breast with her arthritis-withered arms.

Seated on peach-coloured balloon-backed chairs in the sepulchral front room, we pay silent homage to the tick … tock … tick … tock of Grandad's long-cased clock.

It's 1972, and the only light emanates from an ornate glass paraffin lamp.

I sit still until my mouth fixes into a permanent yawn. "Can I go and see if the vegetables have grown, please, Grandad?" He nods. My mother scowls.

At the bottom of the long, narrow garden is a former brick factory from where a laced leather boot with its owner's foot still inside had purportedly landed in the strawberry patch. Grandad Connah was the Chief Engineer who had certified the exploding kiln in full working order two days earlier.

After checking the strawberries for human remains, I clamber over the back garden fence and slip into the vast acreage of spent sand quarries. It's in my DNA to do what I shouldn't, and bored of scrambling along the lower slopes, I climb one of the steeper excavations.

Reaching the point of no return two-thirds of the way up, I freeze, paralysed with knee-trembling fear. I've avoided looking down until now. It's not a good idea given I'm spread-eagled above a thirty-foot drop with a row of spiked railings at the bottom.

With my ten-year-old body shaped in a cross, tightening my hold on the vegetation holding me in place causes the grasses and weeds to come away in my hand, tiny avalanches of grit cascading over the edge.

Legs wobbling, I try to cry for help, but a strangulated moan is all I can manage. Afraid of losing what little purchase I have, the tremor in my left leg becomes a shake, and I begin to slide, bleeding fingernails digging into the dirt as my descent gathers pace. I accept I deserve to die, though I'd prefer something quicker.

It feels like something's leaving my body, and I close my eyes. Will death hurt? Will I be a skeleton before I'm found, flesh and eyeballs pecked at by crows? And then God turns up. No amateur dramatics, just a light touch, a soft applying of brakes, the Lord's presence in no more doubt than my own.

Opening my eyes, I've been conveyed to within a few yards of level ground. It'll take a leap of faith to get me there, but relinquishing what little grasp I have, I scramble up tumbling pebbles. Defying gravity, I make miraculous progress, collapsing a few seconds later, safe, bloodied, but sound.

As I don't have a mother taking care of me, I decide the question of God's existence is best left open.

CHAPTER 14

A few cosmetic changes aside, Stoke Blakely's scenery remains the same. A river flows over the same rocks between banks of ancient earth. Only the people seem smaller.

I ponder what became of Penny and Little Joe, who I falsely accused of doing a pooh on a wall knowing he'd sat on a crab apple. Their only significance to me now is that their images are fading. Then again, at most, they only ever provided a brief connection, reluctant partners in a three-legged race or a canteen chum to sit next to; one lunchtime only.

It's hard to understand how my five-year-old classmates knew to steer away from me. I can appreciate an adult learning from experience, but an infant! Did my fox-like smell repel them?

I've spent forty years trying to forget Joe, Gail, and Jeremy. Their effigies loiter in my conscience, haunting and wailing, but now they're on the wane just when I want to recall them; be a better friend, beg their forgiveness for my unforgivable crime of being.

Clapping my gloved hands against the cold, at least I've cleared my account with Wendy Davies, the post office assistant I stole from. I even tried with Callum, the cerebral palsy boy I mimicked.

The lane I'm walking along will take me to 17 Crow Park Crescent, the family home I grew up in. Its tentacles are pulling me towards it, though I'm uncertain what, or who, is there to greet me.

A rustling in the undergrowth startles me as a blackbird takes flight, sounding its alarm.

Looking left, I see the doorway in the now ivy-clad brick wall that Steve Sharpe escaped through with my Etch A Sketch. The other side of the wall, in the grounds of Colworth Hall, is where I had one of my few successes, and I smile at the memory.

The origin of my status as 'best fighter in the infants' is a scrap with Plop, so-called because his dad secures a job at Stoke Blakely's sewage farm. Despite the treatment works being on the outskirts of the village, an east wind blows the stench into the houses where, like an unwelcome guest, it lingers.

Mr Plop's job as 'Head Shit Stirrer', as we liked to call it, comes with a worker's cottage, making the family's social elevation from pit village to Blakely almost identical to my own. A fact I keep quiet.

Plop is two years older than me and considered so hard and filthy that no one dares laugh at him for taking tomato sauce sandwiches on school trips. He's astute enough, however, not to take my affected swagger at face value and calls my bluff by announcing there is going to be an after-school scrap.

On hearing the fight news, I realise my glory days are numbered. Total humiliation, and a bloody nose, are the best I can hope for.

Trudging between the baying lines – 'fight, fight, fight, fight' – I see my new life mapped out ahead of me. My only friend has jumped ship and is holding Plop's blazer while my nemesis entertains the crowd with an impressive display of bare-chested shuffles. As I enter the fray, the bloodthirsty crowd parts, then reforms around us.

I'm hesitant to put my triumph down to another act of God because, as far as I can tell, it's my own fists that fell my opponent before a teacher arrives. In any event, the next day, Plop and I are bent over Headmaster Dobbs's knee, plimsoll stripes on bare backsides, but as we hobble on the playing fields, only one of our names is chanted. 'DAN-NY. DAN-NY. DAN-NY. Best fighter. In the in-fants.'

Is conflict, the monkey on my back that's plagued me all my life, homegrown, I wonder? Whether it is or not, I'm about to encounter it again.

I check my Omega, then click my fingers as Ben raises his head from a nearby verge and trots over.

"Strange to think you weren't even born when all this was going on," I say, noticing his temples are greying like my own.

Would I be a better person if I'd had children instead of a dog? It's a decision I've made partly out of selfishness and the worry of whether someone who's never felt loved can love. Some risks are worth taking. But for me, not that one.

✸

My 'best fighter in the infants' chest doesn't stay inflated for long when I move from the relative safety of Stoke Blakely to the BIG school on the outskirts of Shidderdale, a declined mining town several miles away. It isn't going to be easy for any of the village children, but I have more to fear than most.

Unaffectionately known as Gulag 13, the BIG school menaces over sooty terraces like the Dickensian workhouse it once was as my classmates and I file through the doors of the new comprehensive system; middle-class innocents shuffling alongside working-class resentment and apathy.

Copying the indifferent expressions on pasty Shidderdale faces, I make it through the disinfectant-smelling hallways to my first Religious Education class. So far, so bad, I've endured nothing more than a jeered 'queer', and as the remark seems to be directed at my new satchel, I shove it behind a radiator.

Keeping to one side of the high-ceilinged corridors, I walk from one lesson to the next, eyes fixed on the floor, copping shoulder barges from long-haired scruffs in untucked shirts and short-tailed ties, though no more than anyone else.

The day crawls through a blur of chaotic stairs, timetables, registers, and somnolent teachers until the bell rings at 3.45 p.m. All I've got to do now is make it to the bus stop.

At the top of the steps, two shiny green bomber jackets are checking the working-class credentials, and pockets, of each boy wanting to go home. A third, slightly shorter though broader, youth leans against a lamppost, smoking a Capstan held between thumb and forefinger.

"Not me, honest," comes every cringing reply.

"Well, when yus see 'im tell 'im 'e's dead. Best bleedin' fight-er in tha shi' 'ole Blakely my arse issie. An' bring us more munee temorra, or you'll git yer teef smashed in? Nah, bog off."

Retreating will single me out, but I don't know any other way to go. Lumbering forwards, I feel the eyes of every Stoke Blakely kid urging me to give myself up. Is the respect I earned for defeating Plop so short-lived that I'm about to be sacrificed? Where's God when you need him?

Slouching off the lamppost, Mark 'Cliffy' Sutcliffe moseys his way along the line, flips his fag end into the throng, and snarls, "Ayup Connah, nice to meet ya."

I fold like a hinge as the first stomach punch comes in. Pretending to be more hurt than I am, I force tears in a bid for thuggish sympathy, but when you're raised on violence, real pain has its own smell.

"*Aw,* look. Posh un's startin' tah cry like a fuckin' faggot. Less gi 'im summat ta rellie cry abaht shall us?" My face is at the perfect height to take the rock-sized fist powering towards it, and I close my eyes.

The eleven-year-old's after-school job lumping carcasses around the abattoir supplements the family's income, and Cliffy's muscles, as does his two older brothers' car ringing scheme, until they're caught selling a stolen BMW to an undercover cop. Or so playground gossip has it.

Cliffy has one known rival. Yeti.

So-called because of his dark whiskered face and long, knuckle-dragging arms, Yeti rests at the top of the school food chain. Even grown men think twice about taking him on, and teachers let him sit at the back of the class with his legs on the desk, ogling *Razzle* and *Mayfair*.

The only potential threat to Yeti's dominance is Cliffy. There's bad blood between them, though neither knows the details of their family's feud, just that they're obliged to carry it on. Who would win the fight to end all fights is the source of endless debate in local schools.

Until the two alpha males definitively settle who rules the roost, Cliffy feels compelled to see off any upstarts such as me, and I can now smell fresh biro ink – he used a compass to tattoo **HATE** between his finger joints during the last lesson – pummelling towards my face.

But the blood-spurting nose I'm expecting doesn't materialise. Instead, I find myself bundled into a semi-circular wall of coats and bags at the feet of yet another chanting mob. "Yet-i. Yet-i. Yet-i."

Angered by the delay in exiting school grounds, along with him not having given permission for anyone to be beaten up, especially by Cliffy, the simian-like Yeti has put his own fist into the side of his rival's head, knocking him and me, sideways.

Barging backwards and forwards, with a flurry of fists and kicks, Cliffy is finally toppled by a jaw-breaking uppercut, a crumpled figure groaning on the ground who Yeti stands over, contemplating whether to finish him off.

I race over to Yeti, extending my hand, which he scoffs at as he walks away, though he does offer me some protection during my twelve-month incarceration in Gulag 13. Having inadvertently found a way to survive, it seems my charmed existence is set to continue.

Where does my good fortune originate, I wonder? Does God or an unknown force acknowledge that having a cold-hearted mother deserves compensation, a positive to counterbalance a negative, a yin to yang? If so, they're wasting their time because the opportunity to fight another day isn't what I need.

CHAPTER 15

I still admire Yeti's, whose real name I never knew, animalistic nature, his exact science of right and wrong, and his ability to defend it.

Why I'm attracted to working-class physicality, I've no idea. Maybe the wrong parents brought me home from the hospital, and I belong on a council estate known to the police; Yeti and Cliffy for neighbours.

It'd be easy to blame Sarah Jenkins, my one-time girlfriend, for leading me into petty criminality, but it's not true.

The defining moment of my shoplifting career is 21 May 1977, FA Cup final day, Case versus Greenhoff, and I've arranged to meet Sarah in the musty upper tiers of Nottingham Ice Rink at 9.30 a.m.

Edging towards me along a row of tip-up seats, ponytail tossing from side to side, she's obviously pleased to see me.

Wearing a glitter mist skirt over a halter-neck leotard stretched over developing breasts, dirty cream skates slung over her shoulder, Sarah looks every inch the cock-teasing thirteen-year-old she is.

I see her out the corner of my eye, though pretend I haven't. Moody and seemingly unimpressed, I maintain a bored faraway stare until she stands on my trainers that I sponged white polish on an hour ago. "*Ow*. Get off. You'll mess my Gola's."

"Serves yer rite fer being soh mardy." Hands on hips, she thrusts her crotch towards my face struggling to suppress a sharp-toothed grin while swinging a carrier bag over my head.

"Wa d'ya reckon's in 'ere, Sulky Pants?" Getting no response, she sticks her tongue out. "Cum on diddums, guess? Ah bin doin' birra shoppin'."

"It's a Tesco carrier bag. You said 9.30. You're ten minutes late."

"Yeah, burrits wurf it. Go on. Bet yer can't guess." Breaking free of her tight-lipped restraint, Sarah reveals a downy snow-white neck when she throws her head back.

I shrug, refusing to play the game I desperately want to join. "What is it?" I reply, scrutinising the bag, which is when the penny drops. "*No way*, not before lessons?"

"Yep. No point 'angin' 'bout. D'ya wanna see warra goh yer or not? Gorra gissa kiss furst."

Most of the things Sarah's pinched are useless. I don't like peppermint creams, special edition eight-inch bottles of Brut, or Batchelors Cup-A-Soup. The Swiss Army knife's alright, though it doesn't have the spike for getting stones out of horses' hooves.

"Wos marra?" Sarah senses my disappointment. "D'ya not like any onnit? Soup's reelly nice. 'Ave it all time at 'ome."

"My mum makes her own," I lie. "Didn't they have an army knife with the horses' hooves blade in it?"

"Ya basturd," she spits, face contorted. "Ya fuckin' stuk-up basturd. Wa d'ya ever geh me? Nowt, tha's woh."

Sarah's ferocity is so exhilarating that I need to compose myself before softening my tone. "I was only asking. Look, the scissors are brill. Ross'll be dead jealous." Her sniffle says I've gone too far. "Don't cry, Sarah."

"Noh fuckin' cryin'," Defiant, she wipes her purple-shadowed eyes and snarls, "Wudn't cry ooer basturd like you."

I pull the knife's blades in and out.

"D'ya reely like it? Gorrit special."

"Yeah, honest I do, but I've got to go and meet Gaz and Rossie now. You could come, but girls aren't really allowed."

"Yus said we wus gonna 'ave mushy peas in Vic Centre market. Pinched-a-pahnd aght me mam's pus pay fer 'em, an' all."

"I know, but I forgot football's on. United v Liverpool in the final. You don't mind, do you?"

"Ya fuckin' cunt," Sarah objects, hammering a skate into the wooden seat in front, an act of pure vandalism I wish I had the courage to do.

"Jus cuz yer rich an' got big haus fink can do wha likes. 'kin' 'ate ya an' 'ope ya die in car crash wiv yer slaggy mam an' wazzie dad."

Yanking loose the embedded skate, Sarah uses its serrated edge to slash the chair's fuchsia-coloured velour, cutting her hand in the process.

Spotting another young couple five rows down who've turned to see what's happening, Sarah pulls back her arm. "Fuck you lookin' a.'"

I put my arm across Sarah's chest even though part of me wants to see the leather boot fly through the air, so she hurls lumps of foul-smelling wadding at the departing pair instead.

Leaping the stairs to the sound of Sarah's cackle, I make my way along Stoney Street, wondering if I love her.

Even aged thirteen, I know 'common as muck' Sarah isn't great for my prospects. She'd drag me down, and we'd end up living on Top Valley estate, drinking Shippos and smoking rollies, pork scratchings for the kids.

I'm barely middle class myself, fully aware the other Stoke Blakely children have a confidence, a self-assuredness I don't possess.

All the same, the Jenkinses and Connahs are unlikely to meet. Sarah has chips every night, me once a week. Our parents would have plenty to talk about if they did get together. I've shagged Mr Jenkins' thirteen-year-old daughter, or rather she shagged me, and Sarah's taught my mother words she barely knew existed.

I admire Sarah's strength, as opposed to my weakness, in dealing with lives neither of us chose, though we both seek the same thing. Do I love her? As far as I can tell, yes.

CHAPTER 16

I continue to debate my feelings for Sarah as I stroll into town to meet Ross and Gaz. She might be lower class, but she's more honest than I am. She doesn't go around pretending to be someone else, trying to impress people, showing respect where none's due.

The people around me confound me, none of whom seem to belong in my life. Sarah, meanwhile, who speaks and behaves according to her nature, belongs in her own skin.

Things are clear in the Jenkins household. Everyone knows who they are, where they're from, and where they'll stay. No unrealised ambitions or la-de-da airs. Sarah's dad brews his own beer and smokes knock-off fags, though it'd be better if he wasn't such a scumbag.

I couldn't live on a desert island with Caroline Curtis, my first schoolgirl crush. Too pretty, too oblivious compared to Sarah's wild, savage nature, we'd have nothing to argue about.

Sarah and I are an unnatural phenomenon beyond laws and convention; my guile, her brawn. Daniel4Sarah4ever, or until we're brought down in a hail of gunfire. Best of all, she loves me with an unconditional, unbridled passion, unconcerned if my heart's yellow or black. She's everything I'm unused to at home.

If we're apart, I twist into a knot, strangulated by the thought of her being with someone else, male or female. Her attention and obedience are beyond my control; my breath not my own until we're together again – and I can ignore her.

I'll never tell Sarah I love her. I don't know how.

I hurry through the Lace Market, whose own industrial heart stopped beating long ago, its red-bricked warehouses and factories decaying from the inside out, along with the junkies they now shelter.

Cutting through Hockley and glancing sideways at the sex shop, I increase the pace along Victoria Street.

Across Market Square, I see Ross and Gary playing Kingie on the concrete lions guarding the colonnaded Council House, a building as neoclassical as the 1920s could make it.

Gary's pulling Ross's leg in a bid to dislodge him from a giant bronze saddle, a fight I'm eager to join, though worry I won't win.

"Ayup youfs, what's up?" I ask, unconvinced by my working-class patois.

"Me, mainly," Ross declares. "This tosspot couldn't get a fly off a witch's tit."

"That makes two tits and a lion then." Delighted with my riposte, I don't leave room for a comeback by adding, "I'm watching the FA Cup final on Jeremy's colour tele, so why don't you two retards get down and get going. I want to get Sarah something."

"Thought you were dumping her cos she's too common," Ross replies.

"Prob'ly will, but she lets me do things that'll never happen to you cos you're a poof."

"Oh yeah, like what?"

"That's for me to know and you to find out." He pulls a mong face and asks Gaz what record he's getting.

"*Smokie's Greatest Hits*. It's just come out, and I'm using my gran's birthday money."

"See. He's the poof, not me," Ross interjects, breaking into song. "*Ooooooo*, living next door to Alice."

Waving his arms and swaying, he warbles on. "Twenty-four years just waiting for a chance to get a second glance of Aliccce's fanny, la, la, la, la, fanny." Heartened by the disgusted scowls of passing shoppers, Ross raises his voice and guffaws: "*Oooooo*, of Aliccce's hairy fanny."

"It doesn't go anything like that," grumbles Gary, making a grab for the taller boy's leg. "Anyway, I like it, and so does my gran, so there."

"*Ohhh*, so does my gran, so there," mimics Ross. "There's only one piece of vinyl missing from my collection, and that's ace kings of rock, Led Zep."

"Dan, what you getting? The Gay City Rollers? Bye-bye Sarah, Sarah bye-bye, you slaaag."

"Don't call her that. I've only got enough dough for a single, probably 10cc, but I've got an idea."

×

Nicking a packet of chewing gum from the Clock Tower newsagents is child's play, and Ross and I elbow each other in the ribs as we run up the Vic Centre's down escalator. "That was so piss-pie easy, Dan. Look, I got two packs."

Gary, who was using the adjacent stairs, objects. "We've proved we can do it, so let's quit while we're ahead. I'm starving."

"No way, José," cuts in Ross. "We're the *three* musketeers, so no more lookout duties for you, Gazzer."

In the next hour and a quarter, we work fourteen shops between the Victoria Centre and Broadmarsh, some twice, accumulating two Famous Five books, several tubs of Play-Doh, and a telescopic umbrella, among other things.

Mid-spree, I contemplate if Muriel, Sarah, or nature account for my need for more, a magpie whose nest is never full. All I know is that once I'm on the slide, it's hard to get off.

I've heard TV psychologists say I want to be caught, to be punished, or that pilfering empowers me, gives me a voice, but in my teenage mind, it's the thrill of going from nobody to somebody with titanium balls; poor man to rich man if only with a carton of Play-Doh.

Woolworths is intended to be our last stop, and laughing as we push each other in front of passers-by, we lean open the double doors. "I still haven't got my 10cc record yet," I grin.

"Bet you wouldn't buy it if you knew why they're called that," says Ross, jumping in front and pretending to masturbate. "It's the amount of spunk a man blows."

"That's disgusting, but I'm not planning on paying for it. Come on. My bus goes in fifteen minutes."

Sunlight reflects off the chrome-framed glass as we enter the gaudy domain of Barbie Dolls trapped behind cellophane wrappers, pick 'n' mix shrimp, nylon nighties, and knitting patterns.

The three of us split up. I bag my 45rpm and a box of Plasticine but arriving in perfume to get Sarah's present, Ross and Gary motion me towards an internal side door. I nod and make a careless grab for a bottle of Charlie. Even without looking, I know I've been caught.

I watch the blood drain, cartoon-like, from Ross and Gary's faces when they see the store detective behind me. Unwilling to be captured alone, I head towards them.

As a walkie-talkie closes in, I'm unsure whether to go quietly and accept that life as I know it is over or make a last-ditch bid for freedom. Coming alongside Ross, we release our bags, trainers screeching on linoleum as we take off. Gary's remained rooted to the spot.

Albeit one man down, we emerge onto Listergate, where I swear to resurrect myself as a wholesome, law-abiding citizen. Change has been a slow train coming, but it's just around the corner from WH Smith.

"*Oi*, you two, come 'ere," commands a gangly man with a walkie-talkie. Everyday life pauses as I await what happens next. Will God rescue me again, give me another second chance?

"Tango Oscar, over. Last suspects apprehended outside Burton, over. Rendezvous with suspect one in security room. Over and out."

Standing before two titans of authority, I wish I hadn't rebelled against adulthood, including my mother. I've lost the battle I was never going to win and should accept my fate like a man.

"I'm Chief Security Officer Bates, and this 'ere's Mr Downs, the manager," Ross and I are informed before being led away.

The security room's a netherworld of flickering screens displaying grainy images of ongoing Woolworths life monitored by a man in an unwashed shirt; rolls of fat hanging over shiny nylon trousers.

"We've got to get out of here before they call the police," I whisper to my two friends between Gary's sobs.

"When they come back, we'll say we're sorry, won't do it again, and will pay for the things we took, plus a bit more if they don't tell our parents."

Three boys with firing-squad stares turn towards the door as Mr Downs removes a handkerchief from his breast pocket, blows his nose, and says, "The police will take things from here. You'll most likely be arrested."

Chapter 17

"**W**e could blame Sarah. Say she showed us how to do it and was going to sell the stuff to her dad's friends – but wasn't going to give us any money," I suggest to Ross across a desk in a windowless room. Gary, whose dad's a judge or something, is being dealt with separately.

"But then she'd get in trouble, and she's your girlfriend. To say nothing about her dad knocking nine bells of shit out of her. Jesus, Dan. Don't you have any morals?"

"Morals won't stop us going to prison, will they?"

The door bursts open, and Nottingham Central's desk sergeant pokes his head in. "Having a nice little chat, are we? You, Sunny Jim, let's see if we can knock some sense into you."

I consider denying having stolen anything, that it was the others but confronted with two dozen exhibits in a Boots carrier bag, I realise it's pointless. Giving a false name and address might work, though.

A cheer goes up along the corridor. 'Glory, glory Man United'. The game's kicked off.

Dabbing the end of a pencil on his tongue, the six-foot-five sergeant enters my list of crimes in a cloth-covered book.

"Right, tie your shoelace. You're going for a stroll."

I'm escorted to every shop I've stolen from, staring at my feet as each item is accounted for and placed in a clear plastic evidence bag. I cope by telling myself I'm an undercover Flying Squad officer.

Alone in the interview room an hour and a half later, the lock turns. And Muriel walks in. Laser-like eyes locked on a specific point on the far wall. Jim offers me an almost sympathetic glance.

Desk Sergeant Hamilton invites my parents to sit down and, in a deep and deliberate voice, explains what I've been up to. With my feet wrapped round the metal chair legs, head bowed, I feel as ashamed as I look.

"Just you wait till I get you home, my lad," Muriel glowers. "You won't know what's hit you."

"Be that as it may, Mrs Connah, I need to inform you what happens next. Once we've verified all the facts, we'll then decide what, if any, action will be taken."

"Do you mean there's a chance he might get off?" Jim enthuses. "Hear that, love? I told you it might not be as bad as all that."

"Be quiet! He belongs behind bars, and I, for one,

won't object if they put him there. No son of yours will ever amount to anything."

Sgt. Hamilton steps in to mediate. "I'm not saying he'll *get off* exactly, but it's unlikely to go to court because of Daniel's age and it being his first offence."

"I very much doubt that," huffs Muriel.

The officer goes on. "Once the case has been reviewed by a social worker and the Assistant Chief Constable, it's possible Daniel will receive a caution rather than be charged. In a week or two, we'll send an officer round to … let's see now … 7 Crow Park Crescent, Stoke Blakely."

"Number *17* Crow Park Crescent," Jim corrects.

"*Um*. We'll put that down to my fingers' and thumbs' typing, shall we." Sgt. Hamilton holds up an enormous hand which is the catalyst for Muriel to swivel her head like a tank turret. Eyes narrowed, lips pursed, hairpins straining.

"But Mum, I…"

"After all we've done for you, my lad. All those Christmas presents, and still, you lie, even to the police."

Clearing his throat while getting up, the sergeant concludes: "Anyway, as I said, we'll send an officer around in a week or so to inform you of our decision."

"Did you say *social worker*?" Muriel's mouth remains open. "We'll be the only family in the village whose son has a social worker."

"The social worker isn't just for Daniel, Mrs Connah. They can inquire into all aspects of family life."

"Are you suggesting this is *my* fault? That I'm a bad mother?"

"That's not my job, Mrs Connah. If you'll excuse me, you're free to go."

The car's silence seems to extend outside, and I watch town centre jewellers become shattered fag machines on boarded-up pubs; second-hand car dealers standing on potholed lots.

"It's not Dad's fault, Mum. It's mine."

"How could you, Daniel? Haven't we given you everything you ever wanted?" The answer's no, but it's the first time I've seen sorrow spread across as much of my mother's face as I can see, tone deflated.

As Jim grinds through the Cortina's gears, eyes fixed on the road, I push my face against a rear window and think about jumping off Vic Centre flats.

"I'll do what Ross says and get some morals, Mum. I'll stop seeing Sarah and might become a priest." Muriel's silence suggests she sees me, as I do, on the road to redemption.

"A good hiding is what you'll get. What was it the sergeant said about sending a police car to the house?"

"He said he'd let us know if I was going to get told off or not. Now I've made lots of promises, can I go to Jeremy's to watch the FA Cup final?"

"It'll be nearly finished, son," Jim answers. "One nil to United last I heard. Pearson scored a corker."

"Will you shut up about blasted football! You don't have the faintest idea what this is doing to me, do you?"

Sensing what's coming, Jim braces himself.

"If you'd been a proper father, *he* might have learned some discipline. How was I supposed to manage with four kids to look after? It's no wonder they're wild."

The whole car seems to tremble in anticipation of an eruption.

"Hell's bells, what have I done to deserve you two?" She pauses, then adds, "What's wrong with you, Daniel?"

"I don't know, Mum. I think you might have taken the wrong baby home from the hospital."

"You'll wish you'd never been born at all by the time I'm finished with you."

Diverting her aim back to Jim, Muriel's voice ups an octave. "And you tell me what they'll think when a police car comes to the door?"

Jim turns a blank face to his wife and, from the back seat, my parents look like two heads on opposing coins. With my pity draining from one and rising in the other, I want to stop time, certain I know what's coming next.

"I'll *tell* you what they'll think."

"Who's that, love?"

"The blinking neighbours, that's who. They'll think our son's a thief and I'm a bad mother. It'll be round the village in no time. We'll have to move."

I smile with the relief of a condemned man whose noose has been lifted. Knowing that my mother cares more about the neighbours than me, my self-esteem takes another knock, but I'm free of all childish pledges. Guilt assuaged, I can do as I please.

"Get up those stairs. And don't think you're having any tea," Muriel scolds, shoving me through number 17's front door. Glancing sideways, the hall clock tells me there are still twenty minutes before the match ends.

A knock on my bedroom door is followed by Jim's face sterner than I've ever seen, hand on his belt buckle. I'm used to Muriel's flesh-smarting leg slaps, but Dad has never touched me, which is both a blessing and a problem.

Straightening himself, I realise where I get my height from, as well as my fear when I notice his hand tremor undoing his black leather belt.

"Your mother says I'm to give you six of the best. Taking things which don't belong to you is wrong, Daniel. Didn't we teach you that much, at least?"

I'm inclined to say they didn't, but when my father appears more of a schoolboy than me and a love I didn't know existed swells in my chest, I don't.

"Why did you do it, son? Is it something *I've* done? Are you unhappy at school?"

My breathing increases to a fit-like shake as I stutter the contents of my eyes and nose into Jim's face when he kneels. "It's n … n … not you, Dad. It's me. There's a devil inside me I can't get out."

A kitchen cupboard slamming downstairs reminds Jim why he's here.

"Well, you're going to have to try harder. Your mother's sick with worry. I've spoken to the sergeant who's not going to send a police car, but you'll get a kind of criminal record, and if you do it again, you might go to borstal. Do you understand?"

"Yes, Dad. I won't do it again, I promise. And I'll try ever so hard at school and stop thinking dirty things."

My euphoria and newly found devotion for my father dissolve into betrayal when he wrenches his belt clear of his waist with his unsteady right hand. "Bend over."

"I think you've learned your lesson, but your mother won't be satisfied until I've given you the strap, so here's what we're going to do. Each time I whack the desk, you cry out as loud as you can. After six, I'll close the door, and you keep crying for a few minutes before getting into bed. But you must stay in your room. Okay?"

"Okay. Thanks, Dad."

WHACK. WHACK. WHACK.

OW. OW. OW.

I count to three hundred, put my pillow under the blankets and climb out my bedroom window. Gripping the ledge of the flat dormer roof, I sidle along the sill past my parents' room, lower myself onto my bum, and inch down the gritty, sharply sloped tiles.

Landing with a louder-than-expected thud on the adjoining outhouse, I hold my breath when the kitchen door opens, my face on the verge of turning blue as I watch Muriel's hands shake the tablecloth. Crumbs for the birds, if not her children.

Easing my thirteen-year-old body around the cast iron drainpipe, I step back, each foot finding a fixing, then jump, dart across the flower beds, leap the hedge, and duck below a row of parked cars to Jeremy's house.

"Who's winning?" I shout, pushing aside my friend's little sister blocking the doorway with outstretched arms. "United, two one. Two goals in five minutes. You've missed it."

CHAPTER 18

"Treat a dog badly, get a bad dog, is what I say, Ben. If they'd told me they loved me, I might have turned out better. Honest, even." My spaniel, who looks like he's heard it all before, lies down, ears flat.

I became an investigative journalist to right wrongs, which is confusing when I commit so many myself. Sometimes being a born hypocrite is hard to live with.

Journalism wasn't my first career choice. Firefighting was. At eight years old, my ambition to be a fireman was sparked returning home from the shops with my parents one Saturday morning.

At the bottom of Carlton Hill, a twenty-foot curl of smoke rolls over the car, dimming the interior that's suddenly illuminated by a flashing blue light highlighting an apocalyptic cloud that sends Jim swerving onto the pavement.

I nearly wet myself with excitement, and I'm halfway to the thirty-foot flames before Jim applies the handbrake. The former Fothergill and Pemberton lace factory is glowing like a Victorian Christmas card.

"Fire, fire, look at the fire! I'm going to be a fireman," I scream, arms pumping, the Six Million Dollar Man. My first job, to rescue any damsels in distress, is halted by a plastic tape strung between two lampposts. Muriel would've preferred it was her shouts that stopped me.

"Daniel, come here, you stupid boy. It's dangerous." Watching the shiny oxygen tanks go by, I want to help so badly it hurts.

"Daniel. If I have to tell you once more, there'll be trouble." Muriel grabs my arm. I'm positive she's more concerned about depriving me of an adventure rather than for my welfare.

With Dad's hand on my shoulder, and Mum standing next to me, it's as close as we get to enjoying a family day out.

Awestruck by the yellow-helmeted firefighters striding into battle, exploding glass tinkling off their tanks, I gush, "Dad, Dad. Can I be a fireman when I grow up? Can I?" I question my choice when one of the planetary defenders is dragged from the inferno, his dislodged mask revealing a charred, bewildered face.

"Is the fireman dead, Dad? Is he? Can I be something else instead?"

Then a crumpled suit arrives in a sun-roofed car who, after presenting his credentials Kojak-style to a policeman, is waved into the action zone, notebook at the ready as he's directed towards an older man with PRESS OFFICER printed on his back.

While watching the journalist dip under the tape, I decide the world is equally served by a pen as an axe.

CHAPTER 19

My vibrating BlackBerry says it's Laura calling.

"*Where* are you?"

"You know where I am, Laura. Walking Ben." I don't respond well to indignation. Laura's the latest girlfriend to fall at my feet, though I suspect she's about to get up and leave.

"I can't believe you left me here with all these people. Jane's the only one I know. It's embarrassing."

"You weren't even out of bed when I left."

"Yes, I was. I was helping your dad, which, as Jane says, is what you should be doing." Her tone is looking for a fight until she softens. "Are you sure your mum was as bad as you say she was? Your relatives seem to think she was really nice – and that you were her favourite."

A rush of exhilaration courses through me before I've got a chance to deny it. "Of course, they do, Laura, but only because she's dead. I'm nearly home, anyway."

The last part's a lie, so I turn my phone off as I kick some stones over my dog's latest steaming whorls of shit.

"Why can't everyone be as loyal as you, Ben? Just because Laura comes from a lovey-dovey family, she thinks everyone else does. Perhaps if she'd been there when I was left to drown in an Irish loch, she'd see things differently."

In my head, my twelve-year-old self is on a family holiday in County Clare. As our Mark III Cortina weaves down an Irish hillside, angry words condensing on the windows cause roadside sheep to raise their heads.

"You should be grateful you're going at all," my father snaps, exasperated by five days of endless rain, arguments, and disappointment. "Carry on, and I'll turn around to take us all back to the farm."

"No, you blimmin' well won't," Muriel jumps in, the smell of blood in her nostrils. "The sheets are filthy, it's freezing cold, and as for those lace curtains, they should be ashamed.

"And when are you going to tell them about that blasted dog *yap*, *yap*, *yapping* all night long? I said we should have stayed in that nice hotel, but *oh no*, you know best, and now we've got another two nights in that fleapit."

"We could hardly afford that hotel's coffee, let alone two rooms," is Jim's attempt to lighten the mood, which Muriel is having none of.

"If you had a proper job, we might."

"Dad, we are going fishing in a speedboat, aren't we? Are we nearly there? I need a wee," I whinge despite knowing Jim's suffering from a forty-eight-hour migraine.

"Will you all just SHUT UP! This endless complaining's making my head pound." My dad's fuse has reached breaking point as he pulls the car alongside a row of hefty-looking rowing boats on a pebble beach.

I watch balls of foamy scum roll like tumbleweed off choppy water while Jane sits beside me, unaware of the maggots inches from her head in my fishing box. My oldest brother and sister, John and Margaret, have long since flown the nest's chaos.

"Dad, tell the man we want a speed boat, not a stinky rower. They're too big, and I don't know how to use the oars."

"How many more times, Daniel? We can't afford a speedboat. This nice man will show you what to do."

"He's *not* a nice man. He looks like a tramp. I'll just stay in the car while you all go off and have a nice time." I add, "I hope you drown," in an only slightly lower voice.

"OUT THE CAR, NOW. And don't be such an ungrateful Smart Alec," is delivered with a smile when Muriel notices a twinkle in the Irish boat keeper's Mediterranean-blue eyes.

I assume the rest of the family is coming with me, though only Jim is opening his door. Even Muriel wouldn't desert her young son on a horizonless expanse of a foreign lake. Would she?

"Come on, Mum. We can all take turns," I try to enthuse.

"Not on your Nelly. I'm not getting in that death trap in a month of Sundays."

"But …"

"Or Saturdays." Self-satisfied and sneering aren't an attractive combination.

My unease mounts as the boatman steadies the vessel against the waves and indicates I jump aboard.

I look for my mother, expecting her to stop the madness, but the Cortina's wheels spitting gravel say it's not going to happen. "See you in two or three ho …" My father's words are lost in the wind.

Shoving me off, the man mumbles something about a life vest under the seat and not to go too far. The sound of icy water squelching from my plimsolls makes it hard to hear.

The lumbering, though rhythmical, stroke I establish takes me out of sight of the landing. Fifteen minutes later, a newfound belief slows my heart to a manageable thump, allowing me to store the oars, stand, and cast a treble hooked pike lure into the troubled waters. The boat's sway forces me to sit down again.

On my third trawl, a tug catches me unawares and, flipping open the reel's bail arm, the twenty metres of line tearing off the spool suggests a monster is charging for the depths. I either risk running out of line or ripping the lure from the pike's mouth by clicking the bail arm shut. I opt for the latter while saying a prayer.

What I don't anticipate is the reel's braking effect that spins the boat from aft to fore, holding it at such an acute angle that waves flap over the side, the additional weight tilting it even more.

I'm equally panicked by the prospect of landing the needle-toothed fish as being capsized – until I realise my lure's snagged on a sunken log or rock. No matter how hard I try to free it, the prevailing wind pushes me further onto the lake, white horses rearing, pins of rain obscuring my view.

When the broken filament pings into the air, cutting a gash in the water's surface, I lurch backwards, feet lifted off the wooden floor as the boat rocks from side to side, me sliding one way then the other along the seat, planks whining, oars rattling.

The pounding in my chest slows when I resume an even keel. It accelerates when I see I'm being washed towards a fast-approaching shoreline, then tipped into the shallows by a side-on swell.

Jostled by unrelenting rolls of water, I struggle to keep upright on the uneven, weed-covered rocks, certain I'm about to drown. Slipping, spluttering, terrified, I somehow find a foothold and fling the floating oars as far as my arms can manage up the shingle beach. Manoeuvring the boat out of danger is too much, so I abandon it, scrambling to solid, if not dry, land.

Shivering, I sit and watch the blue-painted vessel scrape along the shoreline and disappear into a forest of bull rushes. The cold's so intense it's painful, and removing my cagoule, I place it over myself, and I lay down to die, a shipwrecked sailor.

Surprised to be still alive, what feels like an hour later, I raise myself on one elbow, get up, and scan the distance for a house or road, but as I set off in a random direction, there's nothing but marshland under a darkening sky.

Starvation or freezing to death are my only options as I negotiate three rocky bays; then, on the point of giving up, I see my boat. Which means I'm either delirious or on an island.

I climb aboard after wading out to the vessel's protective dock of busby-headed reeds and, bailing out handfuls of water, trap an oar against a boulder to punt myself onto the loch. Instead, I'm repeatedly forced back by wind-driven waves as the smell of peat bubbles up from the lakebed.

Unexpectedly on the move, oars splashing into deepening water, I shield my eyes from the horizontal rain, peer through numb fingers, then row, peer then row, peer then row, desperate and lonely.

The boat keeper waving his arms from behind the wheel of a motorboat, then throwing me a lifeline along with an oilskin coat, is either an apparition or sent from God. He tells me he was doing a final tour of the lake before calling the police, which makes me speculate who they'd arrest for endangering a child's life, him or my parents.

I'm nearly dry, hunched over the man's pot-bellied stove, when the Mark III Cortina crunches over gravel. I run outside though I needn't have bothered when, seemingly irritated and wanting their next cup of tea, Jim and Muriel barely listen to my ordeal. I thank the boatman. They don't.

To this day, I've no idea how I managed to relaunch the semi-submerged boat or why I was allowed to cheat death again. Was it God's way of tormenting me? In any event, being marooned on an Irish loch makes me question if I detest my mother even more or whether I should pity her for being of unsound mind.

Did the incident cause me to view my father as an increasing irrelevance? Yes. Did it make me stronger, as people suggest? No. Will I find any clues at my childhood home about why she neglected me? I'm about to find out.

CHAPTER 20

Rounding a kink in the unmade lane, I'm faced with more twentieth-century progress. Not only have the school's football pitches been sold off, so has Colworth Hall.

The Georgian mansion, along with the family who called it home, was reduced to dust well before my time, but its grounds continued to provide an illicit playground for village children.

Now, something grotesque sprawls across the site. The Hall's acreage of copse, cranny, and lawn is block paved, and I'm glaring at million-pound façades mocking the architecture that went before.

Ben barks at the remote-controlled gates clicking, then shuddering, into action. "When I say 'attack', Ben, go for the throat, okay? Jesus Christ, it can't be. *It is.*"

The Mercedes driver waves in acknowledgement of my stepping aside and jams on the brakes. We're two men of similar age, face on through the side window, and I bend forwards as it glides down.

"*Steve*?"

"Daniel."

"I was just thinking about you as I walked past our old school. Remember how you stole my ..."

"Etch A Sketch?"

"It was my favourite toy ... you were ... but now you're ... the car, the house. Nice suit, by the way. What's it been? Forty years?"

"At least. Your dog's pissing on my alloys."

"Ben. Come here. Jesus, you haven't moved far. Just over the fence, really. The one you jumped over when you nicked my ..."

"Only the Etch A Sketch wasn't actually yours, was it Dan?" I'm positive his smile is more of a jibe even though he's had his teeth fixed. And whitened.

"It was the last day of term, and you were the only one who didn't bring a toy, so school let you use theirs. I was only trying to show you how to use it, but you went mental."

Either he's lost his marbles, or I have.

"That's not true. It was a Christmas present, and you grabbed it, so I chased you ... into here, as it happens," I say, my arm indicating the luxury mansions blotting the landscape. "Who'd have guessed you'd end up living here?"

"Listen, mate, I'd love to stop and chat, but I'm late for a board meeting. Here's my card, give me a call next time you're in town. Sorry to hear about your mum, by the way. She was a legend."

"It wasn't the school's. It was *mine*," I tell Trampo's brake lights. "And how would you know she's a legend?" His card says he's MD of Sharpe Construction. The *bastard*.

I click my fingers to get Ben's attention, and, noticing I'm on CCTV, I flick the Vs and carry on, unsure if *my* memory's false, Steve's, or whether perception is the only truth.

CHAPTER 21

I can almost see number 17, the house where I grew up, but my gaze rests on the bungalow where my best friend, Jeremy Newman, had lived. It had been one of the smartest houses on the estate, but now, behind an unkempt laurel hedge, a shroud of tragedy hangs over it.

Shortly after the last of his three children left home, Jeremy's dad walked seventy-five yards along the railway line and lay down, rumours rife as to why he did it. I've often imagined being inside his head as the train bears down on him, querying whether he was brave or cruel to those he left behind. Relief or pain?

The last I heard, Jeremy had drunk his way through a law degree and qualified, on his third attempt, as a solicitor now buried among secondary case files in a Streatham law firm's basement.

Did I play a part in Jeremy's adult struggles? Shooting him with a Gat gun may have left a mark in more ways than one, though I've no explanation, then or now, as to why I did it. Other than I was compelled to, that is.

I can still feel the chill of the up-and-over garage's door handle as it turns stiffly in my hand; the strain of standing on the tips of my plimsolls and pushing on the flexing metal; the creaks and groans as it opens; instructing Jeremy to follow me in.

As the door clangs shut behind us, I head for Dad's black wooden toolbox, reach behind it, and pull out the gun I bought at the Village Hall jumble sale.

Hanging a crude bullseye on the nail I've hammered into the far wall, I press my eight-year-old weight on the weapon's spring-loaded barrel, take aim and fire metal-ended darts wide of the target.

"The barrel must be bent," I tell my grinning friend.

Casting around for some alternative ammunition, I select a crystal of rock salt used by Jim to clear the winter driveway and place it in the gun's chamber.

Maybe Jeremy's smug smile makes me do it, or I'm compelled by a rotten nature, but I find myself pointing the pistol at my friend's bare leg. Then *thum*, I squeeze the trigger eyeball to eyeball with Jeremy. Wide with disbelief, his face contorts into bewildered distress.

Unable to comprehend what I've done any more than him, I look for ways to undo it, an alternative outcome; to rewrite history. I've learned my lesson, so let that put an end to it doesn't work, so I lift my tee-shirt and implore him to shoot me.

Despite Jeremy appearing unimpressed by my offer, as far as I'm concerned, we're friends again. That is until I worry his yelps of pain will alert onrushing adults. The racket he makes while tearing at the garage door to get out increases my irritation.

"Watch out, or you'll break it, then we'll both be stuck," I warn before adjusting my tone. "Here, let me do it."

"Get knotted, you big bully! My dad's gonna get you for this, *and* I'll tell Mrs Oakley, who'll tell Mr Dobbs to give you the cane. You'll get kicked out of school, and it'll be good riddance to bad rubbish."

I press the gun's muzzle, having re-loaded it, into my midriff, saying, "It doesn't matter if you kill me. Go on." Jeremy inspects his wound, and his sobs recede like a car ticking over as he clambers under the door and limps home.

Sitting on the toolbox, alone in the darkness, I mutter, "I'm sorry" over and over again until Muriel calls me in for tea. Throughout the meal and lying in bed that night, I wait for the police to arrive, debating whether to pack a bag and run or suffer the incarcerating consequences.

As a fifty-year-old, am I full of remorse for shooting my friend or is any experience better than no experience, even for Jeremy? If we're made of memories creating a Viewfinder of ourselves, where would we be without them? The problem is, if God's keeping score, I'm fucked.

The crunch of a frozen puddle's crust tells me the temperature's dropping as I approach higher ground and number 17 Crow Park Crescent. Seeing the source of who I am after so many years is causing my veins to throb.

✕

The house seems less significant than I thought it would, although the longer I stand by the back gate, the more I feel an urge to walk through the door and resume my childhood. I see my mother in a striped apron by the kitchen sink, Jim at the table repairing a Shetland pony's broken leg. In silence.

A sharply pitched roof overhangs the property's London bricks. Next to it, the garage where I shot Jeremy is separated from the house by a narrow passageway. The entire plot sits on a sloping bank of earth.

Inside my nine-year-old head, I'm spying on Caroline Curtis from my bedroom window, one hand down my pyjamas, as she rides her salt-and-pepper-maned horse.

Filling my satchel with biscuits, a torch, and a clean pair of pants, I plan to ask Caroline to run away with me. I hate everyone, and they hate me, so what's the point of hanging around?

Caroline and I would live in the den I'd made in Mr Kowalski's haystack. I'd sneak into the house when everyone was asleep to steal food, and if Muriel bolted the door, I'd break into the school kitchen.

I never did ask Caroline to run away with me, and I'm still crap at talking to women.

Scrubland between the garden and the field is now a neatly trimmed lawn in front of a new shiplap fence. Where I collected caterpillars in jam jars and slayed nettles with a homemade sword stands a gingham-curtained Wendy house, a red plastic slide, and a doughnut-seated swing I'm sure I've seen in a sex dungeon video.

What I think is a sudden movement behind the glazed lounge door sparks a memory. It's the Easter holidays, and Muriel is chasing me out of the house for 'stealing' *her* banana off the dining table. "But I'm hungry," I shout over my shoulder.

Holding the forbidden fruit in the air, I take the corner at full shoeless speed, unaware that the door I'm now looking at is open. The glass shatters, slicing a V-shaped scar on my right forearm that's still there. A physical reminder of Muriel that's outlived her.

Muriel inflicted mental scars on all her children, particularly Jane, whose first-floor bedroom, the scene of a suicide attempt, my gaze has wandered to.

✖

Loony, as Jane's known, is five years older than me. She's always been emotionally fragile and liable to convulsive crying fits and alcohol abuse that her siblings, including me, exploit. I saw her once with an older man on the riverbank and demanded fifty pence not to tell Muriel.

Even as a youngster, I understand Jane lives with the same apprehension about incurring our mother's wrath as a willingness to please her. Her skin's thinner than the rest of us, and while fatefully entrusting her family to care for her, she fails to develop the same protective shell.

As a child, whenever she's in trouble which is most of the time, she instils her coat with magic powers to make her invisible. When it wears off, she hides in the hall cupboard.

Over the years, I've tried to engage Jane in conversations about our upbringing and pool our experiences, but each time she opens the door, she slams it shut again. Assuming the roots are too deep to share, I've pieced together a picture of her life over the years.

Her childhood nervous disposition was utilised by those around her, especially Muriel, whose every angry glance or sharp word was a beating. Being told off, deserved or not, wrings tears of pity, not for Jane but, as she sees it, for those forced to endure her.

Jane's mental and physical resilience collapses, aged eight, when even our parents are forced to seek medical intervention, which results in sleeping pills. Aged nine, she's put under the care of a child psychiatrist who, I overhear, is concerned about his patient's multitude of tics, which her brothers and sister delight in mimicking.

My sister's headmistress suggests special needs tests – 'nothing to worry about, you understand' – though she concedes defeat when no one can establish what Jane's needs are.

As I look back, I suspect my sister's weakness is showing her weakness, leaving her vulnerable to attack, there to be toyed with. I blame our mother for failing to protect her. Jane blames herself.

I can still hear her retching through our partition bedroom wall, the result of another consolatory night on Stone's ginger wine after being dumped by the latest riverbank predator.

Eventually, beyond even fortified alcohol, she stumbles to the bathroom and swallows a bottle of pills. Jim's attempts at regurgitation by sticking two fingers down his daughter's throat are ineffective. I know because I watched through a crack in the door before scuttling back to my room when Muriel, rising to see what 'all the fuss is about', responds to her husband's entreaties to call Dr Crowther by saying, "What will we say? That Jane tried to kill herself! We'll see how she is in the morning."

Hours later, Jane's attached to a hospital stomach pump while Muriel frets over what to tell the neighbours about the ambulance arriving in the middle of the night. Perhaps thankful for the attention, my sister takes a particular delight in regaling all the details to me.

By the time Jane and I have another chat about our upbringing, Muriel is dead, although I accept that earlier this morning wasn't the best timing.

"What are your overriding memories of Mother?" I ask.

"That she was always there for us. If we were sick or needed anything, I mean. Not everyone can say that about their mother."

"You can't be serious?" I reply. "What about all the occasions you were shouted at for no reason, told you were thick and sent to your room for hours on end?"

"Most of the time, I probably *had* done something wrong. I just didn't know what it was." Jane wipes the steam from her coffee cup off the window, and the grating squeak seems oddly poignant.

"That's not true. She picked on you most of all. We all did. It was bad enough for me, but you …"

Reawakened anguish shows itself on Jane's face. I don't want to push her where she doesn't want to go, but I can't make sense of things on my own. What if she's right and my own memories are bent out of shape?

I accept Jane's better off living in her false reality, but shouldn't we be sharing our affliction, comparing our scars? However different we are, we come from the same mould. On this of all days, it's critical I understand who made me, review all the evidence, and then condemn them.

"You don't really know me, Daniel," she responds, biting her nails. "I really *was* bad a lot of the time. I've done some terrible things."

"No, you weren't, and even if you were, which I doubt, it wasn't your fault. It was *hers*. I think she might have been mentally ill. In fact, I'm sure of it."

"I haven't told anyone this before, but when I was nine, I started stealing money from Mamma's purse. At first, it was just a few pennies for sweets, but I kept going until one day – a Monday morning during the school holidays – I took a whole pound." Jane stops to take a breath watching my response.

"You didn't!"

"See, I told you I was bad. I can't even remember what I spent it on. A bottle of pop and a magazine, I think. Something I didn't need, anyway."

"You weren't the only one, Jane. I …"

"Listen before I change my mind. Mother noticed the pound note was missing and said at the dinner table that if whoever took it didn't put it back by the following morning, we'd all be in trouble."

"And?"

"You know the cabinet at the bottom of the stairs, the one she always sat on when she was on the phone? I can see her sitting there now, bless."

I roll my eyes. "Can we get on with it? I'm going on holiday in three weeks."

"Shut up. That's where I left the pound note, in the cabinet drawer, and next morning I was like, 'Oh, look what *I've* found'. Course, she knew it was me and called me a 'good-for-nothing thief'. I wasn't allowed out for a month. Hang on." She interrupts herself. "What do you mean *I* wasn't the only one?"

A smile, a dramatic pause, and I say, "I did exactly the same thing."

"No, you didn't."

I laugh. "See what happens when we talk about things. It makes me feel less of a bad person if nothing else."

"Well, get this. John and Margaret continued to steal, as well," she says triumphantly as more skeletons jump out of the family cupboard.

"So, we all stole," I interject. "Which must mean it was because of our upbringing." Relieved, I feel slightly less evil.

"John was the worst. Saying that, I did once steal a horse. Borrowed one, anyway." Her smirk reminds me of my brother.

"We'll chat about that later, but do you remember when we abandoned you on top of a coal train?" A blank look says she doesn't. "You must do. You nearly got burnt alive in Longlockton power station?" A pained, confused expression suggests it's something she'd rather forget.

"Never mind. But don't you see? We stole because of the way we were brought up. It's not your fault. It's not any of our fault. We didn't *know* any better because we weren't *taught* any better. *And* we weren't loved."

Taking a sip of coffee, Jane watches the last leaves rustle free from the ash tree, rise in the breeze, and fall to the ground. Then, with a slight shiver, she turns to face me, which is when I notice how thin she's grown, foundation and emerald-green blusher her only colour.

"If you tell anyone, and I mean anyone, about what I'm about to say, I'll kill you," she threatens. "I didn't stop stealing. Well, I did for a bit after getting caught but soon started again. Ten and fifty-pence pieces for chips and bus fare into town.

"Then more notes for jewellery, clothes, and drinking money."

I need to appear calm to avoid discouraging Jane, but it's like listening to my own life story.

"You won't remember, but I used to hang out with some older lads, men really, and I had to keep up with them to keep in. Sometimes more than keep up.

"It got so bad I stole some money from a teacher's desk, and ... I hardly dare tell you the next bit."

I give her an encouraging look and say, "I won't be shocked, believe me."

"Do you remember how nice Mrs Simpson, the postmistress, kept a charity box on the counter? For the blind, I think it was? Well, I stole it when she wasn't looking. There, I've said it."

"FUCKING HELL, Jane. I can't believe it."

"See, I said you'd be shocked. You can't get much scummier than that, can you?"

"You wanna bet. I've done everything you've done … except the charity box." I need to rein in the indignation that's taken me aback; an offender turned offended.

"I've stolen organic chickens, a yacht winder, Laura Ashley toilet seats, *and* choir practice money. I even stole a sheep. Actually, that was more Ross."

Intrigued to know if Jane does too, I debate whether to tell her that I continue to steal – screws from B&Q, toothpaste from dentists waiting rooms, supermarket carrier bags – but I fear losing the moral high ground.

She inhales as if about to dive off the high board, and I hoist myself onto the countertop in anticipation.

"You know what, you're right," is something I only usually hear laced with sarcasm.

"There were plenty of times I got told off for no reason, like on a day trip to Stratford-on-Avon when I fell in the river. It wasn't my fault. How could it be – I just slipped but still got into trouble. I had to be rescued by a complete stranger because you lot had gone off somewhere." It's my sister's Irish loch moment. "I could have drowned for all anyone cared … and nearly did."

Jane's off the leash of censored nostalgia, unstoppable, which is annoying when I want to share my own stories. "For some reason, Mother wanted me to fail," she adds, transfixed by the wood pigeon waddling across the lawn.

"Because Mother failed, that's why," I interject.

"Will you shut up and let me finish? Later, when I had my own kids, I don't know how many times she told me they'd never amount to anything, but they're doing alright – apart from Todd getting an ASBO for something he didn't do. Why would he want to nick a garden centre gnome?" Because history's repeating itself is what I want to say.

"Why are you dragging all this up, anyway? Mamma wasn't all bad. Show some respect. We're burying her in a bit, and I, for one, will miss her."

My sister re-shackling herself with rose-tinted spectacles sinks my spirits from rarely achieved heights. Is *she* plagued by false memory syndrome or just a saint?

"Don't look at me like that. It's true. Mother *was* always there for us, on the end of the phone, or willing to babysit. Look how often she got Pa to come round to do some little job or other."

"Oh, I know she had a temper …"

"Surely not."

"But she could also be very thoughtful. I mean, look at all those Christmas presents. The time and money she put into them. She wouldn't have done that unless she really cared about us, would she?"

Christmas Day is my Achilles heel, the flaw in my argument against childhood negligence, and I speculate if Jane mentions it deliberately.

✖

On 25 December, an uneasy truce is declared inside 17 Crow Park Crescent. As a child, I compare it to the Christmas ceasefire between the English and German armies.

On the morning of the big day, the biggest day, confusing quantities of devotion are showered upon us in the form of brightly wrapped gifts Muriel began buying in March.

Naturally, I want to believe in Father Christmas but working on the basis that a bird in the hand is worth more than two coming down the chimney, I develop a search-and-identify the present operation.

Chests of drawers are rummaged through, tops of wardrobes are checked, beds reached under. Most daring of all, I slither through the access hatch into the eaves where suitcases double as hiding places.

More than once, I tremble with fear in the eaves' dark, confined space when Muriel or Jim enter the room. Waiting until they leave the house is a safer option, but waiting isn't the way of a warrior or an impetuous child.

Even as a five-year-old, I know my mission is self-defeating. Not only am I betraying the confidence of every carefully wrapped parcel and the joy on my mother's face when I open them, but I also deny myself the pleasure of surprise.

Is it my twisted way of exacting revenge, to get to her before she gets to me, or did I believe my mother would just keep giving? That there'd always be more

I didn't know about? When this doesn't happen, disappointment breeds resentment.

I become expert at establishing what's inside a box from a shake and a prod, elated if it's something I want, deflated if not.

Under my terms of engagement, interfering with the wrapping isn't allowed. It'd be an abhorrent disfigurement of my mother's care and attention, blurring the lines of morality. Besides, she might notice.

I reserve my last weapon of self-destruction until an overwhelming force makes further abstinence impossible. As a drug wastes a body, I come to understand that my craving to sully my own happiness is absolute and that I should see Jane's psychiatrist.

From May onwards, my mother's purse contains 'The List', a sheet of foolscap paper made tatty by repeated folding. Neat columns detail every present, where it was bought, and its intended recipient, who, more often than not, is me.

The smoking gun is in the final column, where pounds, shillings, and pence reveal, at least to my mind, the true value Muriel attaches to each of her children, which I convert into measurements of love.

If my overall share falls short of my siblings, I inexplicably refuse to eat my dinner or go to bed, silent protests which achieve nothing except a rebuke. Obviously, I believe my own worth to be double that of Margaret, John, and Jim, taking it for granted that Jane's stock will be the lowest of all.

Every year is a facsimile of the one before, with me shouting across the landing at 6 a.m., "Is it time yet?" knowing Muriel won't tell Jim she wants her cup of tea until 8 a.m. "And don't forget to warm Daniel's squash."

The origin of the tongue-cloying drink is lost in time, which is where it should stay. I only tolerate it because I always have done.

The rustle of Jim's dressing gown sees me kick off the blankets and, according to superstition, hop to the bedroom door, slowly lowering the handle. Too fast, and my mother's stocking hanging like an olive branch on the other side of the door slips to the floor.

With its oedipal symbolism and fleshy smell, the stocking's simple offerings – a tangerine, yo-yo, or crayons – offer the purest joy of all, neither exceeding nor failing my expectations as my parents sit on the end of my bed watching my reactions.

From now on, my mounting excitement, like the trembling plug of a volcano, is likely to explode, and if I'm not careful, I'll fall back to earth like a spent firework.

It's imperative that, for one day only, I recognise Muriel's authority, for it is she, now crowned with an auburn tiara of Land Girl curls, who holds the key to multi-room, wondrous extravagance.

From the kitchen, a haze of aromas rises from pans with rattling lids, wispy vapours of flatulent sprouts mingling with roasting potatoes, carrots and parsnips nestling against a turkey so large Jim has to get up in the middle of the night to ensure it's ready, which it often isn't, for one o'clock sharp.

Jim hopes to escape Muriel's wrath, which he doesn't, when he realises he's forgotten the trifle's hundreds and thousands as he spills nets of Brazil nuts and almonds into allocated bowls; tubs of Twiglets hissing like air brakes before being placed next to elliptical boxes of dates with long plastic forks.

But the culinary indulgence is nothing compared to what lies beyond the opaque glass panels of the living room door, glimpsed treasure made more tantalising by glazed distortion.

The Aladdin's cave is out of bounds until Muriel makes her once-a-year calls to whichever, if any, of her five brothers and sisters she's still talking to. Her final task is to rouse her eldest son and two daughters suffering from crapulent heads.

Muriel knows the precise point at which I can no longer be contained, and after releasing me into the nylon-carpeted kingdom, I analyse the towers of presents faster than the blood pulsing through my veins.

On the orange geometric-patterned armchair next to the Christmas tree, branches drooping with fairy-light-reflecting baubles, I seize upon the familiar wrapping of the greatest gift of all.

I prolong the precious moment by pretending not to know what it is and study the handwritten label word by cherished word:

Don't go joining the army
Very much more love, Mummy.

Tearing at the Sellotape with my teeth, the barrel of a Johnny 7 assault rifle that fires life-sized plastic bullets emerges and, glancing up, I return the emotions of a smile from my mother. Jim captures the moment with a flash of his Instamatic camera as King's College carollers sing from the music centre.

I lie belly flat on the hallway floor with my right leg cocked just like Johnny, sighting one of the targets I've lined up on the stair's open treads. The shots need to be quick and accurate, six bullets for six Indians fired in deadly succession, or I'll be a sitting duck.

POW. POW. POW, I shout as a feather-head-dressed chieftain, then a squaw, fall to their deaths inches from where I'm lying. Geronimo – the wild-haired, meanest, bare-chested savage with more than a hundred scalps to his name – is next in line.

"Prepare to die," I tell the Sioux, squeezing the trigger as an imaginary arrow flies past my head and a painful crack vibrates through my finger when the gun jams.

"*Daaad*, Johnny's gun won't work," I moan, knowing it's not going to be my father who replies.

"If you've broken it, there'll be hell to pay. It's no good buying you anything."

"But Mum, it wasn't me. It really wasn't."

"It never is you, is it? If you go to your room, maybe you won't spoil everything you touch. NOW."

As a fifty-year-old man looking back, I despair at the illusion I so wanted to believe. While the food and presents were real, people didn't change, and I'm as confused now as I was then.

Why would a mother neglect her children for most of the year and then overwhelm them with gifts, even if the goodwill lasted only a few hours? And, if only my father had, just once, stood up for me – 'even if Daniel did break it, Muriel, he didn't do it on purpose' – things, and I, might have been different. Instead, I've spent a lifetime telling myself not to forgive or forget, and now Muriel's dead, I intend to continue.

But even now, standing on an earthen step looking at the house where those Christmas' happened, I wrestle with the darkness of my longings, desperate to believe she'd been a kind, gentle mother who'd loved me, that the madness is mine.

I'd swap every breath, possession, and career accolade – every woman I've fucked – to be told I'm wrong, that a short circuit inside my head makes me see things as they're not. But with her gone, there's no one left to answer the one question that means anything to me. Why?

CHAPTER 22

I lower my gaze until it rests on number 17's now disused rear garden gate. It's distressed after years of negligence, though I recognise the rusty nail Jim had missed with the hammer before striking his thumb.

Running my hand along the worn smooth rail, a sliver of wood splinters into my palm, Ben cowering when the gate bangs on its hinges after I kick it. "Sorry, boy." I see the wonky latch still prevents it from closing properly; the pitted metal fitted by my father cold to my touch.

Something's missing, though I'm unsure what until I realise I'm not in the shadow of the horse chestnut tree. Now a stump, another childhood pillar is reduced to nought.

As a teenager, I'd reached into the tree's trunk, pinched my nose, then flinched as a hum of gauzy-eyed bluebottles swarmed past my face. The maggots they deposited in the chicken carcass I left there the previous week would save me eighty pence at the fishing tackle shop. Ten minutes later, though, the neighbour had appeared, complaining of an iridescent invasion in his living room.

My mind races as past events and seemingly insignificant details tumble over themselves in my mind, demanding to be relived.

Huddled against the garage wall, I see Snowy's rabbit hutch home to Jane's beloved pet until it was put to sleep for mistaking a friend's finger for a carrot. The child's mother insisted the animal be destroyed "before it killed someone", which Muriel thought best done by Jim with the back of a spade.

Snowy's passing proved to be one of those unusual events where my father overruled my mother, and, as if it's happening in front of me, I watch my swollen-eyed sister collect her 'only friend' from Jim's arms as he carries it in from the vets.

As Jim lowers Snowy into a rectangle of ground beneath its former residence, Jane recites the Lord's Prayer in a tiny faraway voice:

Oh Lord who lives in heaven Hollowed be your name Kingdom come Give us daily bread Forget our bus pass Your kingdom power and glory For ever and ever Amen

Wearing her best summer dress, she throws a bouquet of weeds into the grave while John sniggers in the background. My sister decorates the grave with garden flowers and a homemade cross, all of which are disposed of when Muriel decides she wants the land for a rhubarb patch.

My mother considers herself vindicated after the vegetable flourishes, providing crumbled desserts, although Jane flees the table each time John claims it tastes of rabbit.

So little's changed about the house that I wonder if I can alter history by walking back into my childhood. If I give the kitchen door a shove, can I sit down with my mother and talk? Really talk.

✖

Until my sixteen-year-old brother swaps the domestic savagery of home for the lunacy of being a live-in care assistant at 'Mapperley Mad House', I share a room with him.

John's last couple of years at Crow Park Crescent seem to pass in a chemical haze as he buys and sells dope until, aged seventeen, he improves his bottom line by growing his own. On our grandparents' windowsill.

I can visualise the day my mother's parents, Reuben, eighty-six, and Mildred Rose, eighty-two, move into what was previously the family dining room. Muriel claims it's to give them "a more dignified end", but her five siblings accuse her of kidnapping the elderly couple from the Poplars Care Home in return for a substantial advance on *their* inheritance.

In any event, the aromatic plants that John convinces everyone are Venus flytraps grow so large they block daylight, remaining there long after Grandad's, though not his wife's, death.

I clearly remember sneaking into my grandparents' room to see Reuben's stiffened body laid out in his Sunday best, the tufts of hair propagating from his enormous ears and nostrils reminding me of a Russian president I'd seen in Madame Tussauds.

Although fascinated by my lifeless relative, whom I've only known in a state of dementia, the same jigsaw purchased half a dozen times, I refuse my own dare to touch his wax-like flesh.

Death and I have an uncomfortable relationship to this day. Unable to comprehend how the living can so easily be erased, gone, I grapple with how a trillion emotions – thoughts, reactions, movements – can simply be extinguished.

John doesn't appear to be occupied by such thoughts as his drug-becalmed manner defeats my mother's attempts to bully him.

One Sunday, when my brother's instructed not to leave the table until he's finished his lunch, he tips the remaining plate of food over his head, gravy furrowing through his pudding bowl haircut.

As a disputed sprout rolls across the carpet-tiled floor, Muriel ignores her eldest son's insubordination and turns her tongue on the weakest link. "Don't you dare," she scolds Jane, whose fingers are on the sides of her plate.

Although my brother tortures me with Chinese wrist burns and two-fingered 'typewriters' on my pinned-down chest, unlike Jane, who lacks the will to retaliate, I exact my revenge by launching flying Kung Fu kicks into his back. Meanwhile, John press gangs Jane into joining his latest criminal enterprise.

She's the one spotted outside the chemist the night it's robbed, shelves stripped of anything which might sell in Nottingham's backstreets by John, who's instructed his sister to "keep a lookout".

On a separate occasion, an incriminating pot of white paint is found in Snowy's hutch after the word WANKER appears in irregular-sized letters on the school wall.

If we children had organised ourselves into a confederacy of friendship, Muriel's divide and conquer policy would've been less effective. Instead, we fought our own battles, the peace ruptured by individual arguments rather than a united front.

Muriel ruled us, her subjects, with the axiom that knowledge was power, the guarding and hoarding of information the fulcrum defining her reign. But I'm now beginning to think her own insecurities knew no other way.

Even now, I hardly know any of my aunts' and uncles' names, having briefly met three and none of a dozen or so cousins. 'Quizzing' isn't allowed growing up, leaving me clueless about Muriel's age until I catch sight of her death certificate.

When she's sixty-eight, we later discover that none of us has been told our mother has advanced bowel cancer. She swore Jim to secrecy and went under the knife to have it removed. In hindsight, the stench of her colostomy bag and restaurant stiffening farts should've alerted us that something was wrong.

Muriel's authority isn't exercised with subtlety, though she could be devious, sons and daughters dissuaded from talking to each other, courtesy of blatant backstabbing.

She alone is permitted to answer the phone but, despite knowing we're being manipulated, we do nothing about it, shell-shocked victims in a propaganda war.

No apologies, no explanations. Muriel's an unopposable, unappeasable chief of a family fiefdom that she ensures keeps feuding.

My mother's sole allegiance, at least for a while, appears to be her older brother, Graham, who becomes an especially violent bone of contention between us.

Chapter 23

Regimental Sgt. Major Graham Jessop is a founding member of the SAS, who I'm beside myself to learn took part in a real-life version of *The Guns of Navarone*, my favourite film starring David Niven.

I only uncover this piece of family history because, after blowing up Hitler's biggest guns, Graham is despatched to Hollywood to drum up support for the war effort, a record of which, a yellowing *Mansfield Gazette* clipping, is kept in Muriel's purse.

"*My* uncle's a war hero?" I query, age eight, when the cutting falls to the floor, and she shows it to me.

"Well, yes, I suppose he is." Her voice is the softest and the proudest I've ever heard.

"My uncle's a war hero. My uncle's a war hero," I chant, charging round the front room. "He killed Hitler and blew up his guns."

"Be quiet. I don't want the neighbours knowing all our business."

"I do. I didn't even know you had a brother. When can I meet him? Where does he live?"

"Australia."

The front-page pictures of Graham – who's as dashing as David Niven – show him being swooned over by starlets. Declaring him to be 'a gen-u-ine war hero', a young Martha Vickers is quoted as saying:

> "I had Graham meet Dennis Morgan and Jack Carson who fight over me in *The Time, The Place and the Girl*, and introduce him to Humphrey Bogart who I appear with in *The Big Sleep*. But I'm afraid Graham did not enjoy himself as much as he should have because we were so interested in him that he had no prospect of being interested in us."

The ageing newsprint account, which remains in my possession, goes on to detail his exploits:

> "On one particular raid on the Benghazi docks, the objective of which was to blow up enemy ships in the harbour, the Sgt. Major, with others, drove into the town in a false German staff car, passed sentries, was charged by the enemy, forced to hide all that day, made the objective the next night and escaped. In a Sicilian operation he, with others, destroyed or captured eighteen guns,

four mortars, three rangefinders and took five hundred prisoners."

I'm twenty and struggling to know what to do with my life when I finally meet my uncle. It's strange to encounter the man whose role I've played in countless childhood battles.

Graham's visiting from Australia, where he's prospered in the dry-cleaning business, and the tall willowy man in a worsted suit sporting the same derring-do moustache treats my parents and me to a swanky Clumber Park hotel dinner.

I've never seen a sparkle in my mother's eye before, and basking in her brother's aura, she gasps at pictures of his ranch-style house and his Aussie wife, Gayle, perched on a wraparound veranda in Audrey Hepburn sunglasses, wide-brimmed hat, and one-piece swimsuit.

I'm convinced Gayle is who Muriel wants to be, especially as, in other photos, there are no children to be seen, just sunlight reflecting off the chrome fender of a running board saloon and an Aboriginal maid wearing a lace cap on wiry, black hair.

Walking into the restaurant, Muriel tells me to speak only when spoken to. "He's come to see me, not you," but Graham shows me levels of interest his sister doesn't know how to, inquiring about my plans as Muriel tuts then interrupts our conversation by suggesting we retire to the lounge for coffee.

Rising, Graham turns to me and says, "If you really don't know what to do with yourself, young man, you could always come to Queensland and work for me."

Euphoria surges through me as I'm presented with a direction in life, free to escape England's claustrophobia and the journalism course I'm failing at North London Poly, cutting the ties binding me to a grey existence.

"If you really mean it, Uncle, I'll be there next week."

"*Whoa*, hang on there, young fella," he chuckles. Seeing my reaction, Graham adds, "I'll tell you what, mate. Finish your education, and then give me a call. Your mum's got my number." I give Muriel an emphatic nod.

"Don't worry, Muriel, love. I'll make sure he's alright, sort him out a car and somewhere to bunk till he finds his feet. You understand it'd involve a lot of travelling, Dan. You up for that? It's a bu-te-full country."

Three months later, clutching a Manila envelope, I'm jumping the last five steps and racing across North London Poly's lobby to the phone box on the wall. "It's me. What's Graham's number?"

"Oh, I don't know. Did you get your results?"

"Who cares? Get Graham's number. Now. I'm outta here, soon as. What do you think it'll be like? Is his house really that big? With a pool? Is his wife nice?"

"I've not heard from him. What grades did you get? All As I hope."

I continue to be shocked by how much she can still hurt me. "All Ds."

"A D's not a pass."

"Yes, it is. Graham's number, if you'd be so kind."

Keen to get on the pool table before the college piss-up goes into overdrive, I accept her promise to search for it later by saying I'll call back first thing in the morning.

A morning becomes a week that becomes a month as Muriel's excuses change daily. His number's either lost in a thrown-away purse, mislaid somewhere in the house, or, finally, that Graham's moved.

Eight years later, I reach for my London flat's phone. Now a Fleet Street journalist, I still want an explanation for why she prevented me from starting a new life in Australia, though I don't expect it to be the most bewildering call of my life.

It's Sunday, and I picture my mother counting the phone's rings before answering, a lifelong charade of pretending to be busy.

As I wait to hear Muriel's affected telephone voice, I admire the floorboards I've spent a lonely weekend varnishing. Various vertebrae object to my endeavours, and I'm not in the mood to be messed about.

The first few minutes of our conversation pass as they always do. Me getting annoyed by my mother's usual petitions of 'when are you going to settle down' furthering my sense of isolation before I attempt to terminate the topic.

"I've told you I'm gay and won't be getting married *or* having children. Have you heard from Graham yet?"

"I beg your pardon?"

"Don't you remember? Years ago, you wouldn't give me Graham's number because he'd become a monk or something, so I wanted to know if you've heard from him?"

"Oh, for goodness sake. You're like a broken record."

"If you tell me, we can move on. Going to Australia would've changed my life instead of being stuck in this dump. I hate England."

Certain I hear a whimper, my tone softens. "What is it, Mum? We've never really talked, and this might be a good opportunity to start."

"You don't understand what it's been like," her voice quavers.

"What *what's* been like? I don't understand."

"Watching you grow up and seeing Graham."

"Do you mean I look like him?" Am I on the verge of an explanation about who I am, some sort of twisted individual born out of Muriel's sibling fetish?

"It's more than that; it's everything. You were the spitting image of him when he was your age and still would be. You walk the same, talk the same, and you both have odd-coloured eyes. Every time I look at you, I see Graham."

I've seen Muriel appear vulnerable in unguarded moments, hunched in living room darkness, a shrunken figure staring at the floor, but now she seems absent, detached from reality even.

That said, I'm unashamed to admit that I hope her introspection is infused with regret for the lives she's stymied. Muriel deserves to wallow, take her own medicine, crouch in repentance, and beg for forgiveness. Maybe then we can all move on.

My vengeful resolve crumbles as it always does, giving way to cheap compassion and sympathy. Is she really so bad? Feeding and clothing me, dusting and ironing, the family car packed with crockery and linen when my parents ease my move to London. And what about her weekly letters? Don't they say something?

Why would I limp home in Friday night traffic, seeking weekend sanctuary from London, if things were so terrible at home? I might not be welcomed with a kiss, but my dirty clothes are laundered, and there's company, of sorts. On Sundays, it was Southwell Garden Centre for lunch. Me trying on a new pair of boots. Muriel telling Jim to pay for them.

I don't leave until the last moment on Sunday evening, Muriel close to tears on the doorstep. Her, 'come back soon', a twenty-pound note slipped into my pocket for petrol money, a bag of sweets on the car seat made it hard to hate her.

Muriel's my first port of call in a storm – another relationship breakdown, a missing cat – although it's impossible to understand why I persist when all I get is heart-stopping coldness. "Get another one, then," is her solution to every catastrophe.

But things are different that Sunday evening as I shift uneasily in my chair, phone in sweaty palm, and on the brink of a hoped-for revelation about my Uncle Graham, an explanation of who and why I am.

Visualising my mother's tears of remorse trickling down her face for what she's about to divulge, I break my vow not to feel sorry for yesterday's despot who's lost her crown.

I've been making promises I'm too feeble to keep since infancy, unable to stop myself crumpling in the face of Muriel's emotional extortion. Fortified by rage, I've immunised myself against her, steadfast in my refusal to let her penetrate my sympathies again, but a week later, I'm stuck in M1 Friday night traffic.

In the here and now of the phone call, I want to reach down the line to console Muriel, to share her desolation, and I press on more gently.

"Why is it so difficult for you to look at me and see Graham, Mum? I thought you doted on him. It's not my fault I look like him; you must realise that. You don't blame me, do you? It's not like I can change my appearance – which, I may point out, you created." My attempt to lighten the mood doesn't work. Silence, maybe a whimper.

"Please help me understand, Mum. I'm not very happy a lot of the time and think it might have something to do with where I came from – if that makes sense, which it probably doesn't. I thought you and Graham were close."

I suddenly catch up with the delay in my thinking. "What do you mean *would be*?"

"Now I'm the one who doesn't understand?" Her reply sounds promising, conciliatory, and almost friendly.

"You said I w*ould* be like him now."

Silence. Apart from the song thrush singing in the background.

"Graham's dead. He died in a car crash several years ago." She's hit me with a sucker punch, and I need a moment to recover.

"For fuck's sake, Mum." I'm back in the ring. "What's going on? You're lying. Why don't you want me to see him?"

"It's true. Graham's dead. I got a letter from his wife's solicitor. Gayle wouldn't speak or write to me directly. I don't even know what he died of, let alone being invited to the funeral." I hear a rustle, a handkerchief perhaps.

"Mum, please."

"I've got to go."

"You're lying," I yell at the cut line.

As a journalist, it's my job to keep on digging until I find some answers. And dig I will.

CHAPTER 24

With my hands on the back garden gate my father made forty years earlier, I contemplate whether my relationship with him will change now that my mother is no longer here. She kept us apart for decades, and breaking the mould won't be easy.

My eye rises from Ben, who's crisscrossing the lawn, nose to the ground, and lingers on my bedroom window, where I see my six-year-old self jump out of bed and swish back the curtains on a hushed winter wonderland.

Acrobatic snowflakes balance on the washing line, my football's a white-hatted dunce in the corner, and red-coated berries glow under a low-lying sun.

Opening the window startles a robin from the bird table, prompting next door's door cat to give me a slit-eyed glare that deserves the snowball I've gathered off the windowsill.

"Dad, *Daaad*, can we go sledging? Can we, *pleeease*?" I shout, sliding down the handrail.

"No, you jolly well can't." I should've known it'd be Muriel who'd respond. "We're late for the shops. Now get dressed – and if you slide down that banister once more, I'll knock your block off."

"Get stuffed, you old bag," I mutter.

Waiting until she's locked the bathroom door behind her, Jim whispers, "Your mother's right, son. Wait till we get back, and we'll go sledging then, okay?"

"No, it's not okay. It'll be crap by lunchtime after all the other kids have ruined it." A flushing toilet snaps us both to attention, Muriel's voice preceding her appearance.

"Mind your ruddy language, Daniel, and get dressed. And don't throw snowballs at next door's cat. And you, Sunny Jim, stop encouraging him." Muriel waves an accusing finger between father and son.

"Hubble, bubble, toil and trouble. Eyes of a cat, ears of a bat," I hum to myself, returning upstairs.

✶

I grip the wooden sides as Jim rocks the sledge backwards and forwards. Then, with one last heave, he digs his feet into the freshly fallen snow, puts his hands on my back, and starts running. "One, two, three." Jumping on behind, he takes the chaffed leather reins.

With our momentum building, Jim shouts how his dad, Alfred Thomas Connah, spent months chiselling and sanding the sleigh's twenty-eight individual parts, applying the same devotional zeal to his son's toy as to his religious activities.

Jim often talks about his childhood, as long as Muriel's out of earshot, giggling as he recalls sitting on the back of his dad's BSA throttling them towards Wrexham and his Aunty Eileen's sweet shop. Dad skinny-dipping in the Trent with his friends at Gunthorpe is another favoured story.

Today in the snow, however, there's no need for father, or son, to recollect because it's more exciting than anything that's gone before, cheering and hollering as we hurtle down the horses' field, modern conveyances fashioned out of brightly coloured plastic, left in our wake.

Released from Muriel's leash, Dad aims for a frozen mound of earth that propels us into the air, carelessly whooping as we land on one rail, certain we're going to topple, swerving round patches of ice worn to mud.

I demand more speed by leaning forward, watery vision blurred, cheeks rouged, throat scorched, my brown and cream bobble hat snatched by the wind as impending disappointment looms. The ride of our lives is nearly over.

But instead of slowing, the sled accelerates us towards the hawthorn hedge, Dad shielding my eyes as we crash through thorns and branches, our chariot smashed to smithereens on stony ground; shattered wood among tangled limbs.

We look at each other's scratches and torn clothing, then burst out laughing. Jim struggles to get the words out as he lays back and roars, "Best not tell your mother about any of this."

✕

As a grown man reflecting on my childhood, I remember hearing my father's infectious chortle less frequently as I got older. Was it because of me, his fourth and unwanted offspring, sucking the life out of him, or was he ground down by my mother's relentless derision?

Perhaps because my happier recollections of Jim are so few and appear so large, they distort reality, creating the illusion that he was a good father. Or am *I* the distortion, an ingrate who always wants more?

I picture my dad's face earlier today, preparing to bury his wife, and I can still see the boy hiding in the creases of old age.

Although Dad's laughter lines are long gone, an impression remains of the young man I remember from early black and white photographs. His eyes, set in shadowy pools under arched brows that meet in the middle, continue to peer out with a trustworthy gaze.

Jim's as complicated as he is simple, thoughtful. And guileless. Even as a child, it was painful for me to watch Muriel reject his cack-handed efforts to please her. If he'd shown his children as much dedication, he might have got some gratitude.

At times, I pity my father. Like me, he's only a product of those that made him, though, even now, his oblivious nature infuriates me because he gave me everything, except what I needed most. To be loved.

Is that fair, I question myself, given he took me sledging, to football and cricket matches? Yes, it is. A child knows the difference between *allocated* and *caring* time. Time spent talking, listening, educating, not watching a clock's hands, fearful of a bigger beast's recriminations.

As an adult standing next to 17 Crow Park Crescent's picket fence, I'm conflicted, knowing that no matter how unsatisfactory my childhood memories are, I wasn't beaten or sexually abused like so many others.

The problem is, I struggle to accept there's always someone worse off than me. We live in our own unchosen heads, not someone else's, our perception our reality.

I can't take my father as he is because he isn't what I want. Am I the son he wanted is reasonable to ask, but who cares? The egg comes before the chicken. Or does it?

My foot's resting on a log that I instinctively try to roll free from its ivy restraints. Am I being confounded, proved wrong, by another recollection of my father? I'm back in 1969, scavenging for bonfire wood.

"Better make this the last one, son. Mother will be wondering where we've got to," aren't words I want to hear.

It'll be the sixth load of loosely roped-together branches we've manhandled down the lane, thrown across the ditch, and heaved over the barbed wire fence into the corner of the horses' field nearest the house since first thing this morning.

We stack the branches into a tepee-like structure, twiggy fingers reaching for the approaching night sky. At the centre, a void ready to be filled with brushwood, paper, and petrol-soaked rags half an hour before lighting on Bonfire Night

The blistering, bruising effort is immense, and while other villagers come to gawp at the emerging pyre, none offer to help. While I resent their lazy indulgence, I'm thrilled that Dad and I create the wonder alone. Albeit in silence.

Muriel's role is to hew a newspaper-stuffed Guy out of Jim's still-wanted work clothes – triangle of felt for a beard, trouser buttons for eyes – which I use to extort *a penny* at strategic locations about the village.

I see my petitions for money as revenge against the parasites who want something for nothing, exploiting a father and son's labours.

At 7 p.m. on 5 November, the acrid smell of burnt treacle wafts from our kitchen, melding into the gunpowder sky as scarfed figures lean into the wind towards the horses' field, a darkened front room illuminated by an indoor firework display.

Jim, unaccustomed to the limelight, strides hesitantly forward, thick cream socks folded over

Wellington boots, and throws a burning cloth towards the papery guts of a seventeenth-century tradition.

The rag falls short, and the damp grass extinguishes its flame, my father humiliated by a communal groan and Muriel's tuts. "C'mon, you can do it, Dad," I shout, wanting to punch everyone.

Sprinkling the retrieved fuse with petrol, Jim sets my world and the bonfire ablaze in a *whoosh* of magician's smoke that sends me leaping up and down as I lead the applause.

Within minutes a flaming glow reflects off nearby windows. And as Muriel hands round trays of jaw-breaking toffee, I pour orange squash, and Jim strolls over to a table made from an old door, we might be mistaken for a family.

Skyrockets, Fountains, Roman Candles, Comets, and Stargazers whizz and bang, each set into motion by Jim. Mittened children swirl figures of eight sparklers while Catherine Wheels whirr dementedly in ever-decreasing circles powered by a screeching tail of phosphorescence.

As twenty-foot flames lick Guy's paper-stuffed head, a coven of bewitched worshippers coo gasps of wonder – '*oooo, arrrr, wheee*' – distorted by the crickle crackle cries of incandescent wood as heaven thunders with pyrotechnical explosions of phantasmagorical light.

"Are you *completely* stupid, Daniel?" my mother admonishes. "You needn't come crying to me when you've got a burnt face." I've already singed my eight-year-old eyebrows by standing too close to the fire, but I don't tell her.

By morning all that remains is a round of scorched earth scarred with shrapnel, an armoury of blackened nails, screws, and hinges, embers pulsating like mutant hearts, into whose heat Jeremy and I drop jacket potatoes, ready by lunchtime.

Something rare, almost extinct, is also created — a happy Connah memory.

✖

There were times when me and my father supported each other before Muriel, usually through the doors of Queens Medical Centre.

I can almost still feel the pain when I slammed my twelve-year-old finger in the car door, though sticking to my theory that any experience is better than none isn't easy as the blood pressure builds under my nail.

My mother replies to my cries for help by saying I shouldn't have been in the car in the first place and turns up the television.

Muriel's lack of concern, at least until *Emmerdale's* finished, has its benefits by giving me something else to think about other than searing pain – like how much I loathe her.

Typically, it's Jim who eventually rushes in from the garden and, after I've passed out in another family car, carries me through the hospital doors, finger pounding.

I yearn to touch the young nurse's black stockings, push up her striped dress, and unclip the buckle on her elasticated belt when she bends forward. My twelve-year-old face peering down her starched apron, pretends to look at her upside-down watch when she catches me and smiles.

Picturing Gina, identified by her name badge, in her jaunty cap and saucy suspenders reminds me of a centrefold in one of Dad's magazines hidden behind the hot water tank.

'Could it really be her?' I fantasise, convinced it is when she touches my knee. 'If we do it in a store cupboard without the light on, she might not notice I've got no pubes.

'Bleedin' Nora, she better not be coming anywhere near me with that syringe. It's massive, and if I cry, she won't sleep with me.' I practically faint as the slender-waisted sex kitten heats the needle with a lighter in front of my face.

"Daniel, can you hear me?" Gina asks, turning to Jim. "Does your son have a problem with needles? I think he might be in shock." I shake my head clear before responding, "I'm alright, but, please, will it hurt?"

The white-hot metal hissing through my nail releases a spurt of blood, splattering over the towel spread across Gina's lap. "You're a brave little boy, aren't you," she smiles. "Would you like a lollipop?"

Ten years later, father supporting son through hospital doors reverses when Jim guillotines the top of his thumb with Muriel's Christmas present, an electric carving knife.

Against tradition and his wife's indignation, the turkey is switched from lunch to dinner when Muriel regales, with misanthropic glee, how accident-prone Jim and I are.

"Remember when you fell off the shed roof?" she taunts her husband. "You were fixing a leak and went backwards over the side like … like Laurel and Hardy." My mother's false teeth come loose in her gaping, malignant mouth.

"I watched it all through the living room window. Come to think of it, you look like Stan Laurel." Then, trailing off in tearful hysterics, she adds, "The last thing I saw was … were your feet in the air … and then … then you … disappeared."

"Yes, and I landed on the greenhouse," Jim retaliates, recalling how his head ached with a concussion. "I could've been killed."

"You could've, would've, should've, but you weren't, so don't take that tone with me."

Jim slumps into submission, teasing his Christmas Day moustache.

"And shave that idiotic thing off. It looks like a giant slug. God knows what everyone thinks."

Exasperated by his subservience, I intervene. "Are you just going to take it, Dad? You're like a human sponge."

My father strokes his moustache, knowing it won't be there for much longer. I can see that the hurt my mother has inflicted is already passing. I either have to back off or take it somewhere no one wants to go except Muriel.

"Talk about nearly died; what about the time I was thrown through the living room window?" I say, summoning a questioning tone.

"Strewth, not that again," huffs Muriel. "For a start, it wasn't a window. It was the French doors. You made a right mess. Second, you weren't thrown. You were playing horses with your father, and the rope slipped. You were sort of … catapulted."

"Either way, Social Services wouldn't have been impressed. Can I have a bit more turkey, please, Dad?"

×

The sun getting higher behind a blanket of winter cloud tells me that if Ben and I don't get a move on, we'll miss my mother being planted in the ground. How different things would've been if she'd given me Uncle Graham's number.

"Would I have come back for the funeral if I'd been living in Australia?" I ask my spaniel, who drools and trots off. "I take it that's a no."

As I turn to leave, I'm startled by a familiar sound behind me. Once I realise it's two branches creaking against each other, it's too late. I'm back in the past, reliving the eventual nightmare of my father's belief he has a genetic aptitude for farming.

CHAPTER 25

Jim's notion that he was born to toil the earth stems from the family tree he's glued onto a piece of hardboard that Muriel wants removing from the kitchen table.

"But we're descendants of Welsh tenant farmers dating back to the 1820s, lov…," is met with, at best, indifference by my mother while Jim increasingly sees himself heaving pitchforks of hay onto horse-drawn carts.

He's so enthused with bucolic idealism that he drags Muriel, who's not averse to a holiday as long as it's in a 'decent hotel', and my twelve-year-old petulant self to various ancestral Welsh villages knocking on doors; beside himself, if a family tie, however remote, answers.

Despite Muriel's protests, I'm convinced she privately relishes how much more 'kept up' she is than the Joneses, though she draws the line at going inside for tea. That is until Jim pulls a rabbit out of his hat.

Lady Tewkesbury is the widow of Baron Edgar Tewkesbury, whose great-grandfather, Joshua, was rewarded by Queen Victoria for services to the mechanisation of the wool industry, an accolade and title that very much appeals to my mother.

Joshua is Jim's great-great maternal uncle, making Lady Tewkesbury a dim and distant relation by marriage. More importantly, as far as Muriel is concerned, Lady Tewkesbury lives in Penymount Hall, a fourteenth-century moated manor house that alerts Muriel's nose to the smell of distinction. I've already installed myself as king of the castle.

Jim pulls our Mark III Cortina alongside an open-topped Jag, spoke wheels winking in the sunlight, outside Penymount Hall early one spring morning. "Are you deliberately trying to show me up?" Muriel barks. "Get this pile of junk behind the stable block."

The mansion's mullion stoned windows appear to sigh when Jim thumps a bronze lion's head against the arched oak front door. "You'll break the wretched thing if you're not careful.

"And neither of you speak unless spoken to. And don't touch anything. And don't slurp your tea. In fact, it'd be better if you two didn't have any. China cups are way too refined for the likes of you." Jim adjusts his tie, disregarding my exasperated glance.

"Can we have biscuits, Mum? Nice ones like yours from Marks and …"

"No, you'll get crumbs everywhere."

Muriel needn't have worried because Lady Tewkesbury has no intention of letting her across the threshold. Stepping outside in a twin set and pearls, she suggests a walk to the Italianate Garden where the baron's buried. En route, we stop to admire an acre of freshly mown lawn dotted with sweet chestnut trees enclosed by railings.

Baron Tewkesbury's final resting place is a small domed mausoleum where his wife asks Muriel if she'd care to pay her respects by popping a rose into an ornate flower holder.

"He was a great cultivator, you know. Thumbs like Hunter wellies. Oh yes, a great cultivator indeed." My mother raises her chin to match the height of Lady Tewkesbury's.

Appropriating a passing servant's secateurs, Lady Penelope uses them to indicate what appears to be a pile of steaming horse muck.

"The baron named this one after me, you know. The Tewkesbury Pink Duchess, he called it. Here you are, dear." She extends Muriel, who semi-curtsies, the eponymous specimen the gardener was told to cut.

"Just pop it in there, yes, that hole there, on the left. No, not that one. Deary me, that's the right." I've never seen my mother flustered, and I'm enjoying it. "There you go. Who's a clever girl? Whoops-a-daisy, you've caught your pearls. So difficult to get the real thing nowadays, don't you find? Would the child like to see the horses before you leave?"

Lady Tewkesbury, who's clearly used to interlopers, confirms our shared bloodline is more diversionary than familial by handing Jim a photocopy of a seventeenth-century document.

Saying she hopes we've had a nice time, the aristocrat turns on her sensible heels and closes the door. Jim retrieves his bow, and Muriel's assurance that we've had 'a delightful time' is cut off mid-flow, along with her full-on curtsy. I want to smash the windows.

"How absolutely divine," purrs Muriel, performing an unreciprocated regal wave out of the Cortina's window. "That's real class and elegance for you." My mother evidently thinks Penymount Hall is where she belongs. "Now get this piece of junk off the baron's drive before someone sees it."

After a starch-laden dinner in our farmhouse B&B, Jim, intent on wringing every drop of heritage from our three-day trip, surprises me by quietly suggesting we go for a stroll.

"Where are we going, Dad? And why don't you want Mum to come?" Keeping secrets from Muriel is one of my favourite pastimes, especially when my dad's a co-conspirator.

"The graveyard."

"*Ohh*, spooky." My sarcasm is laced with genuine apprehension.

Picking our way through the headstones, Jim's torch, that he lets me hold, doesn't prevent us from stumbling over ground elder and wayward setts. An extra cloak of darkness, and moisture-laden air, hangs over the burial ground probably because it lies in the minster's daytime shadow.

Pipistrelle bats dropping from the clock tower, then drawing crazed patterns in the cooling night air, make me half expect to see Scooby-Doo and Shaggy. 'We'd have gotten away with it if it wasn't for you pesky kids,' I snigger Scooby-style. A tawny owl sends a quiver down my young spine, and I scurry towards Jim.

Tearing at the undergrowth as we venture from tomb to tomb, Jim and I could pass for a father and son free of constraint and reprimand.

"Dad, over here. I think I've found something," I holler from an outlying grove where a series of rectangular slabs lie prostrate in the mud, the final ignominy.

As Jim crouches next to me, I notice the veins in his neck are pulsing. Pulling at the ivy, we expose the epitaph on the only memorial still standing:

IN REMEMBRANCE
RHYS GRIFLET CONNAH
BRAVE IN SPIRIT
STRONG IN LOVE
REST IN PEACE WITH GOD
1792 – 1861

Dad and I, both choking back tears, look at each other across the grave.

Neither of us knew at the time that within six months, Jim, Muriel, and I would decamp from Stoke Blakely to pursue the good life that turned out to be bad in Little Haversham.

CHAPTER 26

Passers-by, and unaccustomed postmen, are entitled to think we live a comfortable life. A white carriage gate sweeps noiselessly over a curved gravel drive leading to a Georgian residence, but we only share a postcode with our grander neighbour.

Jim, Muriel, and I – Jane has joined the other two in flying the nest – rent an adjoining property unseen from the road. It's accessed by pushing on a peeling, planked gate set in a high stone wall, our flight from Stoke Blakely to Little Haversham complete.

Ron and Valerie Dorrington, who built the self-contained three-bedroom extension we're living in to accommodate seasonal labourers, reside in the more distinguished property.

An unexpected inheritance, we later learn, enabled the Dorringtons to scale back their farming endeavours and spend more time at the golf club.

No longer needing the hastily constructed pebble-dashed addition, the landed gentry decide to attach a few hectares of stony ground, along with two leaky barns, and advertise for a tenant.

In a pique of uncharacteristic spontaneity, Jim, dissatisfied with his position as Assistant Personnel Manager, chances our family's lot by applying.

What Dad doesn't know is that all the other applicants, one of whom we later meet, were put off by the poor quality soil. Jim, however, goes full steam ahead when the Dorringtons offer to throw in last year's harvest and tell Muriel their glossy "door is always open".

Now almost fourteen, I'm proud of my dad's courage in starting a new life and set about helping him clear the overgrowth choking the backyard. Until I get bored, that is, and find a long-handled axe in an old milking shed with a collapsed roof.

But the self-seeded saplings I swing at, which, having broken through concrete, aren't about to give up easily, brush off my swipes.

On the fifth swing, the axe's momentum carries it into a brick wall, splintering the shaft. "*Daaaaad*, I've got bits of wood stuck in my fingers. It's bleeding. *Daaaad*."

Jim returns from the house with plasters, tweezers, and a pointy black bin liner over his head, two holes for eyes. Collecting his ancient scythe, he makes ghostly moans while chopping at a clump of sedge.

My hysterics seem to send Muriel into barely disguised guffaws, and, leaning out the kitchen window, she tells her 'daft apeth' husband to tend to my injuries and get back to work.

Jim switches to his dad's old shears and, telling me they're at least fifty years old, gives them a testing *snap*. "What was *your* family like?" I ask, hoping for an insight into my own.

"Well, every day, after school," he chuckles. "I ran up Berry Hill Lane, one hand on my cap, the other stopping my satchel banging against my legs, always in shorts, no matter the weather, and …"

"No, I mean, what was Grandad like when you were growing up? He was always quite, *erm*, serious whenever we went." Are we all products of what's gone before is what I really want to know.

"Well, he was certainly a God-fearing man, that's for sure, but rather than shout, he let us know if we disappointed him. I used to think the belt would have been easier to deal with."

"What sort of things did you do wrong? Did you ever steal money out your mum's purse?" I add a 'for example' to throw him off the trail.

"*No*, of course not. Whatever gave you that idea? His sarcasm was the worst, dry as sandpaper it was. I remember being late helping him with some job, and I went skidding round the gatepost in my sandals."

Jim straightens himself and puffs out his chest. "When I was your age, Jim, my lad," he impersonates his baritone father. "My shoes had to last until someone was ready with a pair of hand-me-downs." I clap, urging my dad on. "The Good Lord doesn't like waste, you know."

Jim makes himself small, shoulders hunched, voice snivelling. "I'll make sure these last, Dad, honest." He chortles, then looks sadder than I've ever seen him.

It's as if he's realised he was raised by a man closer to God than his own children, which is when it dawns on me that Jim's not a weak man; he's just been bullied all his life.

Back in the here and now of the farmyard, the present Connah family is more together than I've ever known; lingering in the moment, the air sweet with coconut-scented gorse.

I watch Muriel replace the kitchen window lace curtains with slightly less worn ones from a Crow Park Crescent bedroom. Later, she tries to restore a shine to the encrusted lino floor, and the day ends with the three of us comparing cuts and bruises; crusaders all.

Jim enrols on a correspondence course, filling shelves with introductory guides about farming, but when his tutor, Derek, goes on long-term sick leave, he turns to the Dorringtons, whose glossy door, it turns out, is always *shut*.

My father, family finances already stretched, has to pay an experienced farm hand to help gather the first low-yielding crop and keep the few pieces of machinery running. More than once, I find Jim seated at the kitchen table, surrounded by bills, head in hands.

Muriel's disenchantment with her new life begins with the realisation that there isn't going to be a second glass of sherry in Ron and Valerie's elegantly draped drawing-room, compounded by having to accept the kitchen lino's forever lost its shine.

My mother's summoning of wartime ideals to make do and mend is insufficient to rid mice from the walls, stop draughts rattling the windows, or prevent the *drip drip drip* of rain from cast iron gutters.

Surrounded by cornfields and no village shop, Muriel longs for the communal warmth of Stoke Blakely, eight miles away. This, after a decade of having no one to invite round for tea, just plenty of smiling 'hello, how are you' from people hurrying by. Even if she *could* drive, there was no one to visit.

My reaction to seeing Muriel slide into despair is twofold. The first is jubilation. Her sense of isolation diminishes her anger-driven authority, allowing Dad and me to have the upper hand, or at least not be slapped down by hers.

Removed, forcibly as she now claims, from the little security she'd had, my mother's cast adrift from her now-dispersed family power base.

Finding myself at the heart of the new family dynamic, I'm unsure what to do with the voice I've so long been denied. Then again, in my hands, there might be hope for a normal, if not happy, household.

Or am I nothing but a dreamer, as Supertramp once sang.

Witnessing Muriel flounder in a pit of despondency excites my reluctant desire to help her, to take her hand and lead her through the darkness. I'm beginning to suspect we share the same demons, and imagining us fighting them together is a castle in the air I'd pay a king's ransom for.

I'd sacrifice everything and anything to be the apple of my mother's eye, including my father, who I'm starting to blame for leaving my mother high and dry in the cornfields; previous realisations null and void. My delusion doesn't last long, however.

×

I'm walking double-time, trying to keep up with my mother as she storms over to the barn furthest from the house. "I swear I'll ruddy swing for him working outdoors while I'm stuck inside cooking, cleaning, and looking after *you*."

In a bid to join forces with Muriel, I fire back with what I imagine she wants to hear. "It was ruddy ten minutes ago when you called Dad. Tea'll be ruddy ruined."

Disbelief halts Muriel's stride, Bisto-coloured eyes inflating as she spins to shake my wrist. "Don't you get clever with me, my lad, or you'll get some of what's coming to your father. You're the banes of my life, the pair of you."

I'm uncertain whether my mother doesn't want me, doesn't like me, or is an evil, mad woman. In any event, I seek her approval on whatever terms I can get, and that late autumn day is just one more in a young lifetime of attempts.

The lumpen sky is nearly finished relieving itself of a nine-hour downpour, leaving the farmyard an inch under water, and veering round the corner of the tractor shed, I lose my footing.

A mother's instinct saves me from falling, her grasp jerking me upright before her now permanently makeup-less face. Her frozen expression leads my stare into the barn's wintry light; the only sound the grumbling Massey Ferguson's engine.

"Where's the good-for-nothing blighter got to?" Muriel says with a hint of concern.

As my vision sharpens, the high-wheeled vehicle seems unfamiliar without Dad sitting in the cab, and I search the dripping gloom for his lanky figure. What I'd taken to be the elongated outline of the tractor's exhaust is a shadowy trick. It's Jim's body dangling from a beam.

Assuming it's one of Jim's silly jokes, we wait for life to return to normal, Muriel ready with another snide remark, confused because there's no one to direct it at except me.

Jim may absorb his wife's belittling insults as if it's his lot in life but, looking back, I remember he'd been unusually quiet, going beyond his usual breaking point, which I credited to his concerns about the farm.

Struggling to mend a fractured roof timber two days earlier, I'd watched as Jim tolerated Muriel's accusations of incompetence, despite her refusal to hold the "dirty ladder", without a word of resistance.

What I don't establish until later is that inside Jim's head, it'd been two days too many of questioning self-worth and, by Sunday morning, dark clouds had gathered, his downfall now inevitable. One last chiding remark was all it took to send him clambering on the Massey Ferguson's juddering cowling.

Transfixed in the barn, I imagine my father standing his Wellington boots together, throwing the towrope over the broken beam he thinks he's fixed, and stepping off. Then, as my unblinking eyes move from the timber to Dad's toe poking out of a thickly darned sock, I know I'll regret the last words I'd said to him as long as I live.

"That's not right. You need a bigger piece of wood, for Christ's sake." Muriel's influence isn't good, but my allegiances have changed.

"If you haven't got anything better to do, go and help your mother. She's not the only one who's had enough of you," had been his reply.

Guilt pricks my conscience in the murky twilight. Am I to blame for Dad's death? Of course, I am. I could've done so much more to relieve his suffering, talked to him rather than expect him to engage me, playing a disgruntled child instead of a man.

To this day, as a fifty-year-old walking his dog, I contemplate if I could've allied myself with my father against Muriel rather than help drive him to suicide. "If he didn't have the strength, I should have fought his battles for him," I tell Ben, unable to extricate myself from that day in the barn.

Debating whether to turn the tractor off and assume the man of the house's role, my teenage mind shifts to self-survival, maybe self-pity.

What am I supposed to do now that I've been abandoned to a mother who couldn't care less about me? Although, come to think of it, Jim never said he loved me either.

Three clichéd words have constrained me all my life, shackling me to my lowly sense of self-worth. Don't I have every right to be angry at Jim, knowing what he was about to do and not saying he loved me before he did it?

The only explanation was that he didn't. But couldn't the selfish bastard have said the words anyway, if only to make me feel better?

Muriel eases my head to her breast. Safe in her fabric-softened blouse, I'm back in the womb, protected from the horrors of a world my father has declined to live in.

But, as I stabilise like a storm-battered ship, my mother's left gaping at the reality hanging in the barn, raindrops echoing off the corrugated roof. Others, finding a way through the galvanised steel fall, then hiss on the Massey Ferguson's engine, steam entwining Jim's Wellingtons.

I consider Muriel's careless darning of her husband's sock, noticing that she too appears to be occupied by his big toe poking through the awkward stitches. Does she feel guilty about her husband's death or her untidy needlework? If 'regret' features in her vocabulary, there's no evidence of it.

Knowing my mother, she probably thinks her husband deserves all he gets. His faffing and indecision had driven her to the point of insanity. Or so she's frequently heard to say.

'I bet she's already resenting having to organise the funeral, never mind pay for it.' My own callousness takes me by surprise.

I can practically hear, or think I can, Muriel's thoughts. It was Jim's fault she'd had an eternity of clearing up after others and no money for a new dress, hardly a moment to herself. She'll be better off without him.

I'd like to believe I've misjudged Muriel, but I won't hold my breath waiting to find out.

It occurs to me how slowly time's passing with nothing to do except stare at Dad's toe swaying in the light-streaked murk. He's no longer breathing the sodden earthy air.

Maybe I've got my mother wrong and, in that in her own way she'd loved him, accepted Jim for what he was, a good man trying to do his best with very little. So what if he didn't always succeed?

'What if I was too hard on him?' she might confess. Or am I living inside Muriel's head because I don't know what to do inside my own, numbed by a lack of emotion?

As Jim's body sway slows, my mother closes her eyes, perhaps unwilling to take one last look at his features, and turns me by the shoulders towards the house.

"*What the*?"

A sudden, sharp crack makes us start, each gripping the other as a rasping groan resonates off the shed's planked walls, then escapes through the gaps.

"Dad's turned into a ghost," I yelp as Jim's boiler-suited figure engages in a jerky dance. "LOOK OUT."

I push my mother clear as the fractured roof timber that's finally snapped releases Jim's body, which rebounds off the floor in an explosion of slow-motion dust. Rushing over, Muriel touches the purple-black ligature mark on his neck, screaming when his leg twitches.

"Daniel, quick, he's alive. Your father's alive." Muriel looks to the heavens. "Run to the house, dial 999, and ask for an ambulance. Jim, Jim love, can you hear me? Daniel, wait, he's coming round."

Disappointed to have responsibility snatched from me, as well as lose my mother's attention, our moment of unassailable togetherness gone, I mutter, "He can't even kill himself properly."

'WHAT THE FUCK IS WRONG WITH YOU?' an inner voice thunders, disgusted as much as I am by my heartlessness. "I don't know, but I'm really sorry," I reply.

"For God's sake, Daniel. Stop talking to yourself, and let me have a moment with your father."

"Sorry, Mum, I don't know what I was thinking. And Mum."

"Yes?"

"I'm really glad Dad's alive." I am though being excluded is hard to take.

×

I get halfway to the house before trotting back to the barn, where stepping in a puddle, the splash halts the hushed conversation inside.

Muriel's gaze searches the gloom as I peer through a gap in the planks. Preparing to flee, it becomes obvious my mother can't see me when she returns to cradling Jim's head.

Would I prefer it if Dad were dead? I reconsider hearing him cough, alive if not quite kicking. At least then, I'd have Muriel all to myself, bound in adversity forever.

Am I wicked for even thinking such a thing, envisioning Mother and me soldiering valiantly on, the boy becoming a man behind the tractor's steering wheel, Muriel scattering seed as she walks behind?

The farm would be a great success, and we'd go on the sort of holidays Muriel always dreamt of, buy the Dorringtons' house, and our maid would wear a lace cap. Checking to see if Jim has had a relapse, I place my ear to the barn wall, able to hear most of what's being said.

"What you were thinking of, Jim? Obviously not me. I realise things have been hard, but we'd have got through it; we always have. Is it the farm? Are you worried about money?"

"I can't seem to get anything right, love. Not just with the farm, everything. I've let you down over and over, but Wendy and I, we never ..."

"I told you never to mention that woman's name."

"I know, but ..."

"*Never*, you understand?"

"I've failed at everything; as an engineer; all those years in the church, then dragging you all round those godforsaken places we lived in." A sharp intake of breath says he's in agony.

"And as for being a farmer. What can I say? Head in the clouds, star gazer?" Jim shifts himself, exhaling a long sigh. "But most of all, I've failed as a husband." From my vantage point, I encourage him to include 'as a father' on the list.

"It was so brave of you, Muriel, to come here and support my foolishness. To be honest, I didn't think you had it in you."

"To be honest, nor did I," she smiles. "Although I always did have a stubborn streak."

"I shouldn't have underestimated you."

"I should be used to that by now. By me, not you, I mean. Anyway, what do you say we get you to the hospital. Are you able to drive, do you think?"

"I don't think so, love. My neck hurts."

"Well, we can't call an ambulance. We've only been in the village ten minutes, and they'll never stop gossiping about us."

I'm pretty sure I know what's coming next.

"Apart from the bruise on your neck, you don't appear too bad. I met the doctor the other day, coming out of his house. I'll send Daniel to see if he'll come, and we'll say you fell off a ladder trying to fix the beam. Can you stand up?"

"But he'll see the rope. I'm such an idiot to cause you all this trouble."

"DANIEL." I've stepped in the puddle again. "I know you're out there. Get in here and tell me what you heard – or think you heard?"

"Not much, Mum, honest," I lie, standing in the double-height doorway. "I stepped in a puddle, and it made a lot of noise."

"*Hmm*. Now listen carefully, your father's had an accident. He was fixing the beam and was tying a rope when the ladder slipped. Then the rope, *er*, got caught round his neck. He's alright, but I need you to fetch Dr Lesley. He lives in the house with the black door. Can you manage that?"

"Sure I can, Mum."

"Good. Hurry up, then. Let's try and get you up, Jim. We don't want the doctor to see you in this state. Where's your comb?"

I think about telling Muriel the doctor's not in, but the role of messenger and explaining what's happened in my grown-up voice to the doctor wins out.

×

Obviously unconvinced by Muriel's explanation, Dr Lesley fits a neck brace, tells Jim he's had a 'lucky escape' and calls an ambulance, which takes an hour to arrive. It takes another to reach Queen's Medical Centre, where Dad's kept overnight 'as a precaution'.

Having listened to Muriel repeatedly give her version of events to various family members on the phone, I lie in bed, uncertain if Jim really had tried to kill himself. Fact and fantasy intermingle until I'm unsure which is which.

An accident would be easier to swallow, not least because of the bungled nature of the attempt, but the images in my head tell a different story. Seeing my dad hanging from a rope is as real as the swollen ligature mark on his neck.

The next day, Muriel instructs me to keep quiet about 'the incident', which she claims is the same as Jim cutting his thumb with the carving knife.

"It'll only make him look clumsier than he already is," she huffs before taking my hand. "This can be our little secret, Daniel. You were really brave in the barn." I wait for a congratulatory kiss which doesn't come.

Muriel dismisses Jim's neck brace as 'another unnecessary precaution', though Jane, concerned about our father's demeanour, calls John, who, about to head off to fly fish a Highland trout stream, tells her she's imagining things.

I'm dismayed that my mother and my duplicity, which I'd hoped would re-join our umbilical cord, has no lasting effect. Worse, it feels like a betrayal, though whether of Jim or me for agreeing to keep quiet, I'm uncertain.

In any event, when Jim explains to the Dorringtons that he's giving up the farm for 'family reasons', they point to a clause in the tenancy saying he's obliged to pay for the broken beam, as well as forfeit a hefty deposit.

Penury necessitates Dad re-applying for his old Knitting Lace Training Board job, which, his former boss informs him, is now held by Jim's former assistant. As a gesture of goodwill, however, Jim's offered the newly created position of Deputy Manager of Human Resources on vastly reduced terms.

A few months later, albeit in a less desirable property, we've returned to Stoke Blakely's familiar streets, where Greasy Norma's chip shop is now an Indian takeaway.

In an attempt to remain a cut above the rest, like Lady Tewkesbury, Muriel orders Jim to apply angled strips of lead to the Fairfield Close front windows.

CHAPTER 27

I take one last look at 17 Crow Park Crescent, the 'old house' where I was raised. It's a part of my life I won't see again, and I pity those who've inherited the madness in its walls, much of it my mother's, who's calling me from the grave.

"It's a shame you didn't meet her, Ben. Dogs have a way of knowing who to trust."

A final stroke of the picket fence, and I'm off, melancholy slowing my pace as if the weight of my thoughts is in my feet. I wonder where my childhood has gone; mine and Muriel's history reduced to a scrap heap of recollections, unclear if I want to live in the past, present, or future.

What's already gone is all I have left, or so it feels. Up here, on the edge of the woods, is the last place I remember feeling alive.

It's where I climbed trees and reached into hedgerows for bird's eggs, aborting the life within by piercing their shells and blowing out the yolky contents, sometimes disturbed by the beak or claw of a semi-formed being.

Set back from the lane, nestled in an eerie hollow untouched by daylight, leaves pushed by the breeze sail across Dead Man's Pond as they've always done. It's where, according to local legend, a postman taking a shortcut to the Kowalski house slipped from a log and sunk into quicksand, a handful of letters floating to the surface.

Few village children dared clamber over the barbed wire fence, as I'm doing now, but I jumped at the chance to feed leech-like off the other kids' respect for my bravado.

Rather than savour their admiration, show some humility leading to friendship, popularity even, I scooped up two handfuls of frogspawn then hurled it at my scattering playmates, girls screeching as they tore at the slippery goo in their hair.

As I balance across the same fallen oak, now a palette of lichen, where the mailman fell to his death, I wonder at my need to contaminate my own and other people's happiness. "Is it a case of do unto others as was done unto you?" I ask Ben, who cocks a leg and hurries on.

Why do I retain an unalterable desire to live life to the destructive full, to hang on to the rollercoaster after it's careered off the tracks? To mine an extra millisecond of excitement or because I have no choice?

I'm Daniel Connah, persona non grata who always goes too far, which for me is never far enough.

I circle through the woods separating me from Kowalski's field, late autumn foliage scampering before me like frightened marionettes.

The copse narrows where it joins the unmade lane, and I emerge opposite the stables where Caroline Curtis housed her salt-and-pepper maned horse, Charlie.

Perched on the same metal gate my hands are on now, I watched as Caroline cantered around the paddock in a thin cotton shirt, fascinated by the mechanics of her teenage bra.

The slightly older teenager once let me climb up behind her, pulling my arms about her waist, but it ended badly when I accidentally grabbed her breasts, and she didn't ask me again. Innocent presumed guilty is the story of my life. Some of the time.

The stables are exactly as Caroline left them; only a different girl, doubtless another young boy's wet dream, is shovelling shit.

My early ejaculations were more than the musky beginnings of manhood. They represented an intensity of passion that one day, or so it seems to me, gets swept away in a torrent of compromise and cowardice; the replacement bedfellows of idealism and fearlessness.

Why do we reach an age when making a difference becomes make-believe is a topic I've been heard to mention down the pub once or twice.

I turn left along the overgrown footpath I chased Steve Sharpe along for stealing my Etch A Sketch, narked that he said it belonged to the school. My stride's halted by a PRIVATE sign nailed to a stile, which I climb over.

I'm at the top of the horses' field where the left-to-nature countryside plateaus, a favourite Connah family blackberry picking spot. It's also where I sat as a cross-legged Jupiter in polyester shorts, planning to lock the doors and set fire to the house with Muriel trapped inside.

Today, my chest tightens when I crest the brow of the hill and see a hideous world of cinder blocks posing as Tudor mansions. Me and Ben enter the 'private estate' after I prise apart several recently creosoted fence panels.

I long to hurl abuse at the curtains twitching as we walk by heading towards Crow Park Crescent. "Talk about Pleasant Valley Sunday," I tell my spaniel, who disappears into a shade of giant leylandii bushes ten yards ahead. My "Ben, come here" gets no response.

The resin-weeping branches whipping back behind me mask what sounds like a splash and my spaniel's yelp.

"BEN." I lurch forwards, finding my feet just in time to leap the ditch, grabbing a fistful of hawthorn to pull myself across, hand bleeding.

He's being sucked into a whirlpool that in my day was a tranquil pond, the soil acting as a natural drainage system, but now concrete forces a torrent of runoff water into the ditch.

The stream that had slowly disappeared into the ground now spins with fury, drawing Ben into its mayhem. Coke cans, logs, and plastic bottles thump against the teeth of an aluminium grill, behind which a waterfall plunges into blackness. Mother Nature's been beaten into submission.

My spaniel's head bobs under the water, and I offer up the same prayer as I did forty years earlier for a dying bird. "Please, God, don't let him die. I'll do anything but don't let him die."

Paddling in ever-decreasing circles, eyes wide with fear, Ben's unable to reach my outstretched arm, and when his head goes under, I think about jumping in, but the water's deeper than it used to be.

Flat on my stomach, I stretch in a last attempt to coax Ben to the side, my bloody hand turning artic water red when I pat the surface. "Come on, boy. You can do it."

Apparently assured, he paddles out of his downward spiral, and I haul him onto the bank, dew claws slicing my already broken skin as I hug him.

His gratitude for me saving his life is a shower of icy shaken droplets, but, being as close to a son as I'll ever get, I kiss his forehead and leave him to pursue another scent.

Having given up searching for the bullfinch's grave, I carry on down the lane towards the village.

Greasy Norma's old fish and chip shop, now an Indian takeaway that Muriel said sent the village to the dogs, comes into view, and I appraise my unkindness towards the haggard woman with oil-infused hair.

"Gorrany chips left, Norma?" me and several other boys inquire, putting a foot in the door as she's closing.

"Yes, dearies."

"Serves yer right fer makin' ce many, then. *Ha, ha.*"

Crossing Main Street, I shake some feeling back into my fingers and, ignoring the honk of a lorry's horn, step onto the pavement, put Ben on the lead, then turn left towards the Methodist church where I attended Sunday school.

The gravestones remind me that my own mother's lying in a coffin, and I wonder if her face has remained as hard as granite or is softer now she's at peace. Not that she deserves any. Not yet anyway.

CHAPTER 28

I'm nearing Piggy's off-licence where Jeremy and I glugged on giant plastic bottles of Tizer and Cherryade bought with carol singing money. "While shepherds wash their socks by night, all seated on the ground," we guffaw before ringing the doorbell and trying to appear angelic.

But Piggy's has been replaced by Della's Deli, a bored-looking girl serving the first scones to two silver-haired ladies with rubber-capped walking sticks.

The day's shed its early morning torpor, and straggling commuters can manoeuvre more easily onto Nottingham Road. The junction was the scene of a village fatality when Mrs Roberts was tossed into the air by an Iceland truck, her family's Friday night fish and chips scattered across asphalt.

Housewives are emerging, younger giving way to older on frosted pavements.

Hurrying on, I pass mothers who've completed the school run glancing through 4x4 windscreens at the darkening, silver-blue sky; pregnant rain clouds threatening expensive hairdos.

Sparrows squabble over breakfast crusts in privet hedges as blue tits cling to freshly filled feeders monitored by beady-eyed squirrels and a ginger Tom. I glance along side streets, each stirring a memory: Mad Mary's orchard scrumped for apples, Gary Wilson's house.

I barely knew Gary, which is probably why he invited me to his wedding. The nuptials assumed a sinister undercurrent when his drunken bride revealed she couldn't have children. For reasons unknown, Gary confided in me that he only married her to continue his distinguished family line.

St Helen's Drive is where demented Johnnie Dribbler scurried up and down wittering obscenities, uncared for in the community. A few doors further on, Mrs Patel offended neighbours' nostrils with spicy odours, and when I told Muriel I'd eaten some curry, she dismissed it as 'foreign muck', along with pizza and anything from China.

Where Main Street meets the now steady flow of A59 traffic, I stop at the junction with Beechtree Drive. Three doors along was where my eldest sister Margaret lived with Lenny Shaw, battling to raise two ill-considered children; raised voices and breaking glass summoned the police more than once.

Like mother like daughter, life seems to be an ad infinitum loop — children, then adults, in perpetual motion producing a lottery of winners and losers.

I linger outside my sister's old house. Peering through the window, Lenny could be chain-smoking in his chair, the smell of Woodbine in his stubble and shoulder-length hair.

Lenny didn't belong in Stoke Blakely; he belonged in prison. Shortly after meeting Margaret, he was arrested for handling stolen goods. The charges were later dropped amid allegations of witness intimidation.

Strangely, Muriel appeared to support Lenny instead of banishing him from our family home. I saw her slip him £20 notes on several occasions, though, for what, I've no idea. At one stage, I thought they were having an affair.

The blighted couple's children, Katie and Lee, are thirteen and eleven when Margaret announces she's going to work for 'an old friend' in the double-glazing business. When needs be, which is most of the time, she arranges to leave Katie and Lee with Muriel.

My mother's grandparenting skills haven't yet been tested, and I, now aged twenty-four, fear for my niece and nephew's welfare. But to my bemusement and resentment, on visits home, I witness my mother lavish the sort of attention on them she denied her own children. How and why is unknowable, and it's another Connah family secret gone to the grave.

Jane, who only escaped the village as far as Derby, tells me that within a few months, Margaret's long weekends at nationwide trade shows draw Lenny even closer to our mother – and further from his wife.

The collapse in what remains of the couple's marriage is rapid, my oldest sister confiding in Jane that Katie picks up the pieces of crockery smashed against the wall; Lee sleeping on his friend's sofa whenever he can.

To Lenny, the reason for his marital breakdown is obvious, and he intends doing something about it.

Years later, I meet him in a city-centre pub where he tells me what it was he did. It also explains why I didn't see my sister for nearly a decade.

✱

"Followed 'er all way to Newcastle on Friday evenin' train," Lenny says, jaw loose from several pints. "Watched 'er get off like wer' lookin' fer someone."

Expecting a suave-looking wanker with a bunch of flowers, Lenny's surprised when an older, short-haired woman pushes her way through the crowd, grey pinstripe suit straining at the shoulders and hips.

"Reckoned Mags musta been tellin' truth baht workin' a weekend." In between slurping his Shipstones, Lenny tells me he ambled after the two women, relieved that my sister isn't having an affair.

Following them from pub to pub, he says the hours pass quickly until closing time when Lenny realises he's missed the last train to Nottingham, leaving Katie and Lee alone in the house. "Called yer mam. 'ho went on gottem."

Between long swigs of beer, I learn that he followed my sister and her friend into the winding, darkened streets of the old warehouse district. Finally, they turned into a dead-end alleyway.

"Ya cannie cum in 'ere, pet," he's told through a hatch in a recessed doorway lit by a single bulb.

Shoulder barging the bouncer's rolled-up jeans and monkey boots out his way, Lenny gets far enough inside to see what's going on before a second female gorilla wrenches his arm behind his back and throws him out.

"Loada fanny lickers ther' wor." I'm amused by his politically incorrect descriptions of lesbians at play.

I watch Lenny's older than his years face drop, the last remnants of love appearing to extinguish in his eyes. Hard enough for a working-class lad from St Ann's to discover his wife's cheating on him, but with a woman is beyond his comprehension

"When Mags finally came 'ome," he continues, his gaze fixed on a beermat. "I lost me rag an, sorrie tah tell yer Dan, I 'it her." I empty my pint, asking Lenny if he wants another. I need some time to think, but looking up at me from his stool, he adds, "Birra blood on walls ther' wor when Lee an' Katie cam' dahn see wah wer' goin' on."

"For fuck's sake, Lenny. What did you hit her for?" I'm tempted to smack him until I notice his five-foot-five frame appears even smaller. Plus, he'd still bury me.

I tell him I've changed my mind about another drink, but he continues to talk as I get up

"Packed 'er bags an' left she did. Me, the 'ouse, everthin'. If weren't fer yer mam 'elpin' us raise kids, I'd a topped me sen – them an' all prob'ly." "Suffer Little Children" is the line I remember from Sunday school as the pub door shuts behind me.

Thinking back, when I say Margaret completely disappeared, it's not true.

I found out a few years ago that my mother knew my sister was living in Southwell, no more than fifteen miles away, but she chose to keep it a secret. If I had any thoughts of forgiving Muriel, this alone would prevent it. Divide and conquer her mantra to the bitter end.

It's ten years before I see Margaret again when she reappears crippled by secondary progressive MS in a wheelchair. Her re-emergence was partly due to being safe from Lenny, who lung cancer had put six feet under.

Margaret settles in a bungalow on the outskirts of Stoke Blakely to be closer to Katie, now married with two children of her own. She even begins a rapprochement, of sorts, with Muriel. Her partner Brenda's pension and a host of well-worked state handouts keep them alive.

I visit my sister whenever I'm in town, though I struggle to kiss her dry, misshapen lips, and I avoid glancing at her deformed legs, coughing to mask her death-rattling lungs.

In some ways, I'm jealous of Margaret. Who wouldn't enjoy having their arse wiped without a care in the world? Except to keep breathing. And smoking. And drinking. Which miraculously she does.

CHAPTER 29

evil-eye speeding motorists who I think about stepping in front of while waiting to cross Nottingham Road. Death's always on my mind, especially when I can't dispel an image of Jim's body oscillating in the barn.

Ben's bark causes my gaze to fall on a seven or eight-year-old girl poised to run across the road.

Seeing a break in the traffic, I smile and offer to take the girl's hand. But danger doesn't come much stranger than me, it seems, and, holding a football, oblivious to her winter-ruddled legs and arms, she glares at me and dashes across the tarmac. "What's the point of me trying to be nice if that's all I get?" I ask Ben.

I ruled out having children a long time ago, probably when I was one myself. Unwilling to inflict my personality and heritage on future generations has cost me multiple relationships. I'm likely to lose my current girlfriend, Laura, who, although younger than me, regularly reminds me her clock's ticking.

"But you'll make a wonderful father," she insists, stroking what's left of my hair. An image of me as a family man pops into my head until I remember who I am, and the bubble bursts.

Could I have broken the cycle if Muriel hadn't prevented my move to Australia to live with Uncle Graham? Might I have been able to change who I am, be content, alter my direction, if only by a few degrees? Or was the day I was born already too late?

Ben's keen to reach Wellington Avenue, knowing he's closer to home and breakfast. It's where Stoke Blakely's old money is piled up in Victorian Gothic mansions, low-hanging elms and striped lawns providing work for well-paid gardeners.

The houses' tall brick chimneys and corbelled turrets had at one time overlooked meadows rolling towards the riverbank, but then the sewage farm moved in.

I remember doing my paper round along here, spooked by the oppressive leafy hush and intimidating drives with big cars that never moved, intruder alarms pulsing as they are now. Number 29 was the home of The Bells' lead singer before fame went elsewhere, and he became a builder.

The 1925 village hall I'm approaching was built to lower aesthetic standards than Wellington Avenue, and I glance at the notice board where the posters haven't changed for four decades; Neighbourhood Watch, WI jumble sales, tombolas, and an SB Player's production of *Murder at the Vicarage* exactly the same. Wendy from the post office is going in. Murdered or murderer?

Next door is where my intellectual development began and probably ended. Ross Crawley's parents were scatter-brained, untidy, religious academics who instilled a sense of righteousness in their son, which he interpreted as meaning he could do no wrong.

Ross didn't believe God was omniscient, preferring to think that what the big man didn't know couldn't harm either of them. Whenever times were hard, however, which in Ross's troubled psyche they often were, the Good Lord was the route to salvation.

To me, Ross treated God like an ugly girlfriend; good for rainy day pictures then dumping him when something better came along.

My interest in Ross centred on the profound, as well as profane, questions he posed. As a young teenager, his adult-like mind contemplated the meaning of life, and, in a way, he was my religion, formulating my muddled thoughts into amateur philosophy.

It'd be easy to dismiss our explorations as adolescent angst, but by giving me something to believe in, he probably kept me alive.

The marginally older boy with a mop of conditioned curls quietens my demons by helping me to understand them, and his voice eventually becomes my own. It's okay to think, to challenge, he teaches me.

My only problem with Ross, at least for a while, is that he's taken in by my mother twiddling his tresses and pointing out that he's politer and sweeter-natured than me. "She's really not so bad, Dan. Give her a chance," makes me despair.

Even so, instead of condemning my sullen disposition, Ross and other members of his clique, Leo and Harry, make it cool to scowl. We're anti-heroes, dressing and dancing as we please, defying rugby-playing alpha males in David Soul cardigans. Better still, a new generation of girls takes notice causing us to reconsider our priorities.

If Ross's self-assuredness, the arrogance negating all doubt, fails anyone, it's himself. Absconding when he needs it most, he's left alone on his bedroom floor wrestling with answers he was previously certain of, agonising over whether his path should be straighter. To follow the Lord.

I crave to be Ross's best friend but have to accept it's Leo's role. What's even harder to swallow is that I know Leo's sharper, more thoughtful than me, along with being effortlessly cool. Nonetheless, I resent Ross's lack of discernment.

Staring through my reflection into the Crawley's front room, it's as though I'm in there with Ross and his parents.

Everything's different to what I'm used to: conversation inquiring about each other's day; Mr Crawley conducting Beethoven with his pipe; books rather than arguments about what to watch on TV.

Although Ross and I shared milk monitor duties at Stoke Blakely Infants, it was not until we advanced through the comprehensive system that I cultivated a friendship, though it's not solely to improve my intellect.

I've noticed Deborah Parker going into Ross' form room, but she doesn't arouse my interest until I see her dash to the headmaster's office clutching a music sheet.

"There goes Miss Goody Goody," I'm about to tell my classmates when I notice something about her's changed.

She still has the jaunty, deferential innocence of a teacher's pet, only now, the top three buttons of her shirt are undone, revealing a round of breast. Girl to woman since the last time I saw her, she glances upwards, and her eyes lock onto mine.

Her parents, she later tells me, vexed by their daughter's blossoming charms, demand she be the first girl at Brunswick Comp to wear trousers, which, unfortunately for them, serves to emphasise their daughter's nascent figure.

Over the coming days, I visualise a forest of black curls straining against white cotton panties. In the quiet of my bedroom, the imagery hardens along with my cock.

My inner voice, unimpressed by my post-wank self-loathing, would like to think I've learned that there's more to women than dirty sex, not least because I know from Debs's first blushing 'hi' that she's more placid, though less vital than my first love, tearaway Sarah Jenkins.

Compared to Sarah, Debs does everything too quickly – walking, breathing, giggling, but most of all talking, new words merging into unfinished sentences peppered with trills and exclamations. Debs hasn't grasped that enthusiasm isn't cool, and though it's hard to admit, I find it infectious.

Debs' lavender-scented skin complements her wholesome appearance, though it's at odds with the summer and winter scarves she wears. As English as a country cottage, a 1960s bob frames her rosy features, new tights laddered before leaving the house.

Her personality bubbles with the gift of being uncomplicatedly happy. She's as straightforward as she is unsophisticated, and although she carries me along in the sweep of her rush, Debs' shimmering jade eyes dim when I offend her.

An added benefit of seeing her is that her upper-floor form room resonates with the laughter of mostly middle-class students led by Ross. My own ground-level form room, 4B, is a cauldron of largely working-class thuggery, courtesy of the comprehensive system.

I observe how Ross's dextrous tongue and irreverent humour put him at the centre of attention which, however much I practice, fails to produce the same results for me.

Left with no option other than to join his in-crowd, I hang on to Ross's coat-tail as he holds classroom court. By ingratiating myself into the aesthete set, I'm an outsider who wants to be inside.

Meanwhile, I'm conflicted by my sentiments for Deb, whose rush rather than walk exaggerates the one feature I find hard to ignore; her buttocks.

Each cheek beats heavy time, landing with an almost audible thud that I feel obliged to keep my distance from in public. Simultaneously irritating and endearing, she's a substantial bird singing in my caged heart.

Despite living on the same Top Valley estate as Sarah, the Parkers are aspirational. Their front garden – a picture of suburban formality – scorns their near neighbours' weed-strewn path.

Debs' parents, Geoff and Joan, want to be upwardly mobile so badly they nearly are, but they're held back by their mode of transport; a step-through scooter, craniums protected by 1950s cloth-covered helmets, rather than a car.

It's unfair that Geoff and Joan blame me for coming between them and their daughter. They guillotined Debs's fourteen-year-old apron strings the day they made her play guitar at the school Harvest Festival, leaving her and me victims of finger-pointing sniggers.

I can't deny I encouraged Debs's insurgency, not least by coaxing her fingers round my own instrument.

Sexually, she's a harder nut to crack than Sarah. My first attempt is on a Sunday morning when, having persuaded her to skip church by feigning illness, I wait behind a hedge for her parents to leave.

Lying on her bed, she tells me I look like David Bowie, so I hug her and put her hand on my bulge. We've frequently petted, but it always ended with Debs clamping her legs together.

"No, Daniel. I need to know you love me first," put me in a difficult position. To lie and get my end away or retain a semblance of dignity.

Sexual morality wasn't something I generally worried about, but Debs pleading, virtuous eyes kept me on the right side of decency for once, although I didn't intend to make it a habit.

The Sunday morning things progress spirals me into a panic when, having removed her slacks, I realise I'm wearing the baggy red pants I've been meaning to throw away for two years.

'She's not going to think I'm David Bowie when she sees these,' I fluster, eyeing her now exposed breasts as she unzips my flies.

Debs says she loves me, though I don't know why. Doesn't she realise she's letting herself in for emotional cruelty?

Is my need to dominate women a lesson learned from my mother, not wanting to appear weak like my father, or am I just riddled with insecurity? I question myself without coming up with an answer. Alternatively, I might just be a no-good, heartless bastard by nature.

"Please don't hurt me," Jane implores, eyes swimming, as I remove her own substantial knickers.

"We don't have to do it, you know," I say. "Not if you don't want to." I pray she says what I want to hear. "What if Batman and Robin come back?"

"*Who*?"

"Your mum and dad. What if they come back when we're shag … making love?" I want to wipe away the tears teetering on her eyelids, but I have to retain the upper hand.

"Why are you crying?"

"You've obviously gone off me. Is it because you think I've got a big bum?"

"*Erm*. No, of course not. It's just that … that I want it to be special with it being your first time." I hesitate. "It *is* your first time, isn't it?"

"I'm not a slag like your last girlfriend. It *will* be special, Daniel. For me, anyway."

"Okay, but I need a bit of … you know." I glimpse at my crotch. "Just rub it on top of my trousers for now." I bet Casanova didn't have baggy pants issues like me.

"Why isn't your …you know … your thingy ha…? Is it because you've done it with Sarah and don't want to with me?" The anger in Debs' eyes transitions to self-reproach. "It's because I don't do it right, isn't it?"

Debs' hand has maintained its momentum, and while I want to say something comforting, all that emerges is, "Harder, harder. *Aghh … err*. The last bit is caused by the goo escaping my pants' tired elastic and slithering down my thighs. Pulling my jeans up, I want to go home.

"*Is that it*? Don't I even get a kiss?" Debs says, rolling onto her side. "I suppose you want to go home now." Thank God for telepathic communication.

"Course not. It's just that I've got something to do – with my dad. We're building a bonfire."

"In July?"

The Parker's bathroom air freshener has a new smell to counter as sperm globules stick to my fingers when I shove my pants in my pocket. On the ride to Stoke Blakely, I let the wind carry them into my chemistry teacher's garden. More innocence lost.

I'm close to dumping Debs, but as our sexual relationship evolves, she starts to outperform herself, open to whatever I present her with, including hairbrush handles and a banana that didn't quite fit.

But no matter how much Debs gives, I still want more. The problem is that apart from boys' talk and what's in Dad's dirty magazines, I don't really know what *more* is.

Debs' sexual liberation causes me another difficulty. How does she suddenly know what to do? She must have either done it before and not told me, in which case I'll definitely dump her, or she's been set free by my expert touch, a prurient libido let loose by a master's hand.

In any event, our affair survives two spirited years until, during a Ross-and-his-gang-end-of-school holiday to Brittany, I fall under the spell of a Gallic pout called Pascale.

On the day of departure, I promise Debs I'll be good, and she hands me a tiny, folded card addressed to Mr Grumpy. A hoop-shirted Frenchman is conveying a large gift on a bicycle. Inside, she misquotes Bowie:

"I'd sleep with you, baby, for 1,000 years."
All my love and kisses
Debs xx
PS. No knocking off of others.

The card's still under my bed.

As a grown man walking his dog, I wonder at the way I treated Debs, along with my childhood attitude to sex and whether it's any different now.

My warring parents certainly didn't take the time to teach me about birds and bees, nor were they role models for a loving relationship. Essentially, I was sexually enlightened by Jim's dirty magazines and playground smut.

×

Back inside my teenage mind, I'm alerted by passing remarks that 'my mate fancies you', and it occurs to me that I excite the interest of certain young girls. Why I inflame the desire of a minority of the population while revolting the rest, I haven't a clue, only that I entice the former by offering them nothing and fight in vain for the approval of the latter.

The more I dismiss those who pursue me, the more intense their pursuit, it seems. I'm flattered but could do without male envy adding to my unpopularity. If only I could talk to the girls I like and afford to lose the ones I don't, my life would be bearable. Maybe.

Regardless of my situation, I'm consumed by sex, preoccupied with breast, arse, or the swish of a short skirt. Driving or dining, fondling myself without thinking, I'm a teenage dirty old man. Is my sexual psychology as abnormal as the rest of me?

Nothing's sacred in my deviant world. Every thought tinged with filth, my mind's a reservoir of lechery. Dinner ladies, policewomen, nannies, nurses, midwives, secretaries, all there to be assessed, ruled in or out. A modern man, I'm not.

Does it make me a misogynist? And if I am, is Muriel responsible? Is my hatred for her a curse upon all her kind, caring and sharing beyond me; monkey do like monkey see.

There's no denying I also glow in the presence of masculine beauty; my internet searches black heavy, enthralled by enormous members. At times I'm actually sickened by mammary glands and miasmic discharge, which fuels doubts about my sexuality.

Anyway, is it any surprise I lie to and cheat on women? Wasn't it Eve who committed the original sin, introducing unrest into the Garden of Eden? And continues to do so. My quandary is that I need women because being alone is suicide.

The misfortune of girls like Debs is that they're left to bear the brunt of my nature, a wounded dog launching wave after wave of green-eyed attack. Yet it's with women that I'm true to myself and them.

Once their loyalty is assured, I expose my disturbing nature, revealing my core and encouraging them to do the same. Without a hand to hold, I'd collapse.

As a fifty-year-old man reflecting on my two-year affair with Debbie, I grimace. Then again, given that she soaked up my malice like a paper towel, who could criticise me for not changing tactics that work? Why risk a kind word that might be thrown back in my face?

Little did Debs realise that she held all the cards. If she'd withdrawn her tender-lipped kisses, whispered idolatry, and walnut whips, it'd have hurtled me into a grief-stricken wasteland, and I'd have crawled over broken glass to get her back.

Never apologise. Never explain. Unless the lady turns to walk away has been my lifelong, not entirely successful, motto.

CHAPTER 30

My adolescence is defined by Ross, though as I get older, I try to redress the balance by developing my own thoughts. The consequence is that we become more competitive. We're shadow boxers though his unshakeable self-belief rarely sees me the victor.

A peripheral player who wants a leading role, I slip in and out of my friend's classroom clique, inconsolable if I'm not invited to an existentialist debate in Ross's bedroom. Compensation comes in the form of being asked – do I imagine begrudgingly? – to go on the end-of-school holiday to Brittany.

✳

After a nauseating Portsmouth to St Malo ferry ride, the five of us separate into two groups and hitchhike to St Quentin.

We were expecting a small town, but St Q is nothing more than a hamlet where the only bar long since pulled down its shutters. Our spirits sink even lower when the rented 'house' turns out to be a first-floor flat, crying babies above and below.

My pecking order has Ross and Leo at the top, leaving quick-to-laugh Harry and me vying for middle position, while Keith, a misfit who left Brunswick Comp to sell anything he can find, brings up the rear.

Ross and Leo, whose chartered surveyor mum paid for the holiday in anticipation of her son passing his A-levels, which he failed, take the larger twin-bedded room. I grab the single divan leaving Harry and Keith to argue over who gets which bunk.

Every night after my roommates turn off the lights, I'm forced to listen to Ross and Leo's stimulating conversation through the party wall.

I'm perplexed by Leo's popularity, given that his face resembles a death row mugshot. Soul-stripping eyes resting under hooded brows, nose barbed, mouth slotted, forehead sloping, hair spiked signal danger like a multi-coloured snake.

I like to think of Leo and me as peas in the same diseased pod, both reviled on the catwalk of public opprobrium and constantly under threat from dominant males. We should ditch Ross and form our own confederacy would be my treacherous solution, but his initial interest isn't sustained.

To my regret, the only thing Leo and I ultimately share is the growing realisation that our appearance can have a cause and effect other than condemnation. Glacial aloofness and daring to stand out in a crowd excite impressionable young French girls, it appears.

Our first few days in Brittany are spent drinking Kronenbourg and eating brie-smeared baguettes behind the rain-streaked windows of a nearby, though deserted, village café.

Arguments flare in the flat, mostly involving Keith for not putting his hand in his pocket or the washing up, accompanied by the bloke below banging on the ceiling.

When the rain stops on the fourth day, we venture five kilometres to the nearest beach, where it starts raining again. Ambling along a stream that becomes a river, I try to engage Harry in a philosophical debate, but when he laughs, I wish I'd stayed in Nottingham.

A picture-postcard bar beside a lock excites our interest, but grimy windows and closed double doors suggest it hasn't been open in living memory.

"'Gee Shaggy, hee, hee, heee." My Scooby-Doo impression still doesn't amuse anyone, so I continue. "This place looks haunted."

"Who cares as long as it's serving." Leo's mother found him, aged thirteen, collapsed on the kitchen floor, comatose on cooking sherry. He's barely stopped drinking since.

The middle-aged barman in a white apron, matching shirt, and tightly knotted black tie appears not to hear the old-fashioned bell announcing our arrival. He obviously isn't expecting anyone, and it's as if the glass he's polishing contains the meaning of life. Or at least his.

Over a few drinks, Jacques tells us that before the river silted up, motor launch Parisians ordered champagne and oysters while narrow boaters dined on cassoulet and beer. Back then, not being seen at Jacques's place was a social faux pas. Today it's the opposite.

He agrees to our plans to bring the bar back to life with a shrug, and we drag the table football out of storage, bruising the player's feet with a discarded pool ball. To my amazement, I get the jukebox working by changing the fuse.

"We're Mods," I enthuse. "Except Ross, who's a hippie."

Jacques isn't against us bringing our ghetto blaster, and the bar becomes our private party venue. I throw up in the hole-in-the-ground toilet more than once, the previous night's pizza staining my Hush Puppies.

Word spreads fast about the Englishmen in fishtail parkas dancing to *Poison Ivy*, and the Wurlitzer becomes a posing post leaned on by local youths ordering whatever 'zee Inglish is 'avin' and one for them'.

On the third night, on top of my game, popular and admired, I'm encircled by teenagers imitating my "Green Onion" shuffle, teaching them the words to "Tears of a Clown".

Midway through a ghetto blasted "One Step Beyond" skank, elbows and knees in crazed coordination, I catch sight of a pair of powder blue eyes and flaxen pageboy hair. My deadpan expression belies internal euphoria.

The girl's standing to one side of the makeshift dancefloor, one arm folded across her chest, sipping a luminous drink through a straw.

Dressed as if for school – white ankle socks, knee-length skirt, blouse – she casts me a shy smile before being distracted by a friend.

A rounded face and puppy fat cheeks a favourite uncle might pinch say she might be too young, though the flare of her nostrils, as suggestive as the slightly longer-than-necessary gaze she allows to linger, suggest otherwise.

Then **BOOM.** She smiles, and everything changes, virginal coyness replaced by sexual suggestion, more woman than girl. I reach out a hand, which she takes, and pull her in.

A shout in my ear tells me her name's Pascale and that her perfume's understated; purity and carnal knowledge combined, or so I'd like to think.

Pidgin English, and an unspoken understanding, are enough to share our inner thoughts in a darkened corner before we snog to *Walking on the Moon*.

With her petite frame sitting in my lap, arms about my neck, I'm moved by a different kind of stirring, wanting to stroke and caress rather than defile. Making love can wait. This life or the next, it doesn't matter.

I walk six kilometres the following evening to the Berthou family home, where hours pass like minutes in her bedroom, clothes falling to the floor as we absorb each like mercury.

Pascale's everything I need but didn't think existed. It doesn't matter that her breasts are small, legs shorter than I would like, because her smile illuminates my darkness. Judgement absent; she's silk to my granite.

Swimming in secret seas, we imagine furnishing our Parisian apartment with worn leather club chairs, flea market rugs, and a writing desk with an old-fashioned typewriter on which to write my existentialist novel.

"I know a good market for flea rugs near Paris," she says, cold-shouldering me when I laugh.

"You makes fun of me. *Merde, les Anglais.*" Each word is a knife into my heart, and I apologise with a 'je t'aime' before realising what I've said for the first time in my life.

I nearly die in the pregnant pause that follows, saved when she throws her arms around me and says the same. Convinced my heart's going to explode, I tell her I'll learn French to save misunderstandings.

"Do you like le jazz, Dan*iel*," she asks, brow worried as her father's music leaks through the floorboards. Uncertain what to say, I take a 50/50 chance.

"I love it. Especially Miles Parker and *er* ..." I try to remember what else I've seen in Monsieur Berthou's record collection.

"*Je t'aime*, Dan*iel.*"

"*Je t'aime*, Pascale, but what I'd really like us to do is talk. Really talk."

"*J'adore te parler* Daniel. *Mais* what about *la monnaie?*"

"Don't worry about that. I've got plenty of money," is my second lie of the evening, though I'm struck by the same concern.

"Perhaps you could get a job in a bar." She looks aghast. "Just until I learn to speak French and my book gets published," I add.

I fantasise about Pascale being moved to tears by my words, us making love, then talking into the early hours, our pain and inner demons dispelled in a heartfelt exchange.

Unsure if she's joking, I smile at her coy suggestions of marriage and children. I say 'one'. She says 'four'. I'm uneasy. *Fuck it*. Why not? I'll be a proper parent, unlike my own.

I can't wait to tell Muriel I'm marrying a foreigner. 'A foreigner! Why can't you find a nice English girl, like Deborah Parker?'

What I can't change is the disappointment on Monsieur Berthou's face when he opens the door every evening. He's unused to fresh-faced sternness in his house. I try being light-hearted, but thanks to Muriel, it doesn't come naturally.

I'm positive Pascale's father sees through me, heightening my self-consciousness and fixed expression even more.

The Berthou's featureless single-storey residence on the outskirts of Quimperlé is crammed with hefty Dépôt Vente furniture. A crochet blanket hides a leatherette sofa's fatigue, and a spider plant dangles its creepy offspring from a corner shelf.

But appearance doesn't matter because I'm thrilled by the comings and goings of neighbours, siblings, and cousins. Uncle Georges suggests I visit him in Morocco, where he's doing his National Service as a doctor. He helps himself to an apple in the fruit bowl, carelessly munching and chewing, so I take a banana just to spite Muriel.

The house has the energy and intimacy of a rush-hour train station where people embrace and kiss. I shake manly hands, then offer my mouth to puckered lips aiming for my cheeks, exhilarated by my love for Pascale and her family.

I long to open my arms and express the bubbling emotion fizzing inside me, rejoice in being human after all. Instead, I feel my face shape-shift into a flushed glower, certain my crippling discomfort is seen as angry and hard when I withdraw to the kitchen. Pascale holds my hand, standing on tiptoe to whisper "*j'adore*," though I'm convinced her fervour has waned.

A few minutes later, her best friend, Nicolas, arrives wearing a room-warming smile and the straight-backed confidence of the wealthy. His welcome, or so it appears to me, is that of Monsieur Berthou's future son-in-law.

Shorter and older than me, the trainee dentist reflects the family's glow in his brogues and cuff links, both as shiny as his pelt of dark hair. Abel to my Cain, the BMW key fob he twirls round his finger makes me dislike him even more.

Pascale explains that she and Nicolas grew up together and that her family will love me once they get to know me, but doubt has sown its seed. I search for honesty in her moist eyes, silently imploring her not to desert me, to stand by me in Paris, as we agreed.

As if reading my thoughts, Pascale nods, prompting my own movie star beam, which seems to offend Nicolas as much as it delights everyone else. My behaviour change is contrary to what they've been told, and they respond in kind, finally accepting me as part of the family.

Monsieur Berthou puts an arm round his daughter's shoulders and, offering me, who he now calls her 'ros bif boyfriend', another drink, escorts Nicolas into his book-lined office.

It's taken me eighteen years to realise that I've got to start acting my age and accept girls can have boys as friends. Blowing Pascale a kiss, I smile at my newfound maturity.

✻

Ross, Leo, Harry, Keith, and I, now ex-schoolboys, are returning to Nottingham in two days, and we intend to bow out with a Saturday night bang. Pascale listens as we argue over playlists, me deriding Ross's *Brown Sugar* and disregarding Keith's *We Are the Champions*.

We'd elope to Paris straightway if it weren't for her prearranged trip to see Uncle Georges in Morocco. The thought of us not being together creates an ulcerous ache inside me, our final hours tortuous.

She hasn't yet told her parents about our life-changing plans, though she has deferred taking her English degree at Bordeaux University. Pascale hopes her mum and dad will understand the power of love but worries about putting additional strain on 'Papa's 'eart'.

I'm forced to check my hackles when Nicolas suggests he take Pascale out for 'chocolate *chaude*' at her favourite patisserie. She agrees on the condition they take a lengthy detour to Quimper to buy a new dress, which makes me wonder if she'll exploit my devotion, as well. In the meantime, I've got to get ready to party.

Forty mobylettes are parked outside Jacques' when I arrive just after dusk. Their owners are crammed inside smoking filterless cigarettes and miming "My Generation," each 'oping to die before they get old'.

Mid Baggy Trousers moon stomp in my two-tone suit, I exchange smiles with Leo, dressed in an electric blue and cream boating blazer, who's helping Jacques, and himself, behind the bar.

I freeze, guts alongside the cigarette butts on the floor, when Pascale walks in with Nicolas, who's adjusting the strapless dress he obviously bought. She looks sensational. I wave, though it's hard to hide how annoyed I am. Make that hurt.

The crowd melts away at 2 a.m., and, sweeping his arm across the bar, Jacques tells Ross to lock up when we're done. Nicolas was there each time I tried talking to Pascale, so I left them to it and got even more pissed with my friends.

"FUCK-ING HELL, Dan," Ross beams. "Jacques has only gone and left yours truly in charge, which means we can drink ourselves to death." Jacques giving Ross the keys narks me, especially after I fixed his jukebox.

"Well, don't just stand there, you posing pot of petulance; get me another drink."

The five of us lean against the bar, mesmerised by bottles of brandy, whisky, and vodka hanging between parallel poles behind the bar. "All for one and one for …," we whoop, leaping the counter.

Leo's the first to pull himself up by the wooden poles suspended from the ceiling and press his mouth against an optic, double gin on top of countless pints of lager, followed by me and the others. Whoever throws up first drops out is the name of the game.

Me and Leo are the last men standing until my hand slips from the pole, and I land in a pile of Keith's puke. I know it's his because he's horizontal against the wall.

"*Bollocks*," I shout, flicking a pea off my jacket, and looking up, my vision's clear enough to tell me Pascale's not in the bar. Nor is Nicolas.

I down what I assume is a leftover Coke. It's too late when I realise it's not.

"*ROSS.*"

"What is it, you lanky piece of piss? Want another drink?"

"You've got to get me out of here. I've drunk red wine and am going to be violently ill in about five minutes." He tilts his head quizzingly. "I'm allergic. Where's Pascale?"

"That's easy, my green-gilled chum. She's outside with Nicolas. Says he'll take us home in his BMW if we want. For a Frenchman, he's alright."

"No, he isn't. Now get me home."

Overcome with remorse and longing, I lurch towards Pascale when we get outside, delighted there's an atmosphere between her and Nicolas. I open my mouth to kiss her. But close it again when it fills with vomit.

She casts me a disappointed glance, and I'd be puzzled by her getting into her dad's beaten-up Peugeot if Ross wasn't bundling me into Nicolas' BMW. The others demand the Frenchman crank up the stereo and put his foot down while I wind down the window.

We speed along country lanes where, inside my head, strobes pulse through swirling distorted images to the beat of the bass-driven thud pummelling my skull. Voices screech, headlights flash, grotesque shapes rush towards me, vanishing at the point of impact.

Stepping onto the driveway, convinced we're back at the flat and needing to liberate a bellyful of spew,

I hear a faint warning, a sound from the past I wave away.

Somersaulting through the air bouncing off tarmac isn't what I expect, but neither is thumping off a tree, rolling through brambles, or coming to a halt on the edge of a ditch.

Raising my head, I watch Nicolas's brake lights illuminate, then dim. Which is when I realise the nightmare I assume I'm in is real.

I've no idea whether I pass out for a minute or an hour. The only certainty is that at some point, I'm going to die. I've been here before in a Mansfield sand quarry, only this time there'll be no reprieve.

Lying here, I contemplate what to expect. A pointy hooded reaper, a feather-like descent to a better place, or a spiralling plummet into the fiery depths of hell?

Turns out that dying is more of a gradual seep into a dusky blackness, ashes to ashes, dust to dust as life extinguishes, a final blip about to blacken the screen.

I welcome the release from time's grip, free to roam the stars, one of which flickers, seeming to call me as I drift towards an unknown destination. The absence of trumpeting angels and pearly gates suggests I'm heading where it's hot.

A spark ignites my barely perceptible consciousness, a dazzling blink followed by another until the faraway blueness of a tiny flame burns. Dreamy and slow, as if eternal decisions are being made, my eyes open like a newborn baby, rebirthed. As what, I've no idea.

I categorically reject what I see. It's the trick of an unsound mind. "**YOU DO NOT EXIST**," I shout at the imposter. "I've told you before. **GOD DOES NOT EXIST**." My voice fades with the effort of yelling at windmills.

As when I was about to fall off a sandstone cliff, my redeemer is without form. Just an ageless radiance, a luminosity lifting me onto my forearms and knees, showing me how to breathe. How to crawl.

It can't be happening again. God and I are both stone-cold dead, so who's putting my hands one in front of the other?

"You cruel bastard, leave me alone," I bellow at the heavens. **YOU. DO. NOT. EXIST**.

After a two-kilometre effort, my exhausted knock goes unanswered, so I hammer on the door with a rock until a light comes on. Collapsing, I fill the bucket Ross places in front of me with chuck and abdominal lining, then quietly thank a God I don't believe in but can't deny.

The following morning, Pascale dabs at my wounds as we say our tear-streaked goodbyes. Then, pledges and commitments confirmed, she pins her heart to mine by saying she'll write every day from Morocco.

I hold her not entirely in focus face and tell her I'll count the hours, no, the minutes, until I hitchhike back to Quimperlé in ten weeks. Soon after, we'll move to Paris.

Arriving back in Nottingham, I discover I've secured a place on the second-rate journalism course at North

London Poly I applied for before leaving, which I defer for a year in case things don't go well in Paris. Options are best left open in my 18-year-old experience.

I flaunt the Moroccan stamp at Muriel, then press Pascale's lengthy devotions, sealed with a lipstick kiss, to my mouth before placing them in my bedside drawer.

×

Jim drops me on the M1 slip road almost three months later, then drives away without waving. Muriel doesn't come. She's got a hairdresser's appointment. Or so she says.

I'm the loneliest I've ever felt, directing my thumb at the accelerating cars spraying me with rainwater. Until a National Coal Board lorry hisses to a halt.

Twelve hours later – after getting lost in London, a coach ride to Dover, and an awkward non-English speaking lift to Paris – I'm lying on a Parisian hostel camp bed watching a neon sign flash through the curtains.

The communal toilet at the end of a long corridor is *hors service*, so I piss in the sink, ammonia mingling with mould. But none of it matters because it's done in the name of love, and she's waiting for me at Quimperlé station. Or so I think.

As my train pulls into the riverside Brittany town, I peer through tired eyes at elongated blurs on the platform.

Faces sharpen as the train slows, and I search for Pascale, who I've dreamt about standing on tiptoe, scanning the crowd, then running towards me, arms open, but she isn't here.

Without my friends, I'm exposed, a man out of time, in my Ben Sherman button-down collar shirt, canary yellow tie, and army surplus fishtail parka.

There are no admiring smiles from local youths, just bewildered frowns, and heading for the exit, I pretend not to notice Nicolas toying with his BMW key fob. It'd be an unhappy coincidence at the best of times.

"Ello, Dan*iel*."

"*Oh*, bonjour, Nicolas. I didn't see you there." I lie, scanning the concourse. "Have you seen Pascale?"

"She is not 'ere." A door slams. I flinch. I'm on edge. Something's wrong.

"Pascale, she wanted to tell you 'erself, but …" My eyes follow the BMW key fob he's twirling round his gold-ringed finger.

"*But* what?"

"'er fath*er*, Monsieur Berthou 'e is …"

"I *know* who Pascale's father is. What about him?"

Nicolas runs his hand through his thatch of black hair. I'd do the same, but mine's lying on a barber's floor in Nottingham.

"'e die of an 'eart attack two week ago."

I obviously didn't hear him right. If I did, I'd be having a coronary myself.

"That's not funny, Nicolas. In any event, Pascale would've called me."

"You are not there." I'm not in the mood for this. Even his gallic shrug annoys me.

"Look, Nicolas. I've been travelling since yesterday morning and …" I'm drowned out by a platform announcement I don't understand.

"We are getting ma…" The broken loudspeaker cone above our heads continues to crackle, and six inches taller than him, I lean in.

"YOU'RE WHAT?"

"Pascale and me, we are getting ma*rried*." My pulse rate accelerates from sixty beats a minute to several thousand.

"She ask me give you this." The Frenchman slaps a photograph in my hand, which I drop, then catch. Small victories are what it's all about, sometimes.

"If we both just calm down, we can …" I appeal to his sense of decency. I'll smash his teeth in later.

"I 'ave always loved Pascale, and now she loves me. 'Er moth*er* is very 'app-ee."

I'm in someone else's nightmare where too much is happening.

"Per'aps, you are a little young, Dan*iel*." The 21-year-old trainee dentist's patronising afterthought stings even though he's right. I'm a 12-year-old who needs his mum.

"I don't care if *'er mother is very 'app-ee*. Pascale loves me, not you."

His bicep bulges as he carries his Lacoste jacket, Phil Collins-style, over his shoulder as he walks away.

Fuck it.

I catch up and launch a series of blows into the side of his head.

Or would do.

If I wasn't rooted to the platform. Whether out of fatigue, shock, or cowardice, I'm unsure.

"Pascale's only with you cos her dad's dead." My shout's lost in the station's hum. "You smarmy French… tosser."

An elderly woman, hair coiled like a dog turd, stops and stares at the island in her stream.

I'm a boy out of time. It's 1980, and a stone's been dropped in my rock pool. Crystal-clear water's now chaos.

A shadow of blonde hair flicks behind a pillar. At least, I think it does.

×

I'm unsure I'm over Pascale, even as a fifty-year-old. Certain it was me who fucked it up by getting pissed, maybe I need to stop blaming other people for ruining my life, including Muriel. Who, after all, is dead.

And where does God fit into all this? The Big Man who keeps saving me when it'd be better all round to let me go, to rest in hellish peace with my mother. Now

I've come to rely on him, I'm convinced he's going to desert me when I most need him.

Regardless of the outcome, what I learned from Pascale was priceless. Not only was I wholeheartedly capable of loving someone, I knew what it meant to be part of a family who cared about each other, and if only for a short while, me.

From now on, hope springs eternal. Until it dries up again.

CHAPTER 31

"C'mon, Ben, we're going." As my mind returns to the present, I turn up my coat collar, take a last look at Ross's house, and hurry on. My head's buzzing with childhood recollections, but the vultures are gathering, and I need to bury my mother.

"Jane'll be furious if we don't get a wiggle on." My spaniel's ears prick up hearing a familiar name. "Especially when she finds out I haven't finished my reading."

My sister and Jim insisted I write a eulogy. What am I supposed to say? That Muriel was a great mother who treated my dad like a doormat?

"I wonder if Dad will try to kill himself again now that Muriel's gone?" I ask Ben, though it isn't something I want to dwell on.

I've arrived at the crossroads where my Physics teacher, Greg, turned right instead of left into the village, forever changing our relationship in the process.

We became friends after he'd given me after-school instruction, often in Nottinghamshire's pubs and clubs, some of them gay, about Marxist revolutionaries.

The cool young tutor with the remnants of a fair-haired quiff was an ardent socialist and an amateur photographer. He also claimed I had the makings of a model.

Wanting to revolutionise the world while having my hand crossed with silver and some free clothes was another drop of acid on my already corroded soul. Whether I was born or made bad was something I could account for later.

✕

"You only want me for my body," I joke one summer evening as Greg hands me another pint of lager. We're distractedly watching a game of cricket from The Reindeer's beer garden. "Not even that," he responds, restraining a smile.

Having drunk two halves of shandy to my three pints of Shipstones, Greg suggests we head into Nottingham to check out a new club. "I might even get us in for free."

Married to Joyce, Greg's half the age of most of Brunswick Comp's other classroom relics.

A good three inches shorter than me, with an unmuscular build and no waist, ready laugh, progressive barber, and an incidentally well-chosen pair of Buddy Holly glasses, along with a laid-back attitude to teaching, make him a hit with the students.

The female contingent of Greg's similar-aged colleagues – who, even in my time, have switched from knee-length woollen skirts to denim shirts with two imitation pearl studs undone – is so envious of his easy-going popularity that they fawn over him in the common room then slag him off down the pub. I know because Ross, Leo, and I overhear them on the other side of The Cavendish's saloon bar partition.

"The only reason he wears a tie is that he's got his eye on the headship, the ambitious chauvinistic toad," scoffs Miss Hennessy, helping herself to another glass of Black Tower. "And as for those ridiculous Buddy Holly glasses, he's not a teenager." She's unaware that three of her students have got their hands over their mouths, stifling guffaws a few feet away.

"Buddy Holly *tree* more like!" cackles Mrs Hodge. "I heard he had to leave his last school. No smoke without fire, I always say."

While I doubt Greg's story that he's researching a PhD on the emergent loud and proud 1980s Nottingham gay scene, I'm happy to go along with it. Entry to the best dancefloors in town isn't to be sniffed at; plus, I learn more from him in an hour down the pub than a week in the classroom.

I have the mental fortitude not to look beyond the next free drink as I'm paraded round Nottingham's hedonistic gay meat markets, as long as an unspoken line isn't crossed. Besides, my seventeen-year-old ego isn't averse to a little pandering, even from men in chained leather caps and lederhosen. God knows I get little enough attention at home,

Greg's greeted with kisses in every basement bar we visit and maintains it's taken years to get people's trust. But I can't help sniggering when the head of Religious Education walks in, sees Greg and me together, then turns around. I panic. Greg laughs as if he's fireproof.

Our relationship develops when he says a London modelling agency has offered him a trial-based photography assignment. "They specialise in upmarket menswear. Actually, it's more down-wear," he laughs in his nervous way. "Calvin Klein boxer shorts, that sort of thing." I'm dubious, and his face says he knows it.

"They do polo shirts as well," he tacks on. "Ralph Lauren, Fred Perry, all the top brands – though the real money's in underwear. Not everyone can pull it off if you'll pardon the …"

"Do I get to keep the pants?"

"I'm sure we could sort something out with Adam, the agency owner. We'll have to do a test shoot to see if you've got what it takes, though." My interest sparks his, which dampens when I look away. "It's up to you. If you don't fancy it, there's no shortage of other takers."

"It's not that. It's just that my exams are coming up."

"We could give it a quick go, and if it takes up too much time, we'll pack it in. They might not like your ugly mug, anyway."

Greg finds a recently harvested field fifteen miles away and thinks me posing on a hay bale will make a good shot. I do my best to appear comfortable in a pair of tight, wet-look swimming trunks, worried I'm not filling the pouch, as he sets up his camera.

"*Oi*, David Bailey, hurry up, will you? I'm freezing. And I've got bits of hay sticking up my ar..." My attempt to loosen up goes too far, as usual.

"Over to your left. Too much. Back a bit. Try putting your foot on the bale. No. The other one. Good. That's good. Now lie down." His Nikon doesn't *whirr* the way cameras do on the tele.

"I'm saving up for a motor drive," he tells me. "Now, try one arm behind your head. Relax. Time for a close-up to see the label." I instinctively move back as he leans in. "You need to stay still, Daniel. Great, that's good. Now straddle the bale."

"You sure this isn't for some gay porno mag?"

"Trunks off and bend over."

"YOU WHAT?"

"Gotcha." I notice how crooked his teeth are for the first time as he chuckles. "Now try the Hugo Boss boxers."

Although I didn't see the slides, Greg claims Adam's happy, and there's talk of us all going to Italy in the summer. In the meantime, Greg and I are to continue the good work, and 'yes', I can keep some of the clothes.

Greg hands over the best part of a hundred pounds a few weeks later, saying there's 'more where that came from' if we do some interior shots.

There's a problem when Greg says Adam doesn't want to stump up for hotel rooms, so we settle on my teacher's semi-detached home instead. His wife, Joyce, is on a lecture tour.

We switch to the conservatory, from where I can see the top floor of Brunswick Comp, when Greg says his Habitat couch 'isn't sexy enough', ducking when the next-door neighbour hangs out her washing.

"*Shit*. Did she see us?" I worry, astonished and reassured by the risks Greg takes.

"I don't think so, but we'd better move upstairs," he replies. "Fancy a drink?"

"A large brandy should do the trick." I'll be pissed in no time.

The guest room's too small, and I end up on the marital bed, being stared at by Joyce. It's not a flattering photo, though few are. Last summer, Greg invited a few Sixth Formers and almost liberal colleagues to a house party, further increasing his popularity, and introduced me to his wife, whose larger-than-life presence wasn't matched by her personality.

When Greg asks me to open my legs, modelling a pair of boxers, I worry I'm revealing more than you'd see in a Littlewoods catalogue. So I think about the money and concentrate on being the centre of attention. Besides, what's wrong with giving someone a bit of visual titillation if it's their thing? I reassure myself.

My exam revision suffers from the late nights and lost weekends, though it's worth it. Not only do I benefit financially, the secrecy cements Greg's and my relationship. *No*. It's more than that. It's an intimate, intellectual friendship.

I've begun my great unfinished novel – an existentialist attempt to make sense of my life – and my sixth form tutor encourages me, offering insights and amendments. Journalism, he agrees, is a good fallback position.

At home, Muriel insists I'm wasting my time and should focus on getting 'a proper job like being a doctor'. My father, Jim, naturally agrees with her.

Greg's extra-curricular lessons, referencing Marx and Guevara, stimulate me beyond the kings and queens of England, and as long as Greg doesn't touch me, I regard it as time well spent. The way I see it, I'm getting more than I give.

During a country pub drive, he says he's concerned about my mock exam results but coolly states he knows how to ensure I don't fail the real thing.

"How? A brain transplant?" I sound more dismissive than I intend, and he looks offended.

"Come for a Friday night drink, and I'll tell you," he teases.

I'm three-quarters sloshed in a red-bricked cellar gay nightclub when Greg next brings up the subject. "You know your exams are in two weeks, don't you?"

"Like I'd forgotten! I'm going to do so badly it's barely worth me taking them."

"Even if I know a way to pass them?" Smug doesn't suit him.

"Like what? You become psychic and give me the answers."

"I was thinking more like the questions."

"That's not funny. I'm fucked if I fail my A-levels."

"And thanks to me, you're not going to." He brushes my knee as he slips a large manilla envelope under the table.

Greg claims he's got a 'queer contact' on the examination board, who supplies him with two of the three upcoming Physics and Sociology papers in return for an unspecified favour.

"*Fuck me*," I say, peeping at the Cambridge Examination Board headed paper, knowing I've got two out of three qualifications in the bag. I'd hug Greg, but I don't want to encourage him just in case he's after something I don't want to give.

My complacency turns to despondency in the examination hall when only one of the supplied questions appears. I leave school with a single C in English Lit, which, later on, scrapes me onto an HND journalism course at North London Poly.

In my 18-year-old experience, when things can't get any worse, they do. And, after apologising about my exams while driving me home from a conciliatory pub crawl, Greg indicates right instead of left into the village.

"What you doing? This goes down to the river," I slur as the last streetlight reflects in my now former teacher's glasses.

"I fancied a bit more of a chat. You don't mind, do you?" Greg says, parking his Volvo behind a car rocking on its suspension springs. I laugh when a male hand shoots up to protect the occupants from our headlights.

"Looks like those buggers are having a good go at it," I say, instantly regretting my word choice.

Greg's unusually quiet in the starless gloom then shifts in his seat. Something's not right, and I search for the door handle I can't find, fearing this is the moment I get my just desserts.

The mechanical *click* that breaks the silence causes my out-of-sight fists to tighten, which uncurl when I realise Greg's adjusted the handbrake.

"You made me jump," I semi-laugh. "I should be getting back before Mother Dearest locks me out."

The next *click* has a hollow echo, as in one deft movement, Greg unbuckles his seatbelt and slides an arm across my back, then uses his right hand to try and convince my thighs to part.

Slamming my fist into his head isn't easy in the confined space, and my hand glances off the headrest. A flurry of flaps and blocks follows until I find myself at the front of the Volvo extracting my boot from its radiator grille.

Twisting my foot loose while hurling insults at Greg's shadowy figure in the driver's seat, I notice a rat scurrying along the riverbank, which somehow replaces anger with loneliness.

I walk to the open passenger door intending to kick it, but Greg's portrait of shamed indignity under the courtesy light prevents me. "You shouldn't have done that," is all I can manage.

"I know, but I thought …. Get in, and I'll take you home." I hesitate. I'm nothing if not a pragmatist, but the five-minute drive takes an eternity.

Reflecting on our relationship three decades later, do I feel preyed upon, groomed? The answer is 'yes'. And 'no'. I gained more than I lost is the way I see it. Regardless of his motivation, Greg showed me the sort of kindness, even love, my parents didn't know how to.

Given that Greg can't help who he is any more than I can, might it not be said that I abused the abuser? Perhaps I should find him, tell him that my solitary A-level, along with some fast-talking, got me into journalism, after all. Who knows? "There might even be some free pants in it, Ben."

Chapter 32

Ten minutes from home, where extended family members are assembling for my mother's funeral, I'm alarmed. Two swaggering carpenters with low-slung holsters are coming towards Ben and me. 'Hands in or out of pockets?' is a quandary that's vexed me all my life.

Although I resent how the way in which someone walks defines them, it's a social regulation I rarely risk breaking. I've long since realised that appearance is king and that it can work for or against me.

My own inherently pendulous gait is an insolent stand against the tradition that Englishmen must keep their hands in their pockets unless they're hard enough to withstand a challenge, which I'm not.

It's taken me years to formulate a guideline that if the approaching threat level is high, i.e. a stronger male, both extremities should be hidden and shoulder sway minimised. If the threat level's low, however, such as female or elderly, I'm free to strut like a redneck cockerel.

The two approaching builders, pistols and fists at the ready, at least in my imagination, clearly suggest danger, and shackled by convention, I slide my hands into my pockets.

I've no idea why but I'm intrinsically frightened of people. Even the smallest are capable of inflicting pain with a snide remark; my external armour of unshakeable self-belief and physical presence, which in itself attracts unwanted attention, is an illusion.

Aged twelve, I trembled when a classmate said, "nobody likes you", and, thirty-eight years later, it still keeps me awake at night, exacerbated by the vilification I've accumulated since.

The carpenter danger passes, and a few yards ahead, Ben tugs on his lead, eager to cross the road. He knows his breakfast is only moments away, and the spaniel gives me a dirty look when I make a turn.

Around the corner is where Simon Duxley lived, who I haven't thought about in years, which is odd given how much time we spent together. He was supposed to come to Australia with me to work for Uncle Graham.

Simon was in the year above me at Brunswick Comp, where we hated each other. I saw him as the Punchinello of a rugby-playing, cardigan-wearing clique of toy men who tolerated him because his wit was sharper than theirs.

It wasn't until I moved to London that Simon and I became close, having established we had near-identical record collections and rode motorbikes. Yet, despite the years of being almost inseparable, to this day, I still don't know if he's gay, straight, or hermaphrodite.

Not knowing if Simon prefers the hard or soft option restricts our friendship, as far as I'm concerned, not least because it limits our conversations to barstool banter and who's top of the league.

Honesty and the intimate ties that bind are missing, which probably explains why we drifted in and out of each other's lives until we lost contact altogether. I heard on the grapevine that he's now a successful music producer in LA.

When I initially arrived in London, Simon clearly didn't want to introduce me to his friends, and we arranged to meet at the Soho Brasserie, which had the advantage, for me at least, of being surrounded by sex shop window displays.

✽

My affiliation with porn begins aged nine when I discover a copy of Dad's *Fiesta* magazine hidden behind the hot water tank. The bagful of Swedish publications I later find under a hedge, wide-open images to transcend the everyday further broaden my mind.

Things progress, age sixteen, when I take my first steps towards Nottingham's only licensed sex shop, veering away when confronted by its metal grilles and black-painted windows.

Shopping for sex in the 1970s is done under the threat of feminist attack, and I walk past Private's intimidating frontage on five consecutive Saturdays before pressing the buzzer.

Buttocks clenched, legs buckling, I'm terrified of being spotted by friends, teachers, or neighbours, which also increases the thrill.

I admire my own bravado, my pleasure-seeking individuality, but worry about my lecherous nature and why, if my disdain for Muriel makes me despise her sex, I desire the charms of the female form, albeit in subservient positions?

After what feels like an eternity, Private's intercom admits me into its starkly lit rows of metal shelves stacked with 18R magazines. Disappointment displaces elation when I see that opaque cellophane hides everything except the crowns of indiscriminate women's heads.

A tattooed and nose-pierced assistant seated on a stool behind a glass cabinet with nowhere to put his legs eyes his only potential customer, me, then glazes over again, which is when I move to the video wall.

From a distance, *Chitty Chitty Gang Bang*, *Pussy in Boots*, and *King Dong* beckon, but the bent double models' only bits of interest are concealed behind inky blobs. Stills on the back of the VHS boxes, while explicit, are so small they could be passport photos.

Self-disgust and morality muddy my mind, and my craving for indecency switches to a yearning to change – to be good, and leave my Private hell behind me, so I mope into a newsagent to buy a consoling Toffee Crisp.

While waiting to pay for my self-congratulatory treat, I notice a revolving rack of filth at the rear of the shop. I want to be disgusted but seedy sexuality is more exciting than morality, and the dependable names of *Rustler, Hustler,* and *Whitehouse* lure me into the shadows. They might not be the shooting stars of an adults-only shop, but they're a step up from reticent *Penthouse* pets with hands over their vitals.

The string-vested shopkeeper is poring over a crossword puzzle, and I wheel the rack out of sight to devour the illicit pages, happy as a pig in shit. Finally, I untuck my shirt and stuff two magazines down the back of my jeans.

Walking stiffly to the counter, fantasy meets reality when I squeeze sideways on behind a fanciable female customer. Problem is, I'm not sure I can tell the difference anymore.

My next sex shop challenge comes aged eighteen when I definitively move to London. Getting to grips with Soho's pleasure domes is an entirely different proposition demanding precise environmental conditions.

My always identical routine goes as follows:

Cruise the principal streets until I'm drawn by a flash of obscenity in a window or a grunting soundtrack.

Check means of access and whether there's any security to negotiate.

Ensure no women or policemen are in the vicinity. If so, give the premises a contemptuous look of revulsion and keep walking.

Repeat the operation ad infinitum until the coast is clear, then plunge my hands, prayer-like, into the beaded curtain.

Unscathed inside Erotica's bunker, my shoulders drop along with my arse cheeks.

I begin by stroking a 12-inch dildo's 'realistic' textured length, wondering if I can somehow pass it off as my own. Then, turning, I stretch for the blow-up doll suspended, angel-like, from the ceiling; fleshy cherried lips there for the taking until I'm distracted by whips, fetish outfits, and chains.

But the Holy Grail of grime, drawing me as if a metal filing to a magnet, is the airless rooms where spunking spectaculars play on tired screens, grunting males relieving themselves in the darkness. Before I've left, I know I'll be back for more, often within the hour.

✖

Because being alone in a bar isn't an option, I've ensured I'm fifteen minutes late meeting Simon at the Soho

Brasserie. Problem is, I can't see him in the cheek-to-cheek crowd, and my stomach's beginning to flip.

'What if he isn't coming?' I fluster, wiping my palms on my Levi 501s. 'Wait a second, has he dyed his hair blond and been down the gym since I saw him a year ago? It sure as hell looks like it.'

Schoolboy tricks never die, so I tap one of his shoulders, then duck to the other side.

"Been pumping iron, have you, mate?"

"*You fuckin' what?*" I'm being glared at by a muscle-brained jock.

"Sorry, I thought you were someone else. Only you're not." I back off, Uriah Heep-like.

Convinced everyone is judging me for being Johnny No Mates, I exaggerate my head movements, search out recesses, and check my watch. 'I'm definitely not here on my own' is the message, reinforced by sticking my head out the door and looking both ways.

'What's the matter with you?' an inner voice demands. 'Stop being such a wimp, go to the bar and order yourself a drink like a normal person would.'

I make it to the counter, where the aproned barman won't acknowledge me. It's a good thing because I don't know if cider's in or out, and I don't want to step out of line.

A glance in the mirror tells me my hair's flopped forward instead of being swept back, so I fumble for my comb that's not there. *Shit.* My barnet's made a bad day worse.

I'm eventually served a bottle of what everyone else is drinking; only they don't seem to be gobsmacked by the price.

Now I need something to casually lean against because sitting in the only available chair will make me stand out. "There must be something wrong with him," I hear them whisper. "Pretend you haven't seen him." I don't blame them. I'd do the same.

Lighting a cigarette is the last card in my self-conscious pack. Realising I don't have any is a bonus. I can now fill ten minutes finding the machine, asking for change, unwrapping the packet, tapping one on the box for no apparent reason, then, slowly, very slowly, light up and inhale the head-swimming fumes. Then I can spend another five minutes learning how the Marlboro Lights are going to kill me.

Where can I look so as to avoid accusing stares? Thank God, that bloke left his newspaper in the rack. *Bollocks*, it's yesterday's. If Simon's not here by the time I've finished this rip-off lager in a pretentious bottle, I'm leaving.

"Simon, over here, mate. Good of you to turn up," I laugh across, turning heads, jiggling the embossed brown bottle with an unpronounceable name.

"Get the beers in, son." His forced smile says he's embarrassed.

My social paranoia is so chronic that on a bad day, I steel myself to go out – eat, shower, gel my hair, then get back into bed, unable to face what lies ahead.

I contrive to see my few friends singularly, unwilling to lose their attention by mixing them together. It also marginally increases the chances of having an interesting conversation. No one gets naked in a crowd is another lesson I've learned over the years.

The word 'party' makes me shiver, partly because I'm so rarely asked, intensifying my sense of unpopularity, which compounds my terror of talking to unknown people. Thus, I spiral into ever-increasing circles of anxiety.

Admittedly, the presence of an attractive girl might add a frisson of sexual interest, though it's tempered by the fact that I'm incapable of communicating with her.

The women I've loved the most I haven't spoken to. For which, I've got my controlling conversation-less mother to thank.

CHAPTER 33

Regret plays a leading role in my life, though it doesn't extend to Muriel's death.

Even now, as I take a final walk round the village where I grew up, her image, in my mind's eye, is already partially decomposed. The rats are gnawing at her rather than her gnawing at me.

When, in about an hour, I watch my mother being lowered in the ground, how will I feel? Relieved that the weight holding me down for five decades has been lifted or destitute?

All Saints Church is a short hearse drive from the family house, which is where I'll be in five minutes, but what if I just keep walking, then drive back to London, avoiding all pretence? It's not as if they care enough to send out a search party.

I watch a postman empty the pillar box across the street, everyday news and life-changing letters tumbling over each other into his sack.

Cars cough in the chilled air, unwilling to start, housewives cursing. Who I assume to be a sales rep adjusts his tie, fixes his smile, and enters the chemist.

Would life have been easier if I'd stayed in Stoke Blakely? Could I have tried harder with my parents and friends, swopped righteousness for the need to be right? Or would I have become my mother, consumed by a lifetime of 'what ifs', children obstinate obstacles to happiness?

The swish of a passing seventeen or eighteen-year-old girl's orchard green skirt transports me to a scene of excruciating regret.

✳

After inveigling my way into Simon's circle of friends, I'm included in their tradition of celebrating birthdays in foreign cities. I choose Paris for my twenty-fifth.

Under pressure to have a good time, or at least not an awful one, I want to take a girlfriend along as insurance against The Black Dog snapping at my heels.

There's an awkward silence when I tell the others I've invited Kath, a reluctant choice, but such is the expediency of time.

The reasons for the others' animosity, it seems to me, are varied and valid. Simon would rather have male company; Jez is a hard-drinking, heavy-smoking man's man; and Phil is so unhappily married that the last thing he wants is to have a woman around.

I've only prepared the ground when I say I've asked Kath because I haven't. And I'm not looking forward to it.

I hear her phone ringing, which I know she'll be rummaging for in an enormous designer handbag, probably while wearing oversized Joan Collins sunglasses.

We met in the office, by which I mean I saw her magnificent mammaries the day she wore a full-length, elasticated dress. I'm News. She's Fashion, and I watch her 'where's my phone?' charade fifty times a day. Blonde. Ditsy. Fun up to a point.

Perched on the edge of an unused office desk upstairs, I'm psyching myself for the charm offensive of my life, which, if I pull it off, will mean I'm in for heaven. And hell.

Hell is the depth of grovelling required to recover the ground I've lost by picking Kath up when times are hard then dropping her when someone less tiresome comes along.

My ploy of 'treat her mean keep her keen' has worked for two-and-a-half years, but the last time didn't end well. "Don't ever come near me again. Ever. Do you understand?" were her parting words.

My situation is particularly awkward because Kath makes Deborah Parker's hyperactivity seem like a plod. Three years younger than me, Kath is so pleased with her own inanity that she laughs rather than talks making conversation impossible.

Heaven is her melon-sized breasts with organ-stop nipples and long, silky legs that stretch to a shaven pussy that contrasts with the salon-styled Debbie Harry hair on her head. "Anyone can see I was born to be fucked," she once told me. So I did.

She's finally answered her phone, and so far, it has taken forty-five minutes of my admitting to being 'a lying cheating scumbag who absolutely doesn't deserve her' to win her round.

"So you'll call in sick and be on platform four at nine o'clock tomorrow morning? That's platform FOUR at NINE O'CLOCK tomorrow morning. Got it?"

"There's no need to shout. I'm not stupid, you know." I beg to differ is what I want to say.

"Mum says I should have nothing more to do with you. And if you mess me about one more time, I'll cut your balls off. Is that clear? I said, IS THAT CLEAR?"

"Yes, Kath. So see you on platform four at nine o'clock tomorrow morning."

"Can we drink champagne under that tower thing, babe? Did I tell you she's changed hairdressers?"

"*Who?*"

"My mum, of course. Remember I told you about the one who goes out with the married footballer?"

"No. Platform FOUR. NINE o'clock. Tomorrow."

"*Oooo, Paris.* How romantic. Course, I'll need some new shoes."

"Just make sure that, you know, down below is … sorted."

"You dirty old man," she hee-haws. "I should grow it long like a raspberry bush so you can't find it."

✸

The five of us unwind in a Friday evening stumbled-upon bistro; clichéd candles in wax-sculpted wine bottles and accordions. Even I enjoy myself, though I'd prefer it if Kath let go of my hand.

I fall asleep with my head on her golden orbs, cleaned of a well-executed blow job, and I feel a degree of contentment. I've come, but Kath had to work hard because I find sex with someone I'm not mentally attracted to difficult.

On Saturday, we all meander along the Left Bank, lick ice creams on ornate metal benches, and manage the top two floors of the *Musée d'Orsay* all before lunch.

To stay in the cliché theme, we dine on Pernod, steak *frites*, and Beaujolais, during which Jez empties a carafe of red wine on his own, and his references to Kath's tits turn into a crude attempt to grope them. Anyone else I'd have punched, but Jez has replaced Leo as the person I most want to be.

Afterwards, Kath and I stroll narrow backstreets on our own, gasping at prices in *chi chi* shop windows, and when she slips her arm through mine, it occurs to me we might work as a couple, but then she speaks, and the fantasy dissolves.

During dinner in a *Les Halles* restaurant with arrogant service and undercooked food, I react to another of Kath's fatuous remarks by snatching my hand back from under the table.

My mood flattens further when Jez polishes off what's left of the wine I was going to have and announces he's off to score some coke. From where no one knows because he's never been to Paris.

With his Jack Nicholson smile and a few drinks inside him, Jez is everyone's favourite Scouser. But one glass too many transforms him from raconteur to belligerent, worse when he's halfway through a gram of Charlie.

Jez and I usually connect at the point of optimum E-high, my first pill his third, exchanging depravities and insecurities in nightclub chill lounges until sunrise.

It's what's lacking in my friendship with Simon, and I'm unmoved by coming between the two men who were mates long before I came along. I have to steal the only friends I've got, and I want Jez as *my* best friend and no one else's.

Simon does what he does best now that Jez has left the restaurant and gets my birthday party going by ordering another round of Calvados and flourishing the gold-embossed business card of a *Marais* nightclub owner.

"Pete from work's been," he announces. "They play the hippest tunes in town, and with this, my friends, I might just get us on the guest list." His energy's contagious, and everyone's spirits shift through the gears.

"Now neck yer drinks, let's find a cab, and show Birthday Boy how to have a good time." When Simon tips his glass towards me, it's as warm as the brandy slipping down my throat, and I feel bad for betraying him.

Simon flashes the club owner's business card at a bouncer half an hour later, who tells us to get in the queue. "'*Pete from work's been, and I'll get us in on the guest list*'," I mock, annoyed at being parted from another fifty-franc note. My emotions are like riding a rollercoaster.

The club is as empty as I feel until Kath takes my hand, and we gyrate across the small, circular dance floor towards the bar where Simon and Phil are ordering drinks. Jez is still missing in action.

"Watch it. You'll have the buttons off." Kath's grabbed my Ben Sherman collar.

"What about that dance you promised me? These Johnny foreigners haven't got a clue. Wait 'til they get a load of me."

I resist being dragged towards last year's mirror ball disco, saying, "I'll dance when they play some decent music – not before." I'm incapable of not being a miserable old git, which annoys *me* more than anyone.

The slowly filling club is unresponsive to the DJ's attempts to enliven it, so I lean into the booth and, returning to the bar, the bass-heavy beats of Frankie's "Relax" rebound off the walls.

I take Kath's hand, leading her to join Simon and Phil centre stage, where we sing the words into each other's faces while twirling cigarettes above our heads. Kath and I trade grins when I gaze at her tits bouncing in time to the music.

Turning, I'm entranced by the slender calves under a knee-length apple-green skirt, bare feet in cardinal-red pumps, coming down the stairs. Madly, unfeasibly, the love of my life, who looks like a 'Sophie' and reminds me of spring, has arrived.

A thin, pink leather belt defines her trim waist, hips broadening to curvaceous, a palmful of breast in a creamy lace bra, its strap provocatively exposed on an olive-skinned shoulder. Even Sophie's white tan line, suggesting a reluctance to go topless, contrives to be sexy.

We catch each other's glance before, coy, shy, yet confident; Sophie looks away then runs her fingers through her thoroughbred's sheen of chestnut hair swept to one side.

Stepping backwards to allow Sophie and her two male companions to inch past, the wide-eyed 'thanks' of her hazel brown eyes thrill me more than the previous night's blow job.

The sway of her thong-bearing arse is almost too much to bear, though the rush of blood isn't lust; it's devotion. However implausible, she's Pascale times ten.

Sophie dances to a different tune, languidly sliding up and down grief-stricken notes that only she appears to hear. Hips writhing, Frankie isn't for her.

"*Fuck you*." Kath interrupts, then storms over to the bar to down rum and Cokes with Jez, who, typically, has reappeared.

"Now then, Dan, me old mate." Jez's bellow says he's marching on Colombia's finest.

"Wanna hand these beauties over to me?" His head's next to Kath's chest. "You'd like that, wouldn't you, Kath, love?"

"Yeah, be nice to be with a real man furra change," she slurs in reply. "Preferably one who can get it up." It's a low blow, but I deserve it as I slump into a chair set back from the dance floor.

I fail to cling to people even after chasing them down. The lucky ones escape relatively unscathed, while those I ensnare are stripped to the bone before I push a fistful of fingers down my throat to purge the taste. Revolted by their flaws and limitations, my need to feed equals my need to fast. Whichever way I play it, it's a losing hand.

Should I reach for the stars in a Sisyphean struggle to reshape myself, fight on, or end it all? If I continue the way I am, exhausted by public censure, I'll be toppled like the statue of a fallen dictator. Am I hostage to my mother's ill fortune, or is it my misfortune to be her son? Nature versus nurture. Or a toxic cocktail?

I emerge from my reverie to find myself in eye contact with Sophie. Are her Persian cat lines dancing for me?

Or is she simply warming up for the main event? An Alpha male black as Africa, ten-inch dick and pendulous balls banging against muscled thighs? The only one who can rightly dream of entering her.

I wry smile, thinking Sophie might be interested in me, only to see her smiling back. All I've got to do now is go and say 'bonjour'. Or is it 'hi'?

Then again, what if she's just humouring me? That she's with one of the two geeky youths. Or both. In any event, my schoolboy French is pitiful. *Shit*. What do you do with a girl's attention when you've got it? Lose it, I suppose.

I tell myself to get a grip, return her smile and head over there. 'Sophie, I presume?' isn't going to happen, so I opt for a less committed nod of the head, then worry she's looking at someone behind me.

What's happening? *Go. Go. Go.*

Free of his humourless wife and her shitty-arsed dog, Phil is chancing some more moves on the dance floor alongside Simon, and they're about a yard from Sophie.

Sparking a Marlboro Light, I down the dregs of the nearest glass and shoulder my way over, an overconfident smile illuminating my face as I shout above the music, "Matey boys, back in the groove." Appearance and reality are different things.

Aware I'm crossing the line between cool and being a prat, I restrain my exuberance before casting a nonchalant glance around the room, and it settles on – the back of Sophie's head. "*Bugger*. She's not interested."

"You're talking to yourself again, Dan," Simon's voice crashes in. "D'you want a beer?"

"No, not really. Don't look now, but you see the girl with her back to me?" He looks.

"I told you not to look."

"How can I see her if I can't look?" Simon toys with me and then sees I'm serious. "Do you mean the one in the apple-green dress?"

"Yeah, the French one with the two blokes?"

"Fancy a threesome, do you?" He gets another glare. "She's English."

"WHAT? That means I can talk to her."

"But you won't, will you? I'll get the beers in."

We're so close I can feel Sophie's body heat. It's the electric moment where everything, or nothing, happens.

All I have to do is wipe the scowl off my face, ask her to dance, then speak, but I need more time. One last heel turn, and I'll move in.

Losing my balance, I build the slip into my dance routine and spin as Sophie heads for the exit. I'd smack myself in the head if I didn't think I'd miss.

Simon and Phil, tired of awaiting the outcome of another failed Connah conquest, want to go. The fact Jez and Kath have already left tells me that my popularity matches my mood. Sub-optimum.

I'm determined to open my mouth and heart to Sophie outside, but our two groups stand apart in angled rain cutting across streetlights until unspoken love walks away.

✕

Along with Pascale, Sophie's loss pains me to this day. She prompts maudlin moments when I contemplate what I've let slip from my grasp; the 'what ifs'; the 'what might have been'.

As a middle-aged man, I want to know who's responsible for my reticent nature, the provenance that disables smiles and forbids 'hello's'. My bitch of a mother I'm on my way to bury, that's who. All I've ever known are arguments and silence.

My greatest regret of all? That's easy. It's living with Daniel Connah.

Chapter 34

"Excuse me." I'm trapped in the past, staring at Simon's old house, unaware I'm obstructing the pavement.

"Oh, it's you again. You must think I'm following you," Wendy Davies chirrups, putting a hand over her mouth.

"I did wonder." My reply's more accusatory than I intend.

"You asked me if I knew where Callum lived, the boy with cerebral palsy you mimicked in front of his mother."

"You told me he died," I hesitate.

"He did, but Mrs Duxley knows where his mother lives."

"Simon's mum? Funnily enough, I've just been standing outside their old house."

"Really. Well, it seems Maureen kept in touch with Leslie and …"

"Do you think resurrecting the past might not make matters worse, Wendy?" I've no need to apologise to

Callum's mum because, as far as I'm concerned, I've already been absolved by Wendy.

"Yes, yes, it was silly of me to mention it. Muriel's funeral must be about to start. Say hello to Jim for me. Goodbye, Daniel." Wendy's short, quick steps take her in the opposite direction.

Taking a last look at Simon's house, I can't remember the last time I spoke to him – or Jez, Ross, *or* Leo. "Unlucky for you, it appears you're my only friend, Ben." He pants, then wipes strings of drool on my jeans.

My mother might have been a cow, but, as Jane said, she was always there, a voice at the end of the phone, a constant. Now there's no one I can depend on, including Laura, who I'm certain is about to dump me. I visualise her at Fairfield Close sympathising with a group of strangers about a dead woman she's never met.

I check my watch, put Ben on the lead and quicken my pace. 'You'll be late for your own funeral,' Muriel used to tell me. It seems she got it the wrong way round.

Moments from home, I can almost hear my brother and sister apologising for my absence to family mourners balancing another biscuit on their saucer. Distant relations curious about my whereabouts will pose veiled questions about my whereabouts. 'Is Daniel coming to the funeral? He's not unwell, I hope.'

Once a deliberate ploy, being late is now an unalterable habit that I attribute to acute self-consciousness. And paranoia. Of being alone in a public place. I didn't stop believing that everyone was looking at me until I was forty-five.

Up until then, I made certain of my late arrival by deliberately underestimating the time required to get there. Then, if by accident, I arrived early, I conjured a list of diversionary tasks, usually involving a sex shop.

I enjoyed my tardy notoriety – Wilde was right, the only thing worse than being talked about is not – but the joke fell flat when friends compensated by arriving later still, or not at all.

The way I see it, time's dictatorial parameters are the problem. Without its incessant *tick,* we're neither late *tock* nor early. Controlled by clockwork gods, we're blind to time's hands snuffing out the impulsiveness of everything it touches. And so *is* becomes *was*, which is death by any other name.

Time's incapable of standing still, putting its feet up and taking a breather, but leaving what behind? A fleeting impression of a life or an indelible being that goes on living in ghostly perpetuity. Laura says it's not normal to think about these things. It's one of the few things we agree about.

Perhaps a personality disorder makes me see time's onward circular march obliterate all before it, ceaseless unlike the paltry coming and going wind or retreating tide. But, that said, I do have rare moments of clarity when I feel I belong in a time and place, an improbable sense of being connected, if only for a minute or two.

As if close to grasping time's meaning, its reasoning, I'm coupled to other selves in the same space, though in different ages, past and future. I assume it's why I'm drawn to streets I lived in decades earlier, wiping dirty windows to catch a glimpse of myself.

My last moment of lucidity was twenty years ago when my vision cut through the clouds like a searchlight.

Arriving home too early to be drunk from a party, I slide open the doors of my flat's roof terrace, smelling the residue of a summer's day, supplemented by honeysuckle, in the night air. Beyond the back garden is an acre of forgotten land reclaimed by Mother Nature, fox cubs tumbling in the undergrowth, childish screams scratching at the sky.

A growing elation tells me I am precisely where I need to be, while the presence of unknown others – confident that someone, somewhere, is contemplating the same star, experiencing the same emotions – assures me I'm not alone. Is there another me, another tortured soul calling, or someone telling me it doesn't have to be that way?

The chaos of selves, enlightened by why and who they were and settling themselves into one, clears my mental haze like mist from an early morning forest, releasing me from solitary confinement.

A being, sentient or not, is reaching out, and it's as if I see my young self in a mirror; only a different boy is on the other side. I'm unsure why I think he's foreign, because he doesn't speak, but we're two youngsters inside each other, waiting to unite.

Everything exists according to a greater scheme designed to unify us, me aching with excitement knowing I am so close, willing a missing element to perform its role.

But our union uncouples as quickly as it forms. Line disconnected, the boy's image is replaced by the daunting realisation that I have an unoccupied hour to fill before I might, or might not, sleep; a sentence to be served with my old cell mates, isolation and discontent, an iron band tightening against my brain, each empty second another turn of the screw. My greatest fear is that it keeps turning, an incessant incoming tide.

I'm an enigma to myself, which, when I'm stable, reassures me I'm an individual, a standout face in the crowd rather than part of a whole I detest. The rest of the time, it hangs like a noose about my neck, my craving for company so great I can hardly breathe, feelings of inadequate separation blocking my airways.

I do what I can to break the silence – work, watch TV – but whichever darkened corner I try to hide in, loneliness finds a way in.

Yet should I stumble across human warmth, a throng of thousands, or one, the only solace I long for is my own, urging the clock's hands to quicken to save me from other people's minutiae. But when they accelerate, I grieve their loss, demanding more time to spend with others. Life is an unwinnable crusade against myself.

CHAPTER 35

Ben doesn't need directions. Across Main Street, left, right. Food. The difference is that he knows what awaits him. I don't.

"*Bugger.* John's over there. Has he seen us?" A beckoning wave tells me he has. My brother, suited and shiny-shoed, a red carnation in his lapel, clearly isn't happy.

"Where the fuck have you been? Jane's furious, and, come to that, so am I. These stupid shoes are killing me."

"Is something happening?"

"Ever the smartarse."

"And *you're* turning into Jane. There's an hour or more before the hearses arrive."

"You're not even dressed."

"What's wrong with going like this?" I sweep my arm across my drool and mud-spattered jeans. The Red Lion opening its doors excites my thirst. "Fancy a quick pint, John? I've got a few things on my mind."

"As long as it's not another one of your 'what's the meaning of life' conversations," he replies, leaning over the bar, trying to get served while I grab a table.

"Your IQ couldn't cope if I did," I shout, falling short of my brother's sarcasm. "It's Dad I'm worried about."

"That's unlike you."

"What if he tries to top himself again?" I say. John's raised eyebrows tell me I've put my foot in it. I forgot no one else knows about Jim's suicide attempt.

"I hope the rain holds off," I remark. Judging by the look on my brother's face, my diversion isn't working. "We should give Jane more credit, you know. She does a lot to keep Dad going."

"You know about him trying to top himself?" John's face is the colour of his carnation. "But I thought *I* was the only one who …"

An awkward silence needs breaking. "So did I," I reply. "Only I didn't know for sure until you just confirmed it."

"What the hell are you talking about?"

"Mother told me it was an accident so many times I started to believe it. What a fucked up family we are." I feel devastated for Dad, whose darkest hour I've treated like a joke. Making it all about me is even worse.

"Sorry to break it to you like this. It's just that I …" I've never seen my brother, whose gaze is fixed on a Home Ales beer mat, appear helpless. "You're right, Dan…iel. Weirdly, Jane seems to think we're normal."

"I wouldn't be so sure. I talked to her this morning, and even she's beginning to think we're a bunch of weirdos." I take a breath and a swig of lager. "You know I was there, don't you?"

Before the words are out, I'm back in the barn, the *hiss* of raindrops hitting the Massey Ferguson's engine, Jim's body dangling in the gloom.

"*You're joking*! Why didn't you tell me? I'm your brother, for Christ's sake."

"In theory, but it's not like we've been close. Mother Dearest, the twisted old cow, saw to that. Maybe we could try and change that." I look hopeful. John looks away.

I tell him what I heard and saw in the barn. How Muriel cradled Jim's head, his swollen neck purple. That I'd hoped it marked a new beginning for us as a happy family.

"She told the doctor, and me, that Jim had fallen off a ladder," my voice quavers. "I knew what I'd seen, yet she tried to convince me otherwise to the point I thought I was going mad." I'm ten times more affected than I thought.

"Jim's 'accident' was 'our little secret', she said, and that I mustn't tell anyone." I wipe my cheek with the beer bottle.

"Problem is, John. Keeping Dad's suicide attempt secret all these years, as well as the way we were treated, has really screwed me up. I can't seem to form relationships, especially with women."

My brother's expression says he's unused to people opening up to him.

"I tried to pretend it didn't upset me. I even laughed about Jim not being able to kill himself properly. I'm either insane or a really bad person."

I'm pleased to share the load I've carried for forty years though I'm unsure John, given his repeated unfolding of knees and arms, wants to hear it. "How come Muriel told you what happened, anyway?"

"She didn't." I'm convinced my brother practices being inscrutable. "I coincidentally became friends with the doctor, and he told me it was a load of bollocks about it being an accident."

"Did you confront Mother?"

"You're not going to believe this, but she told me that no one else knew and that it would be 'our little secret'."

"For fuck's sake, it's no wonder we're so fucked up," I say, swirling my Pils bottle.

We sit in silence until he downs his pint and asks me if I want another. Standing at the bar, I notice John's hair is on its way to a bald patch which I presume is where mine's going.

Returning with his real ale and my 'poncey bottle of lager', a furrowed brow suggests something's on his mind.

"Seeing as all the skeletons are coming out the family cupboard, do you know about Wendy?"

"The postmistress who isn't? Yeah, she's been following me all morning. Why?" John casts me a look that says, 'I wasn't going to tell you this, but ...'

"Please God, no. *An affair? With Wendy?*"

"Not exactly. But she's the reason you left the village. One of them, anyway."

"This gets weirder by the minute."

My brother, oblivious to the irony of continued family secrets, makes me swear not to repeat to Jane what he's about to tell me. "She'll only get upset" is his reasoning.

He coughs and says the village gossips thought Jim's visits to the post office were too frequent, he and Wendy too friendly. Dad's late post given preferential treatment.

The rumour mongers' suspicions, the way they saw it, were confirmed when Jim was seen leaving Wendy's maisonette late one evening. What they didn't know, John informs me, was that Wendy had locked herself out, and Dad, who happened to be passing, helped her break in.

"So Mother got it into her head that people were laughing at her behind her back, which was roughly when Dad had the bright idea of becoming a farmer and dragged you off to live in the middle of nowhere."

"Dad spent a lot of time in the post office posting Ma's letters to me abroad," I pitch in, indignant.

"Come to think of it, I remember Mum telling Jim in the suicide barn that she never wanted to hear Wendy's name again. It also explains why Gail Mills asked me if I'd seen Wendy." I glance at John, searching for a reaction that doesn't come.

"Well, well. Fancy Dad playing away. Then again, he was married to Muriel."

"Don't get carried away with your newspaper headlines. The so-called affair almost certainly never happened. Anyway, Mother wasn't that bad."

"Don't you start. I had an earful of that from Jane earlier. You need to take your rose-tinted off." I glance at my watch. "Shouldn't we get going?" I say, emptying my Pils. "Sis'll be doing her nut."

"Ever the drama queen." My brother's joke is at odds with his serious manner. "Maybe you're right ..." I'm intrigued, but John can't help but add 'for once'. "And we should make more of an effort to see each other." I nearly fall off my stool.

"You and Laura could come up to Scotland. Maybe do a bit of fly fishing." I'm moved by him putting himself out on a limb.

"That'd be really nice, John. Thanks. But we'd better skedaddle."

Turning into Fairfield Close, I release Ben, who bolts across the cul-de-sac and up number 9's rippled concrete drive, where several cars are parked. Looking up, I see Jim at the bedroom window. I'll straighten his tie when I get in.

I see the phone cabinet through a side window. Its slide-out seat is where Muriel took my calls; the most significant was when I asked why she prevented me from visiting Uncle Graham in Australia. The line and what was left of our relationship died that day, though I still don't know why she did it.

The clatter of the back garden gate, through

which I'd taken a succession of girlfriends for Muriel's disapproval, alerts my presence to an unknown face in the kitchen.

Muriel's attitude towards my latest girlfriend changed as soon as the relationship failed. "What have you done with that nice Deborah Parker? I always liked her."

"No, you didn't."

"It's time you stopped all this gallivanting around and settled down. Start a family."

"I can't. I've told you, I'm gay."

The garden's layout, split-level lawns and flowerbeds haven't changed, apart from the pond's goldfish were speared by a heron. What's different is that since Muriel died, Jim hasn't cut the lawn, and the greenhouse is turning algae-green.

My six-foot nephews, propped against the garage as if holding it up, extinguish their cigarettes in the water butt, then play-fight with Ben.

"Alright, Uncle Dan, found any scoops? Mum's looking for you." I raise my eyes skywards. They shrug, arms open. "We'll feed Ben if you like."

Jane's up to her elbows in washing-up suds. Her daffodil-coloured marigolds clash with her dislodged navy-blue hat. The unknown woman I saw smiles at me and carries a plate of Garibaldis into the lounge.

"Those biscuits look, and I'm sure taste, like cardboard," I say, about to adjust Jane's feathers before she bustles me out the way.

"Shut up. Dad got them. Anyway, where the hell have you been? It's one thing being late, but for your own mother's funeral, for God's sake." Picking a thread of cotton off my coat, she adds: "Go and get ready." I fiddle with the radio. "NOW, Daniel."

My father disregards my, "Morning, Dad. Are you okay?" So I leave him to adjust his own tie in the hall mirror until a different image of him hanging from a rope flashes across my mind.

"Do you want me to help you?" I ask, staring at our reflection. He barely seems to notice me. My sadness is as deep as his, though for different reasons. It's another opportunity lost to reach out and touch.

Through the crack in the lounge door, I see Jim's older sister, Harriet, chatting in hushed, respectful tones, though why people lower their voices to speak of the dead is beyond me. I should say 'hello, thanks for coming,' but I've only met Harriet once, and I'm not even sure that's her name.

Terry, Jane's husband, is sitting in Muriel's old chair who'd have a fit if she knew. She thought him too dark-skinned to be 'one of us, Italian or something but definitely foreign'. I wave, point at his chair and mime 'dead man's shoes'. He laughs and, with a pained expression, holds up a Garibaldi.

Laura brushes past me with a crumb-scattered plate. "You okay?" I ask, offering her a kiss she doesn't want.

"You should keep an eye on your dad. I found him crying in the other room and didn't know what to do."

"For what it's worth, nor do I," I reply. "You won't believe it, but John's invited us to Scotland."

"*Hmm*," is her only response.

Jane fixes Dad's tie and points him towards a cup of tea. "Any chance we could finish our chat while I get ready – and finish my reading?" I can't help but wind her up.

"What about? Oh no, not Mother again. Alright, but you'd better make it snappy. The cars will be here in ten minutes.

"What do you mean *finish* your reading? I thought you did it ages ago."

"Only kidding," I lie. Jane's glare says she's dubious. "Come upstairs in five and help me do my hair. Think Morrissey quiff."

"Very funny."

"I'm serious."

The conversation doesn't go where I want it to. I need to delve into the emotional debris of our lives. Share resentments about being left to live in a world that demands decency when all we've learned is rejection and duplicity.

Having been pursued into childhood psychosis, and overdose, by our mother, Jane must understand what I'm talking about more than anyone, but she doesn't want to excavate old ground.

According to my sister, our mother isn't to blame; she is. Jane, the child, is responsible for her own mental breakdown, and adult Jane is guilty of visiting the sins of the mother upon her sons. Though I reject my sister's self-assigned culpability, it appears amnesia is her coping mechanism.

"*If* you've repeated some of the same mistakes with your own kids, and that's a big *if*, it was all you knew. You haven't neglected them the way we were. You'd be locked up if you had."

I'm almost pleading with Jane to see sense. "Mother picked on you, we all did, because you were vulnerable, the weakest link. We called you Loony, for God's sake. It was unforgivable, and I'm sorry."

"Great, so now I'm Ann Robinson. Look, I've already told you I did a lot of bad things. Normal children don't go around stealing charity boxes, do they?"

"You're right, they don't, but it must tell you something that we all stole – you, me, John, Margaret. None of us is *normal*, and the reason why is obvious. What if some of us still do steal?" I'm uncertain if she hears my admission, though she's gone quiet. It's as if we're playing moral chess, each wary of conceding our queen.

"You shouldn't feel bad about things that aren't your fault, is all I'm saying, Jane. You must see that."

"Not really. I know Mum put me down, told me I'd never get anywhere, but what if she was right? I'm not exactly Brain of Britain, am I?" I stop myself from throwing my hands up, just in time.

"I did get upset when she said things about my kids, though." Maybe we're getting somewhere as she stares out the window obscured by her coffee cup steam. "She was always telling me to leave Terry and get myself a flat. I'm sure she thought he was common. You know how snobby she could be."

"That's *exactly* what I mean, Jane. It was all about control." I dial back my enthusiasm that seems to startle her. "She was unhappy in her own marriage and didn't want you to be happy in yours. I often wondered why she didn't leave."

"But you're forgetting all the good things she did."

"*Like what*?"

"Like being there when we needed her, taking us to the doctor, babysitting, that sort of thing. Why are you going on about it now, anyway? It's her funeral, for Pete's sake. Show some respect."

"That's the problem. I don't think I can. She didn't care about me, so why should I give a toss about her – dead or alive?"

"Of course, she cared about you. I always thought more so than the rest of us. At times, I envied, even hated you." It's like playing chess on LSD unless it was all part of Muriel's strategy. Divide and drive them mad.

"Listen, Daniel. I know you're struggling with Mother's death, but can you behave if only for Dad's sake? I'm worried what he might do." It'll push me over the edge if Jane knows about Jim's suicide attempt, as well.

"Yesterday, he told me he's unsure if he can live without her." The window squeals as my sister wipes away a circle of condensation. "Blimey, the cars are here. Get your skates on."

In the doorway, she turns to face me and adds, "You know Dad blames himself for the crash, don't you? That Mother would still be here if it weren't for him." She turns to go. "By the way, Laura's really nice. Look after her."

"But she wants kids, and I …" I don't tell her Laura's decided to catch an earlier train back to London.

"And remember. Respect, Daniel."

CHAPTER 36

I put my pen down. My hands are trembling. Muriel's eulogy amounts to no more than a few scribbled words, mainly because I can't get a picture out of my mind.

Muriel's lying cross-armed in her coffin – make-up applied by the undertakers, mouth decorated with her favourite lipstick, Jaeger blouse, Hermès scarf. She's not dead. She's never looked better. And I'll tell her so when she opens her eyes. Whatever she's done, I want her back.

The story of her demise unravels in my mind.

It's eighteen months ago, and I'm working on a story about a cabinet minister embroiled in a children's home scandal when the phone rings. "It'll be the lawyer telling me the minister's threatening to sue," I tell Ben, who's asleep on the Peter Jones rug Muriel bought.

"*Yes.*" As a Fleet Street journalist, I'm obliged to bark when I answer the phone. It makes us feel important. "Oh, it's you, Dad. Can I call you back? I'm on deadline."

His hesitation says something's happened. "Everything alright?" I ask, checking my watch.

"An accident? Are you and Mum okay? If it's not serious, why is she being kept in? A spinal injury sounds pretty serious to me. Shall I come up?" I'm torn between seeing my name in the paper and seeing my mother.

"Well, if you're sure, but let me know if anything changes. I can be at Queen's Med in three hours." Am I a bad person for thinking Muriel's getting what she deserves? Yes.

Is self-aggrandisement an acceptable reason for not being en route to the hospital? No.

How will I feel if my mother dies before I get there or, God forbid, turns into a dribbling cripple, like my sister, Margaret? I can't be expected to kiss two sets of distorted lips.

On the other hand, if Muriel's departure is imminent, which, given Jim's inability to face reality, is likely, there'll be no one left to explain who I am. My 'why' would elude me forever.

I needn't have worried because Muriel isn't ready to concede defeat, and a month later, on Christmas Day 2002, Jim, John, Jane, and I gather round her hospital bed, urging her to open her presents.

"What's the point?" she responds as a fluorescent tube flickers overhead.

At the nurses' station, I hear one mutter to another, "Sum people jus' ain't got no gratitude," though her colleague's more to the point. "Talkin' 'bout Mrs

Sunshine over there? Been 'ere a week an' not a single please or thank you. She don't deserve no visitors dat for sure. *Um, hmm.*"

As more weeks go by, Muriel's morbidity shows no sign of retreat. Unmoved, if not irritated, by her husband's near-permanent bedside vigil. When Jim's there, Muriel ignores him, and when he leaves, she complains of being abandoned and uncared for.

Dad returns home solely to sleep and cook his wife meals that she mostly refuses to eat. The 'disgusting' hospital food was thrown in the bin on day one.

I suspect, partly to get rid of her, the doctors decide to transfer my mother to Sheffield's spinal rehab unit forty-five miles away. And so Jim's daily routine becomes even more exhausting; his reward more abuse. To be fair, Muriel also dishes it out to the doctors and nurses.

She insists she wants to die, pretty much hourly, until a handsome no-nonsense consultant of last resort comes to see her.

Amazingly for a seventy-something-year-old woman, Dr Salah's bedside manner arouses a glint in my mother's eye. Coincidentally or not, for the first occasion in several months, Jim's instructed to find his wife a hairdresser.

'Dr Omar', as she prefers to call Dr Salah in a nod to Omar Sharif, tries to convince his patient to take a few steps with the help of a Zimmer frame.

"Not on your Egyptian Nelly. I wouldn't be seen dead with one," Muriel protests. "That's fine," the surprisingly obliging doctor replies. "I'll order you a wheelchair instead."

It takes a fortnight's worth of persuasion, mainly from Jane and John, but our mother ultimately concedes – on one condition. That the wheelchair's 'not NHS'.

To my amazement, on trips from London, I alone am permitted to push my mother along the hospital's corridors in a 'temporary wheelchair', almost running past the wards where I know Muriel will point out other 'inmates'.

"He's only here because he hasn't gone anything else to do. There's nothing wrong with him," sees me offer apologetic shrugs to horrified relatives, then hurry on.

Muriel makes some reluctant progress, and Dr Salah discharges her into a self-contained 'halfway house' within the spinal unit's landscaped grounds. It's been a long six months for everyone, and it's hoped the three-day trial goes well, which it doesn't.

Relaying our mother's even greater despondency in an afternoon phone call, I get the message that Jane thinks I should visit Sheffield.

The next four hours are spent fighting my way north in Friday night traffic, though I'm partially motivated by the perverse pleasure of engaging with an enemy whose power is waning.

"Does anyone else find the word 'mother' almost impossible to say?" I ask my asleep passenger, Ben, who opens, then closes, one eye.

A brunette pulls alongside in a Mercedes SLK, and my glimpse is met with her giving me the finger before putting her foot down. She's got more power than she thinks.

*

I've been house-hunting in SW France for the past few weeks and haven't seen as much of Muriel as my conscience tells me I should. Parking my Citroën next to Jim's hire car, I see the halfway house is actually a flat.

Winding the Picasso's window down a few inches for Ben, I dread the reception I'm going to get from my parents when I get inside. Anger's likely to rank highly, I know.

I enter the flat without knocking and see the price Dad's paid for his unwavering devotion.

Gaunt frame hunched over a medication chart on a worn-out settee, the plate of food he's been unable to persuade his wife to eat congealing in his lap, he looks ten years older.

Muriel's still in her temporary NHS wheelchair, and my heart aches as if for two wounded animals.

They still haven't seen me, and I contemplate leaving them to self-destruct, but something stops me. Not love, surely, but something makes me bound into the room.

"Right then, Ironside. Gis-a-go yer wheels."

Muriel spins in her chair, primed with invective, seeking out the voice that dare humiliate her.

"Who the blazes is calling me Iron…?" She looks me up and down. "I might've known it was you. If you've come to laugh at me, you needn't have bothered."

"But you're going home soon, you loveable bundle of joy; my Bakewell tart of uncomplaining sweetness; you font of irrepressible optimism."

"Shut up, can't you see I'm not going *anywhere*? Have you any idea what it's like being stuck in this thing? I'd rather be dead."

"But Jesus doesn't want you for a sunbeam just yet – or probably any other time. He's not ready for your force of positivity." I begrudge my congeniality, confident it won't be reciprocated.

"That's enough," Jim snaps. "You're only making things worse if that's possible."

'Four hours in gridlocked traffic for this!' I say to myself. 'Jesus, what's that smell? It's as if twenty people have farted in a crisp packet.'

"Now look what you've done," Jim remonstrates. "Help me get your mother to the toilet." I'm nauseous just thinking about it and tell them I've got to move the car.

In the age it takes Muriel to emerge from the bathroom, supported by her husband, I've nearly mastered pulling a wheelchair wheelie.

"Get out my chair, you little …"

Whoaaaaaa. My skull thuds against the lino floor, and, dazed, I see Muriel trying not to laugh.

My mother's restraint is concerned with not wanting to appear amused, a lifelong habit, rather than any concern about my welfare. She's a martyr who rejoices in her own suffering.

"Don't help me or anything, will you?" I grumble, pleased to get some sort of reaction.

"Serves you jolly well right," she says, a tear of sadistic delight rolling down her cheek. "You always were a good-for-nothing. Now *give me back my chair* – if you haven't already broken it."

✖

Muriel disregards the neighbourly waves greeting her return to Fairfield Close, tutting at the ambulanceman's appreciative wave. A week later, she shuffles from the kitchen table to the sink, blaming Jim for getting in the way when she drops a plate.

My parents' marriage has been short on highlights from day one, trajectory downward, and I don't know whether to admire their resilience or despair at them staying together. Compounding the tragedy is that their lives had brightened before the car accident that broke my mother's back; hope dashed.

CHAPTER 37

When the government winds up the Knitting Lace Training Board, Jim, aged sixty-two, despairs of ever working again.

My trips home are more regular after another relationship breakdown, and I witness my father descend into depression and, for once, maybe because I know how he feels, my heart goes out to him.

Every morning, Muriel tells my father he's under her feet, so he scours the *Evening Post*'s Situations Vacant columns in the library, then goes down to the Job Centre. En route, he knocks on any old clients' doors he recognises, but they're always on the phone.

Rejected by what's left of Nottingham's textile industry, the Civil Service, and the local Nat West, Jim lowers his sights until even Asda has no use for him pushing its trolleys.

Coming downstairs one Saturday morning, I find

him sobbing at the dining room table, head in one hand. I catch the few lines of type he has in the other as the notepaper falls to the floor.

Dear Mr Connah,
We are sorry to inform you that the sales position you applied for has been filled.
Yours sincerely,
Spudulike

I notice a Plymouth postmark on the envelope, next to a pile of other 'no longer a vacancy' rebuffs.

Dad's decline raises my concerns about his suicidal tendencies, and I suspect that when even Muriel reduces hostilities, going so far as to offer Jim a cup of tea, she's also fearful.

Seven months later, voice barely audible, chin stubbled, Jim announces he's been offered a government job scheme interview that he isn't going to attend. "What's the point?" he says, though he does when, remarkably, my mother encourages him.

"You never know, Jim. This might be the one," is the closest thing to affection I've heard in their house for years.

Trades for Life is another Tory initiative designed to get the unemployed back to work. I see it as a cynical attempt by Norman Tebbit's 'on yer bike' brigade to massage the spiralling jobless figures, but my political stance isn't thought helpful and causes several family rows. Regardless, I'm delighted for Jim when he lands the job.

His role is to use his personnel experience to recruit a small team of professional tradesmen who'll teach a bunch of unqualified participants how to build or plaster a wall. Either that or their dole money's slashed.

Jim also has to find projects for the 'volunteers' to practice their newfound skills, which isn't easy when even landlords with near-derelict buildings don't want a group of 'layabout scroungers' on their land.

My own view is that Dad's pent-up motivation blinds him to the programme's underfunded political manoeuvring, though I'm impressed by how well he deals with society's underprivileged underbelly.

In a twist of fate that seems to pass Jim by, he recruits his old Training Board boss, Gerald Dowell, as his deputy. Between them, they manage to convince Wollaton Hall to let Trades for Life restore the collapsed Elizabethan boathouse in the far reaches of the grounds.

It's an 8 a.m. start, and by 9 a.m., two-thirds of the workforce hasn't shown up. At 10, Jim decides it isn't worthwhile unloading the pickaxes and calls it a day, all of which he relates to me in a downbeat early lunch.

"Maybe they got the day wrong," is the best I can manage – until I have an idea. "*Or* they need a bit of encouragement, like a bacon sarnie. It'd definitely get me to turn up tomorrow."

Jim calls every name on his list, using a long-forgotten sense of humour to chivvy, implore, and bribe fifteen grumbling recruits to gather in Wollaton Hall car park at 8.45 a.m. the following day. Intrigued, I decide to see if my plan works.

✗

Cannabis wafts through my open car window as I watch half a dozen sixteen-year-old youths blow smoke rings from Lonsdale hoods.

I want to tell them to pack in their 'fuckin' this' an' 'cuntin' tha' baht 'avin tah carrie shitload-a-shovels bleedin' miles away'. But Jim doesn't appear to need protecting as he jokes with several ageing Teddy Boys chuffing on Players No.6 and gobbing greenies.

Nearby, keeping their distance, two older hat-and-scarved enrolees stamp their lace-up shoes and camera frame their hands at a pair of great crested grebes on the fog-blanketed sixteenth-century lake.

My gaze shifts to a shirt-and-tied, duffle-coated man in his mid-sixties, who I take to be Gerald. He's standing at the car park entrance extending 'good morning' smiles to two short-skirted, gum-chewing teenage girls as they teeter across the frozen tarmac in high heels. After Gerald ticks off their names on his clipboard, each girl takes his arm as he shows them the way.

I wander over, noticing Jim's got another problem: none of the three instructors has arrived. A cheer goes up when Gerald, having been despatched to discover where the tutors are, says they're fourteen miles away at *Woodborough Hall,* scratching their heads while staring at an immaculate boathouse.

At this point, one of the younger lads legs it into the car park clutching a large white paper bag. I hear mumbled complaints 'baht ther' bein' no brahn sauce' on the bacon sarnies from a nearby café, but there are the beginnings of a group.

Trades for Life becomes a national success story under Jim and Gerald's stewardship. Newspaper pictures appear of acned youths brandishing plasterers' floats alongside girls in hard hats and steel-capped boots.

Nottingham's disused railway station is converted into a Virgin gym, dovecotes and ice houses restored. Ministers sent to shake Jim's hand cite his achievements as an example of what the government can do to help those willing to help themselves.

Muriel's snorts of derision – unhappy her husband's hogging the limelight – quieten when she appears in the *Daily Mail* closer to 'real class' Michael Howard MP than Jim.

I congratulate Dad on his promotion to Regional Manager, and although the salary remains pitiful, he's content doing what he's been put on God's earth to do; helping others, if not his children.

It occurs to me that his life's come full circle from his days in the pulpit. Only now, he works alongside his congregation in builders' boots rather than a cassock.

Muriel, too, seems to notice a change in her husband that she finds hard to disparage. He's the same 'faffer', fretting over whether he's locked the back door, but he's also concerned about her need for a new hat or evening out.

I observe my parents' relationship develop, if not to levels of devotion, then degrees of goodwill, foundations I'm sure will crumble with the slightest provocation, which comes in the form of a brown envelope three years later.

But, to my astonishment, our parents take Jim's latest redundancy in their stride, me angered more than them by the closure of another government scheme. Aged sixty-five, Jim's grateful his working life's been extended at all, and Muriel's delighted with his generous payoff.

After a shaky start, my mother, apart from being riled by her now-retired husband's need to be *doing* and his John Player Specials 'stinking the house out', rub along reasonably well.

I'm helping unpack the Saturday morning shop when Jim hands his wife a tin of M&S chunky chicken that he isn't allowed to eat because it's Muriel's and says: "*Hey*. Why don't we go for a pub lunch instead of having the usual cold cuts? We haven't done that for ages."

"Can I come?" I ask, smelling a free lunch. I accept I'm too old to sulk when my request is denied, but I do anyway.

"If you mean to the dirty old Fisherman's Arms, I'd rather have Spam." Muriel's dismissal of Dad's attempt to please her narks me, though he's not deterred.

"How about the Saracen's Head, then? You used to like going there. Further to go, but it's worth it."

And so begin trips to country pubs and stately homes. There's a stumble when Jim runs out of petrol on an excursion to Ingoldmells, but he reprieves himself by booking them into a four-star hotel, bathrobes and disposable slippers in the wardrobe.

I'm further astounded when Muriel lets Jim take her hand at a family gathering, which I imagine, for my father, revives wartime memories of cloakroom trysts with his fiancée. Muriel, I suspect, dispels images of the barrel-chested US colonel who never returned.

I'm invited to an Italian trattoria, once dismissed by my mother as 'foreign muck', where Jim gazes at his wife and says, "What with the redundancy money and my two pensions, we're not badly off, you know. I was thinking we might stretch our wings a bit. Go abroad, instead of Wales."

"Oh, you were, were you?" Muriel's bark is less ferocious after two glasses of Riesling. "Where did you have in mind, Bongo Bongo Land?" I cringe on behalf of the passing black waitress.

"No, not quite, love."

Muriel bristles. The L-word remains a sentiment too far.

"I was thinking more about Denmark."

"As in Lurpak? Who the blazes goes on holiday to Denmark? The neighbours won't have heard of it, so what's the point?"

Jim's 'dirty old man' glimpse at the pornography on display in Copenhagen airport doesn't go unnoticed by Muriel, she later tells us, but otherwise, their first foreign excursion appears to be a success.

Opening my Christmas present of a miniature mermaid reclining on a sliver of 'genuine' harbour rock, I put it to one side and say, "Denmark's the most boring place on earth. How could you possibly have enjoyed it?" Their knowing looks suggest they're in cahoots. "Please don't tell me you went to Legoland! You did. Didn't you?"

After celebrating their Ruby wedding anniversary in Venice, my parents continue to broaden their horizons for the next ten years. My siblings and I notice that now Muriel's getting more of what she believes she's entitled to; there's far less bickering.

Except for *Coronation Street*, *Emmerdale Farm*, and anything with Charles Dance in it, the television is switched off in favour of a game of Scrabble or a stroll around the village – until Darcy Campbell has a row with her boyfriend, and Muriel exchanges an airline seat for a wheelchair.

✖

Blonde, straight-A student Darcy was halfway down a dip in the A168, arguing with her boyfriend on her mobile. She was in the middle of the road doing 70mph. Jim and Muriel were travelling in the opposite direction. Or so the police accident investigation officer, who I'm sitting a few feet away from, Dad and Jane, either side of me, tells Nottingham Coroner's Court.

As a journalist, I've spent too much time in these places. Jim and my sister haven't spent any. Also, unlike me, they don't have their suspicions about coroners who, I've often thought are more concerned about not rocking any boats than the truth.

I briefed Jim yesterday about what to expect at Darcy's inquest. Her mother and boyfriend will be there giving evidence, along with a likely army of lawyers, because I've made compensation noises to our solicitor.

In my opinion, we've got a strong case against Darcy's insurance company to pay damages for Muriel's suffering and future medical costs. But to stand any chance of success, we need the coroner to record an 'open verdict', which means he needs convincing that Dad didn't cause the accident.

"But I don't want to cause the poor girl's mother any more torment. Imagine what it's like to lose a nineteen-year-old daughter, Daniel." While I understand Jim's mindset, I'm concerned he's not steadfast in supporting our cause.

"I can't begin to think, Dad, but someone should pay for what Mother's been through. Who knows what she's going to need in terms of wheelchairs, special beds, etcetera. It's what insurance companies are for. It's them we're after, not Darcy's mum."

The next day, the first traffic officer on the accident scene is called to give evidence, followed by Jim.

I worry about my father as he climbs into the witness box. His hand shakes when he grips the rail, and he's spilt vending machine coffee down his shirt. The coroner tells him to take his time and relay what he can about the crash.

Jane, her face etched with concern, gives me an accusatory stare about what we're, by which she means me, are putting Dad through. I'm conflicted between avenging Muriel's death, journalistic endeavour, and whether I'm being a selfish, vindictive bastard.

Letting the case go would be by far the easiest option, but perceived injustice is a red rag to my bull, which I accept contradicts some of my other character traits. Hypocrisy reigns, I guess.

John, who considers the claim an unnecessary burden, is down from the Scottish Highlands, keeping an eye on Muriel at home. I'm used to battling alone, but my family's antagonism makes it harder.

Dad opens his mouth, then closes it when he spots Darcy's mother with the same aquiline nose and similar coloured hair as the picture of her daughter in the *Evening Post*.

Mrs Campbell is dabbing a handkerchief against her clearly sleepless eyes in a washed-out face, and Jim stutters, says he's sorry, something inaudible, and that all he can remember is seeing Darcy's Escort coming over the hill and ploughing into it.

My heart sinks, for Jim as well as me, as he leaves the stand after some perfunctory questions, and Jane accompanies him out of the courtroom, her arm round his now 28-inch-waist. Her glower says I should leave, as well.

Not yet ready to concede defeat, I watch Sandra, my de facto sister-in-law, stride into the witness box where she swears to tell the whole truth. She's as tough as the Gateshead council estate she comes from. If anyone can be relied on, it's her.

The fact that on the day of the accident she and Margaret had been lunching with my parents at Southwell Garden Centre was unusual. It was the first occasion they'd sat down together since my sister returned from abandoning her two children and husband, Lenny.

Sandra relates she was following my parent's car after the get-together.

"We were looking forward to putting our feet up when this bright red car came over the hill on the wrong side of the road," she addresses the coroner, firm and direct.

"*Jim*, I shouts. *Swerve, man.* Not that he could hear me, but it was too late. An almighty fuc… *BANG* there were."

Sandra explains how she slammed on the brakes, rear end wobbling, and skidded to a halt yards from where Jim and Muriel were embedded in a soft-top Escort.

As if on autopilot, Sandra says her legs 'felt funny' running towards the two vehicles as steam billowed from my parent's concertinaed bonnet.

I can see her reliving the scene in her head as she discloses how, with one foot on my parents' Vauxhall Vectra's bodywork, she'd yanked on Jim's door until it 'crunched open'.

My seventy-five-year-old father was confused, though awake, Sandra says. Looking across, she remembers Muriel's unconscious head resting on an airbag, false teeth in her lap.

My sister's partner states she ran past motorists on mobile phones to the far side of the Escort, where, strangely, she recalls the twisted frame of the car's cabriolet roof poking through the fabric.

Unable to see the driver, Sandra says, although relieved, she thought it was a miracle they'd got out.

Apparently confused, Sandra surveys the ceiling. Which is when her knees buckle and a collective gasp says the courtroom thinks she's about to faint.

The coroner, whose handlebar moustache belongs to another era, inquires if Sandra would like to take a break, which she declines.

Regaining her composure, the Geordie takes a sip of water and, almost inconsequentially, adds: "The lass's head was in the footwell." This time, I join the collective gasp.

A loud sob seems to shake the room as all eyes swivel toward Darcy's mother rushing through the double doors, which swing shut behind her. I feel for her, though she's not in a wheelchair like my mother.

I respond to Sandra's glance with a nod, knowing what she's about to say.

Seated in an ambulance, she recollects hearing 'a terrible screeching sound' and, throwing off a thin cotton blanket, watches two firemen cut Muriel's legs free, sparks flying.

I fix my gaze on the herringbone floor when Sandra recounts how my seventy-eight-year-old mother was lifted clear of the tangled metal, oxygen mask over her face.

In a broad northern accent, Sandra describes how a kneeling paramedic was brushed away by Jim, who, raising a hand at the helicopter angling his wife towards Queen's Medical Centre, roadside vegetation flattened, mimed, "Please don't die, love."

Next, the coroner calls the doctor who pronounced Darcy dead at the scene, 'head unfortunately decapitated'.

"In the other vehicle, a Vauxhall Vectra, I believe, an elderly lady was suffering from life-threatening spinal injuries," the clinician matter-of-factly says, adjusting his tie.

"So I arranged her immediate evacuation by air ambulance." His interest stops there. Mine doesn't.

Sitting in the panelled room of this nondescript

building opposite the train station, I watch Darcy's boyfriend take the stand. Short and stocky, his biceps contour through a tight, squirrel-grey suit jacket.

The coroner, who's checked his pocket watch more than once, asks the witness what he can recollect of his last conversation with Darcy.

"In your own time, Mr Ellis, and remember you're not in a court of law. We're here to establish the cause of death, not who, if anyone, is to blame." I disagree. Culpability is everything.

"It's all my fault," he blurts. "I knew she was driving, and if I hadn't called her, she'd still be alive."

"Just try to remember, as best you can, what was said during that most unfortunate telephone call, Mr Ellis."

The boyfriend falters, takes a breath, then lowers his head. "I accused her of being in the student bar every night with her ..." He hesitates, shame etched on his face, and adds, 'with her poncey mates'.

Eyes brimming, he continues. "We argued for a while, and then I accused her of sleeping with Josh." The coroner raises his Denis Healey eyebrows like a question mark. "He's one of ... was one of Darcy's uni friends.

With his anguish silently echoing off the custard cream-coloured walls and tears streaming down his face, the twenty-three-year-old lifts his head and says: "She told me she wasn't shagging him, that I was impossible, and that I should go and lay some bricks, or whatever it is I do. Then ..."

The boyfriend puffs his cheeks and exhales. "Then there was a bang, and the line went dead. I'm sorry … I …" A young woman, perhaps his sister, gets up, takes his hand and leads him away.

I'm on the verge of weeping myself.

As the coroner shuffles some papers and then taps them on his elevated desk, I wonder if he's immune to the daily conveyor belt of grief. Peering over his spectacles at those of us still here, experience tells me he's about to record his verdict.

"This is the very sad case of Darcy Campbell, a nineteen-year-old woman whose life was cut tragically short in a car accident. She almost certainly died on impact, and it's safe to assume she suffered, if at all, very little."

"Unlike my mum," I mumble. I accept there are no winners, but, for me, Muriel's the biggest loser.

The coroner might as well don a black cap as he draws breath.

Accidental death is not what I want to hear, and the glare I give him as he exits through a side door is intended to say, 'You haven't seen the last of me.'

CHAPTER 38

I wince as the hearse catches the kerb and topples a display of carnations on Muriel's coffin. In the car behind, my father, brother, Jane, and I are about to follow my mother onto consecrated ground.

An avenue of low-hanging beech trees scratches the Dorchester's roof, seed cases that a gardener, who doesn't look up, continues to rake, crunch under our wheels. It seems the man's head's bowed by thunderous clouds rather than respect.

All Saints church comes into view as we inch forwards. The tip of its spire, struck by lightning, crashed to the ground the day I stole the collection plate money. Convinced I'd incurred God's wrath, I waited to be punished, renouncing my sins, but when nothing happened, I decided it was a coincidence and took another threepenny bit.

Pulling alongside an oak-framed porch, Jane nudges me towards an earnest, young-faced vicar who hides his inexperience with an impression of gravitas that only age can bestow. We shake hands. He's stronger than he looks, handsome even.

As I walk down the aisle behind my father, I can smell eight hundred years of misery in bear-black oil paintings infused with incense. Jesus's bleeding heart is exposed in a statue, nails hammered into his wooden flesh.

Muriel, reposed in the Co-op's second most expensive casket borne by pallbearers, edges towards the altar. No longer a teenage May Queen, she's Cleopatra carried by subservient slaves, though she's ignored by stone-dead knights missing arms and legs who've seen it all before.

Most of the pews have been moved out of sight in a bid to make the nave appear full. For my mother's and appearances' sake, I regret the number of empty spaces despite the congregation being bolstered by several villagers hopeful of a free sandwich in a nearby pub – though none of Muriel's extended family.

"Not a single one do you hear." had been Muriel's final instruction to Jim. Her concern was unwarranted because, as it turns out, her siblings were already dead.

When I pressed Jim, mid-funeral arrangements ten days ago, he told me my mother's family were once 'close', though he described his wife's relationship with older brother Graham as 'devoted'. Further details, despite my persistence, weren't forthcoming.

From what I've pieced together over the years, it appears a decades-old rift lingered from when Muriel's five brothers and sisters accused her of stealing *their* inheritance. Though Jim strenuously denied it, she had, they said, 'kidnapped' their mother, Mildred Rose, and husband, Reuben, from the Poplars Care Home in Mansfield.

Muriel's scheme, according to her siblings, was for Reuben and Mildred to live with us in Crow Park Crescent while Mother pocketed the money from the sale of the elderly couple's house. If true, I can't help but admire Muriel's ingenuity and wonder if it's where my tendency to covert what isn't mine originates.

In All Saints church, my oldest sister, Margaret, debilitated by MS, is at the far end of a second-row pew beside Sandra, who doesn't look far from death herself. I can tell by the way my sister's rocking in her wheelchair, muttering, that she probably wants a cigarette – and a glass of Blue Nun. Margaret doesn't 'do' being kept waiting.

Sandra, whose face is obscured by a lace veil, shushes Margaret under the seemingly disdainful gaze of a stained-glass angel dulled by dirt and musty autumnal light.

Organ notes thunder off the fourteenth-century roof as Muriel advances towards her creator, but the shorter than the rest pall-bearer tips my mother forward as she's lowered onto a trestle table draped with a purple fringed cloth.

Half smiling at my mother's final indignity, I admire the stalls where I'd sung as a choirboy before being asked to leave for repetitive farting, a consequence of spending my school lunch money on chip shop mushy peas. The vicar tapping his microphone returns me to the present.

Jim had bargained with the recently ordained Reverend Hughes for as close to a non-religious service as the cleric's conscience would allow – a hymn for the Almighty followed by a favourite song of the dearly departed.

I watch my father say the Lord's Prayer through gritted teeth, then warble "Morning Has Broken" slightly more cheerfully. His antagonism towards the church, which increases with every birth, death, and marriage he attends, makes it hard to imagine him as a former vicar.

Dad's insistence that I write a tribute on behalf of the family has caused me considerable unease. How can I tell the truth without offending those who believe, however incredulously, in Muriel's divinity? My last-minute solution is to deliver a largely off-the-cuff tribute laden with double entendre.

Stepping up to the lectern with as much solemnity as I can muster, I clear my throat and, probably too loudly, project:

"Our mother, the self-styled Queen of Stoke Blakely – and no one was sure how firmly her tongue was in her cheek when she said it – like God, moved in mysterious ways. She raised us as best she could and was always there for us. I think anyone who knew her would agree, Muriel Connah was unique."

Jane's front row frown says she knows exactly what I'm doing.

Retracing our steps along the aisle we've not long come down, we're accompanied by a crackly 1936 recording of Richard Tauber's "Somewhere a Voice is Calling". Jim says it was Muriel's favourite, though it's news to the rest of us.

My mother's about to be buried in reclaimed flood plain rather than original sacred ground, and ancient headstones guide us from the old cemetery into the new. I see Margaret give her ex-husband, taken by lung cancer, a disinterested squint.

When Lenny was laid to rest ten months ago, there were only a handful of neighbours, but such is the pace of Stoke Blakely's decline that he's now surrounded on all sides. Some graves are decorated with flowers, others with photographs of those gone and nearly forgotten.

The pallbearers swing Muriel towards a freshly dug mound of fertile, though stony, soil, exposed worms squirming.

Glancing into my mother's grave – a watery pit, her reward for lifelong servitude – I want to join her because now she's dead, I don't know what I'll do without her.

So far, Muriel's passing has been an exercise, a sequence of events directed by convention and Co-op Funeralcare, which left me unmoved. I tried to have feelings, to force tears, but they wouldn't come.

The accident, Mother's time in hospital, her learning to walk again, and the funeral, all happened at a distance, a place just beyond my emotional range. Even arranging the flight from France, where I now live, felt like an inconvenience.

Until this moment, I didn't know if I was inhuman or unable to face reality.

Muriel deserves better than mud walls and three inches of water for a final resting place. I watch a beetle trying to avoid the same fate, clambering out, only to fall in again. It's futile, but at least it's alive.

People don't seem to understand that the woman who breathed life into me, a goddess among mortals, doesn't belong in a claggy mausoleum, regal flesh left to rot in a wooden ossuary that itself is decaying.

Or am I distorting reality, rewriting history in an instance of grief rather than waiting to see what the cold light of tomorrow brings?

While my mother deprived me of what I most wanted, a door that was always open is now closed. With no one left to turn to in a crisis, to answer my cries for help, however scornfully, I no longer know what's real: love or hate.

For every foot of rope lowering Muriel into the ground, for every crow's caw in the chestnut tree, for every grain of soil rattling off her casket, I shed an unseen tear. Wishing I could hold my dad's hand, a new relationship to recompense for what's gone, I know it's pointless because my mother's irreplaceable.

And so, I'm left to reconcile fifty years of bitterness with a woeful sense of loss, oscillating between two conflicting emotions.

My mother damaged everyone around her, but if she was malignant, why do I want to resurrect her? Is it to fill the emptiness she's left behind? A connection, no matter how fragile, lost? Or is Muriel's ultimate spite to leave me wanting more? She who laughs last laughs longest.

And if she was the devil incarnate, who's to blame? She, along with the rest of us, was bequeathed a nature handed down from previous generations, each contributing a defective gene. Does that make God responsible? Is He the guilty party?

And what of her parents' contribution? Are they accountable for nurturing Muriel's mordant personality, a childhood spent caring for a polio-stricken sister, a lack of confidence masquerading as aloofness, ill-equipped to join in? Like mother like son.

Wasn't her life one of expectations dashed? Jim not the suitor she hoped for, her letters to the US colonel unanswered; unrequited. Next came deprivation in Glaswegian slums, followed by four children: me, the last, the full stop at the end of a lengthy sentence.

I flinch as Muriel's pine container splashes into her waterlogged burial chamber, christened perhaps for the first time. Cleansed, if not absolved, of her sins, at least she left a mark, an impression, which is more than can be said for most people.

My unsatisfactory conclusion as I say goodbye is that I pity, admire, and loathe her as much as myself. How can I blame her for abandoning me to loneliness when she endured a lifetime of her own?

×

Tramping back through the graveyard, passing the whalebone arch that'd fascinated me as a child, and on to Nottingham Road, I catch a glimpse of my mortality in the speeding traffic. One step, and it's over.

The sandwich-inspired mourners are disappointed when we scramble into taxis and head for a memorial lunch in a nearby country hotel. I smile at the irony. Muriel had always wanted to dine there, deterred by its prices.

"Eleven pounds fifty for a prawn cocktail? I'd rather starve," she exclaimed every time we went by. I suspect the real reason was that she worried her airs and graces, her exaggerated cut-glass accent, would be found out among the wealthy clientele.

The hotel meal goes tolerably well, most likely due to the free bar Jim's provided that's caused thirteen family members to be less sombre-eyed. I'd still put money on none of them wanting to be here, though.

Dad cuts a lonely figure at the head of the table, and, while watching him, I make small talk with someone I think is a cousin. I nod in agreement that Muriel's 'gone to a better place', though neglect to mention I wish I could join her.

I'd prefer to be alone with Jim, John, and my sisters, supporting one another, affirming natural bonds, being a commiserating family. But as my gaze shifts from Margaret spitting out the food spoon-fed by Sandra, to John, who'd rather be fly fishing in Scotland, to Jane, who has her own family with no need for ours, I know Jim is my only prospect.

In Fairfield Close that evening, I return from the kitchen with two cups of Horlicks and sit in my mother's chair. Twelve hours earlier, I'd placed my hands where hers had worn the orange geometric fabric and do so again.

Is it my imagination, or can I feel her presence, a warmth I rarely felt when she was alive? Glimpsing at Jim, illuminated under a reading lamp, I reach for the photo album and turn once again to Muriel and my toddler self on a windswept beach.

Showing the picture to Jim, I say, "Do you remember this, Dad? We were on holiday in Southport, though why I'm wearing a girl's bathing suit is anyone's guess." He refuses, or is unable, to meet my eye.

"Do you suppose we were a happy family? I mean, do you think Mum was happy." I persevere, aware that time and opportunities are running out.

"What sort of a question is that?" Jim's tightening neck muscles tell me I'm walking on barely formed ice. "Of course we, and she, were."

"Are you sure, Dad? Some of our family holidays, for example, were a bit, sort of, well, tense, weren't they?"

"Are you trying to rob me of my memories now, as well, Daniel? Is that what you want?"

"Honest to God, I don't." My fifty-year-old heart tells me to stop, but I press on, in need of answers. "I know we had some good times, and they're worth a lot, but there were some bad ones as well."

"What on earth do you mean?"

"There were lots of arguments. Mum shouted a lot, mainly at you as it happens." I've lightened my tone, but Dad's face says it's not working.

"You couldn't put a foot right. None of us could. And I was just wondering if it was because she had an un..."

"You don't know what you're talking about. Your mother and I didn't argue. Not having much money caused a few problems but we always enjoyed ourselves. Ask Jane." I would if I didn't already know her answer.

"I didn't have a very good time in Ireland when you abandoned me on a loch." I try not to get riled. "I nearly drowned."

"*What* loch?"

"Don't you remember? I thought we were *all* going, but you and Mother left me on my own in a rowing boat. I was only twelve and had to be rescued."

"I hope you're not suggesting she was a bad mother – and me a bad father?"

"She never told me she loved me. Neither of you did."

"Look at the pictures." He raises himself and jabs several photos with his finger.

"Can't you see how much she cared for you?" His hair appears whiter than it did this morning, perhaps because I'm disturbing a fantasy romanticised by death.

"I know you've had a tough day, Dad, but I'm leaving tomorrow, and who knows when we'll be able to talk again."

"There's nothing to talk about."

"There is for me." I take a deep breath. "Like, why didn't Mother want me to go to Australia to live with Uncle Graham? Did something happen between them? Years ago, she told me I was a lot like him – like he was living inside me or something. Is that why she didn't love me? Because I reminded her of him?"

"Graham was … He …" My life depends on Jim going somewhere he doesn't want to.

"There are some things even I don't understand, Daniel. Things were said. Anyway …" I'm losing him on the brink of revelation, just like I did with Jane.

"Now's not the time to be dredging up the past. Your mother's dead, for Christ's sake."

"But …"

"I said, NOT NOW."

"What happened in the barn? Why did you try to…"

"**NOT NOW.**"

"It's never going to be now, is it, Dad?"

CHAPTER 39

As winter advances, on infrequent visits home, I witness the mood darken inside Fairfield Close, along with Jim's mental and physical deterioration.

I lay in bed listening to him relay the day's events to Muriel each night, afraid I'll hear my name. 'You'll never guess what Daniel's done now, love.'

My father's nightly sign-off is always the same, "Sleep tight, Muriel, and I'll see you in the morning." What he doesn't know is that I'm having almost as much trouble letting my mother go as him.

I've seen Jim scrape the depths of despair, pinned down by rejection and furious words, but never the lifeless wretch he is now.

With gangrene-coloured veins prominent on parchment-like skin, he's a cadaver beyond comforting words as he sits on the marital bed stroking Muriel's nightie. Does he know it'd been closer to her than him, I wonder?

Almost a year after the funeral, I find Jim sorting through my mother's belongings, separating charity shop stuff from rubbish. Jane, who's come over for lunch, declines Dad's offer of Muriel's dresses, which is when he calls me into the bedroom.

"Do you know what's in this old cash box? It was in the back of Mother's wardrobe." *Nottingham Savings Bank* is written in gilt lettering on a black metal case. "It's strange that I haven't seen it before. I can't find the key."

"Why don't you go and make us a nice cup of tea, Dad? You look worn out. I'll put these clothes in the car." I've smelt an opportunity.

Shaking the cash box, a dull thud suggests it's full, and I search for the small unlabelled key I remember finding in Mother's bedside drawer years ago. But there's a problem.

"*Dad*," I yell through the wall. "Have you cleared out Mum's bedside cabinet yet? Would you like me to do it?" I'm a fisherman casting a line; subterfuge for bait. Why? Because it's a cheap thrill.

Jim sticks his head round the door. "She didn't like me going in there, so I put everything in a cardboard box for Jane to go through. It's in the garage. Why?"

"No reason, but I could do with that cuppa; I'm parched." I collect the cash box and head outside.

Scattering the drawer's contents on the garage bench, I use a screwdriver to sift through panty liners, spare dentures, and a tube of KY jelly.

"Where's the old bag hidden it?" I ask Ben, who's followed me in.

Bingo. When I unfasten a spectacle case, an inch-long barrel key jingles onto the concrete.

The cash box springs open to reveal bundles of discoloured bank books eager to be released along with a burst of mould spores. Sneezing, I check the last page of the latest book.

"*Fuck. Ing. Hell*. There's over fifteen grand in here."

Nineteen-sixties handwritten entries give way to 1970s golf ball printed entries; laserjet in the '80s. It's a historical record in more ways than one.

Monthly ten-pound deposits in earlier books progress to twenty pounds, then thirty, and so on over the years.

"Was she blackmailing someone or on the game?" I try to dispel an image of Muriel dressed as a Mapperley Rise hooker. FUCK. I know exactly what it is.

"It's the friggin' housekeeping money. And Child Benefit. And any other cash she could get her thieving hands on. No wonder I didn't get fed as a kid. She stashed all the money in here."

Pulling up an old weaver's stool Jim 'borrowed' from a Trades for Life renovation project, I try to make sense of it all.

What was she going to do with fifteen K? Search for her wartime colonel, or fund an escape route? In which case, why didn't she flee when I came along.

Or was the money Muriel's greatest concealment of all? A lifelong fixation maintained to the bitter end. Manipulation through stealth.

Either way, I've got a father who won't talk to me and a mother who, despite being dead, is still fucking with my head.

My gaze returns to the cash box.

Under some legal papers, books of Green Shield stamps, and a beaming wedding day photograph of Jim and Muriel, is … every childhood birthday and Christmas card I ever sent her. Bizarrely, there's nothing from my brother and sisters.

My head's spinning. Why did Muriel keep *my* cards and no one else's, not even Jim's? I'm reluctant to trust her again, but could it mean she cared about me, loved me, even? Is she begging for forgiveness from the other side? Finally repentant.

At the bottom of the box, an airmail letter, weighed down by decades-worth of secrets, is stuck to the metal. Prising it free, my pulse quickens when I see it's from Graham.

Dear Muriel,

It was good to see you again after all these years. Nice to finally meet Daniel too. He's turned out a strapping young fella. What might have been I wonder if you'd let Gayle and me adopt him? Still, best not to dig all that up again. You made a decision, then changed your mind. Gayle's never forgiven you nor likely to, I'm afraid. She hit the roof when I got back to Melbourne and said I'd invited Daniel to come and stay. Hope he didn't take it too hard when you told him he couldn't.

Speaking of forgiveness. Our brother and sisters didn't take it too well when I told them I was going to see you. People say blood's thicker than water, but it's not half as thick as money! They still think you swindled them over that business selling Mum and Dad's house. I've gotten over it, but that's probably because I've done alright for myself. Between you and me, I've helped one or two of the others out over the years.

It comes down to this. Ida and the rest don't intend building bridges anytime soon, and they've given me an ultimatum. Either I stay in contact with you or with them. It puts me in a difficult spot, but I don't have much choice. It's either the sister I was closer to growing up than all of them put together, or two sisters and a big brother who, having bred like rabbits, have given me nine nieces and nephews to think about. I'm sorry, love, but what with Gayle and everything else that's happened, I've got to stick with them.

Maybe one day everything will blow over, but until then, I've got to say goodbye.

Yours
Graham

The letter slips from my hand. I can't and don't want to believe what I'm reading.

Adoption! Was she seriously going to give me away? How old was I? One, two, five? Assuming I'd even been born? The stool creaks. I'm trembling.

Graham must've written the letter sometime after he took us out to dinner at the Clumber Park hotel, some thirty years ago.

Thirty years for Muriel to tell me what happened. Was she ever going to? Did she get close the night I called her from London?

Does Jim know about the adoption? Did he prevent it, or did neither of my parents want me?

Then again, Graham did say Muriel changed her mind. And that's what I've got to hang on to. For now.

×

Was I born or made bad? It's hard to say though I've realised our natures require nurture. And an unloved child will always suffer.

As for God. What can I say about the Man who, perhaps in a case of mistaken identity, kept me alive?

I could deny his existence. Or grasp at straws and believe that inner strength got me through fifty years of torment.

Can my newfound resolve help me change? Let's hope so.

BOOK CLUB QUESTIONS:

In *A Corroded Soul*, Daniel blames his mother, Muriel, for many of his character traits. He's particularly affected by feeling unloved. Is Muriel in any way accountable for her son's questionable behaviour?

Do you think Muriel is responsible for Daniel's difficulties forming relationships, particularly with women?

At what age, if any, should Daniel take responsibility for his own actions?

Daniel begins taking money from Muriel's purse, aged five, then progresses to shoplifting. He says he steals because he wasn't listened to as a child and that it empowers him. Is stealing ever understandable/acceptable?

Muriel lives a largely unfulfilled life. Her US colonel doesn't return after the war, for example, which, as she sees it, forces her to marry Jim. Do these dashed expectations justify the way she raises her children?

Is Muriel mentally ill/depressed? If so, does it mitigate her behaviour?

Daniel's sister, Jane, was abused more than any of the children, so why does she have a more forgiving attitude towards their mother? Is Daniel an unreliable narrator?

Daniel eventually sees his parents as products of their own backgrounds. Muriel, for example, had to take care of her polio-stricken sister, and Jim's father was emotionally distant. Who do you think should break the cycle?

Daniel, in modern parlance, is groomed by his Physics teacher, Greg. Daniel says he benefitted from the friendship because, unlike his parents, Greg supported him. Is Daniel wrong and Greg simply a sexual predator?

Ultimately, we learn that Muriel considered letting her brother, Graham, who lives in Australia, adopt Daniel. Would it have been better for everyone if she had?

Do you think that, in her own way, Muriel loved Daniel?

ABOUT THE AUTHOR

Peter Woolrich is an award-winning investigative journalist. The Channel 4 documentary *The Dying Rooms*, about babies being left to die in Chinese orphanages, won him a BAFTA nomination and led to him being banned from China and Hong Kong. During his career, he's had a meat cleaver, a machete, a baseball bat, and a gun pulled on him.

He largely gave up his journalism career to concentrate on his lifelong ambition to write books. *A Corroded Soul* is the first in a planned trilogy.

Peter has lived in the Far East, Australia, and across Europe. Originally from Nottingham, he now lives in Harrogate, North Yorkshire.